Also by
SUZANNE ENOCH

The Handbook to Handling His Lordship

SUZANNE ENOCH

St. Martin's Paperbacks

THE HANDBOOK TO HANDLING HIS LORDSHIP

Copyright © 2013 by by Suzanne Enoch.

All rights reserved.

For information address St. Martin's Press, 175 Fifth Avenue, New York, NY 10010.

ISBN: 978-0-312-53454-7

Printed in the United States of America

St. Martin's Paperbacks edition / April 2013

St. Martin's Paperbacks are published by St. Martin's Press, 175 Fifth Avenue, New York, NY 10010.

10 9 8 7 6 5 4 3 2 1

For Kelly-Leigh Proellocks, who suggested the name "Nathaniel"
For Elizabeth Butler, who gave me "Stokes"
And for Christina, who came up with "Westfall"
Congratulations, ladies—you made a hero!

Chapter One

The idiotic ways in which people deluded themselves, against all better reason and judgment, had long since ceased to surprise Nathaniel Stokes.

He, for instance, did not view a well-documented meeting in the middle of Hyde Park at the height of visiting hours as discreet. Neither would he have thought that wearing an enormous yellow hat and an unseasonably heavy cloak lent itself to being unnoticed, but then he hadn't arranged the rendezvous. That honor belonged to the elongated face and plucked triangular eyebrows beneath the hat. And the black-gloved fingers sticking out from the enormous black coach's window and beckoning him closer, spiderlike. Ah, very subtle.

Of course he'd taken his own precautions in order to ensure that the residents of London in general, and Mayfair in particular, saw the portrait of him that he intended. Therefore, as he swung down from Blue, his dark gray gelding, he adjusted the pair of glass-lensed spectacles that bridged his nose and pulled his ebony cane from its well-fashioned holster in his saddle.

He needed neither, but required both. Or rather, his particular brand of hobby required, he'd learned from careful observation, a certain air of both absentmind-edness and trustworthy gravitas. Spectacles did that with a minimum of discomfort, while the cane made him look harmless—especially when accompanied by the slight limp that tucking a button into the bottom of his left boot elicited. No one else needed to know about the razor-sharp rapier tucked inside the ebony wood—but *he* knew about it. And how to use it.

"Lord Westfall," the female beneath the hat whispered, ducking back into the shadowed recesses of the coach, "do join me."

And then there was the largest part of his disguise. Nate found it ironic that Mayfair's blue bloods had found him worthy of hearing their darkest secrets only after he'd become the Earl of Westfall—not because the title wasn't legitimately his, as an army of solicitors had deemed it to be—but because of all the disguises he'd ever worn, this one of aristocrat had the illest fit. And it also seemed to be the only one he couldn't take off and set into the wardrobe at the end of the day.

Favoring his left leg, he stepped up into the carriage and pulled the door shut behind him. "Are you certain your reputation is safe with me, Lady Allister?" he asked with a smile, removing the dark blue beaver hat from his head and setting it on the posh leather seat beside him.

The dowager viscountess giggled, color touching her pale cheeks. "At my age I shall risk it," she returned, still using the same conspiratorial whisper she'd assumed for each of their half-dozen conversations. "Were you successful?"

Nate nodded, reaching into the wrong coat pocket and then the correct one to pull out an old, gold-rimmed ivory brooch. The carving was rather delicate, the silhouette of a young lady with an elongated face and high-piled, curling hair. "I leave it to you to decide if you wish to know where it was located," he said, handing it into Lady Allister's black-gloved fingers.

"Oh, dear," she said, gazing at the small thing before she curled her fingers around it and clutched it to her bosom. "I hate to be sentimental, but it is the only image I have remaining of my younger self. The fire took the portrait my father had commissioned. By Gainsborough himself, you know."

"It's a lovely piece. The craftsmanship, and the subject, are remarkable." That seemed to be what she wished to hear, anyway. As he'd spent the past week looking at half a hundred of the things as he trailed one small brooch across central England, he wasn't certain how qualified he was to judge at the moment.

Light blue eyes lifted to meet his. "I will only ask this: Was it sold from my son's possession, or stolen?"

He'd discovered the answer to that question early on. Gambling debts and an overreaching lifestyle had rendered the current Viscount Allister with a less than desirable quantity of funds. As he looked at the damp eyes of Allister's doting mother, he settled his expression into a frown. "Stolen, I'm afraid. A group of young brigands who've already been seen to justice for other crimes."

The woman's shoulders lowered. "It's as he said, then." She cleared her throat. "And your fee, Westfall? You have certainly earned one."

"Twenty-five pounds, as we agreed, my lady."

"In exchange for your efforts and your discretion."

And there the word was again, as rarely as it was actually spoken aloud. He couldn't imagine anyone else would care a fig whether Lord Allister had sold his mother's brooch or not, but she'd convinced herself that her entire family's reputation rested on his silence. So be it. "Of course."

She handed the coins into his hand, briefly gripping his fingers as she did so. "Thank you, Lord Westfall."

Nate opened the coach's door. "And thank you, Lady Allister." Then he grimaced for effect. "Ah, my hat." Reaching back, he retrieved the last bit of his disguise and descended to the ground.

He stepped back as the coach rolled away. The first time a peer had asked him to find something, he'd made the mistake of attempting to perform the deed gratis. After that had nearly sparked a duel with the fellow, he'd realized his error. If he didn't ask a fee, that meant a client—as he'd come to call them—owed him a favor. It meant that, however trivial the deed or misdeed, he held a piece of their privacy, their reputation, over them. Payment for services rendered made them even. And so whether he required the additional income or not, or whether the fee matched the efforts he'd made or the expense he'd truly gone to, he named a nominal price and they paid it. And the dearer the secret they felt the need to protect, the larger the price they demanded he ask.

Pocketing the blunt, he stowed his cane and swung back up on Blue. Whether the dowager viscountess believed his talk of the brooch's travels or not, he'd said what she wanted to hear. Sometimes that seemed to be of more import to his clients than the recovery of the missing item. It meant more lies heaped upon his head, but after the life he'd lived and some of the tales he'd told as a consequence, some of the truths he'd told that cost men's lives, improving the character of someone's son or cousin or uncle hardly made a dent.

The front door of Teryl House opened as he climbed the top step. "Welcome home, my lord," Garvey said with a nod, stepping aside to allow him entry. "You have a letter on the hall table, and a caller in the morning room."

Nate retrieved the missive and broke the wax seal. "Who's here?" he asked the butler as he unfolded the note to read through it. Evidently his younger brother had earned an enforced holiday from Oxford, the idiot. He barely glanced at the details; it wouldn't be the truth, anyway. *That,* he would have to learn from Laurie face-to-face.

"He didn't say, my lord."

Ah, another one of those. Nodding, Nate shoved the letter into a pocket. "Send in some tea, will you? And we'll need a guest room made ready. Laurence is coming down early for the Season."

"Very good, my lord. It will be splendid to have Master Laurence about again. He's quite . . . lively."

Nate wasn't certain that he would have used the same adjectives, but he had no intention of bantering with Garvey over whether *lively* and *splendid* or *bothersome* and *complicated* were the more appropriate terms. "Yes, it will," he said aloud, and finished removing his gloves and hat to hand them over to the waiting butler.

Generally he preferred to know with whom he was conversing in advance of a meeting, but in all practicality such a thing was a luxury. And he did enjoy the process of discovery, after all. With that in mind he resettled his spectacles, tapped his cane on the floor, and pushed open the morning room door.

His caller stood before the front window, his gaze on the street beyond. With a swiftness bred from equal parts practice and necessity, Nate tallied him up—highly polished Hessian boots, a dark green coat of superfine and not a wrinkle or crease across the square shoulders, a large signet ring on his right hand, the stance of folded arms and braced feet. Neatly cut blond hair and the closest shave a face could have. A man accustomed to people looking at him, and one with money enough to appear in the manner he wished.

"Good afternoon," Nate said aloud, pulling the door closed behind him.

The figure turned around, lidded dark eyes regarding him with the same thoroughness he'd just used on his visitor. "I've heard some things about you, Westfall," the fellow finally said, in an accent that bespoke southwestern England. "Are they true?"

"That's a rather broad canvas," Nate returned in his best tone of cool, slightly distracted indifference. "Would you care to elaborate?"

"Certainly. Who am I?"

Ah, a test. At best he had only a passing acquaintance with his new peers. Given his visitor's age, attire, and speech patterns, though, he would put the man as either Viscount Delshire or, taking into account his visitor's obvious arrogance, the Marquis of Ebberling. Considering the way the fellow had arrived at the house without giving a name, however, coupled with the suspicion with which most of his clients regarded his powers of deduction, Nate only squinted one eye and adjusted his spectacles. "Have you lost your memory then, sir? I'm acquainted with several competent physicians. I have a penchant for finding things, but a person's memories . . . Hm. That would be an interesting endeavor. Fascinating, even."

"Never mind that. I'm Ebberling—the Marquis of— and I wish to engage your . . . services."

On occasion, Nate thought in passing as the tea arrived and he gestured Lord Ebberling to a chair, it would be pleasant to be surprised. The nice sort of surprise, though; not the firing-of-a-pistol-in-his-direction kind. Once the footman left, he poured himself a cup and dumped two sugars into the mix. "What is it you've lost, then, Ebberling?" he asked, noting that the marquis sat squarely in the center of the comfortable chair, his weight balanced and not an ounce of slouch in his posture.

Considering that he'd once avoided being shot because he'd noticed that his dinner companion kept one leg around the side of his chair rather than on the floor in front of him, Nate took account of everything. And from what he could tell, the marquis had lost something valuable. Vital, even. And he wasn't happy about going anywhere for assistance in locating it.

"What assurances do I have of your discretion, Westfall?" Lord Ebberling asked, ignoring the tea.

"I like finding things. The what and why of the task don't actually concern me. And since I wish to continue in my hobby of finding things, I have no intention of betraying the confidence of anyone who hires me. Does that suffice?"

For another moment the marquis eyed him. "I suppose it will have to. Very well, then. Five years ago, my wife hired a young lady to serve as a governess to my son, George. Three years ago a very valuable diamond necklace vanished from my wife's dressing table, along with the governess."

"A stolen necklace," Nate said with a nod. He was becoming a bit weary of hunting for misplaced jewelry, but London's *haut ton* seemed to have very slippery fingers. "I think I can manage that."

"That isn't quite everything," the marquis countered, sitting forward an inch or two. "The afternoon Miss Newbury disappeared, my wife was killed in a riding accident." He cleared his throat. "Actually, the horse returned to the stable without Katherine, and everyone went searching for her. We found her in a ditch, her neck broken. It was only afterward I realized that Miss Newbury hadn't been among the searchers. When I returned to the house, her things were gone, along with the necklace and the girl, herself."

"So you think this Miss Newbury murdered Lady Ebberling?" Nate asked slowly, studying his client very carefully. Hands clenched, jaw tight, eyes lowered—anger. Deep anger that this governess had escaped without paying for her misdeeds.

"The physician said Katherine's fall was possibly an accident. What I *think* is that something untoward occurred. Perhaps Katherine saw Miss Newbury with the gem, or . . . I don't know. But if you can find the diamond necklace, then perhaps you will also have located Rachel Newbury. And I would pay three thousand pounds to recover one or the other."

Four years ago, Nate's annual salary from the Crown had been three hundred pounds. Today, as the Earl of Westfall, his annual income was somewhere in the realm of eight thousand pounds. In theory he would have offered all of it to find the killer of his wife, certainly. But he would hope that the man he hired wouldn't accept it. "My lord, three thou—"

"And another five thousand pounds if you deliver her to me and allow me to contact the authorities."

To Nate both that comment and the amount of blunt being offered spoke volumes. Ebberling wanted to find that woman very badly, and when he did, Miss Newbury would likely never reach the authorities. If Nathaniel meant to be squeamish, however, he'd missed his chance a very long time ago. And he knew quite well that women were perfectly capable of being vicious and murderous. In some ways they were deadlier than their male counterparts, because who would suspect them of such foul deeds?

Above—or below—the morality of it all, the prospect of hunting down someone who'd vanished into the shadows three years ago fascinated him. For God's sake, he could use a damned challenge. He awoke some mornings with his mind feeling positively mossy.

"May I ask why you've decided to embark on this venture now?" he queried, settling his spectacles as he did when he wanted to look particularly unthreatening. "It has been three years, as you said."

"I was patient for a very long time," Ebberling replied, "waiting for Bow Street and the local magistrates to do their duty. But now I've made plans to remarry. The idea that the woman who may have had something to do with Katherine's death—who stole from me and betrayed my trust—is still somewhere in the world perhaps waiting to do harm to me and mine again is intolerable. I won't have that hanging over me any longer."

It seemed as good an answer as any. "I'll need whatever information you can provide me about this Rachel Newbury. Age, appearance, breeding, education, birthplace—any of it could be the key to discovering her whereabouts," he said after a moment. "And that of the necklace, as well."

Ebberling nodded. "My wife hired her, of course, but I do know her present age would be somewhere between twenty-three and twenty-five years. She was a tall chit, with an air about her, as if she thought herself just a bit more clever than everyone else. Brown eyes, yellow hair that seemed to want to curl every which way, though she always wore it in a perfect knot at the back of her head. Pretty enough, I suppose, and very proper. And I recall that she had a fondness for strawberries and liked to ride. And read. She always had a book in her hands."

Standing, Nate walked over to the writing desk and pulled free a piece of paper. "I'm a fair hand at drawing," he said, finding a pencil and taking a seat again. "I'll make an attempt at sketching her if you'll guide me through it."

"Excellent," the marquis returned, finally reaching for a teacup. "Rycott said you were the man for the job."

The name startled him. "Rycott?" he repeated, facing his new client. "You're acquainted with Jack?"

"You mean do I know you served Wellington as a spy?" Ebberling countered, filling his cup and then moving over to the writing desk. "I have my connections. I required someone who could successfully complete this task. Jack Rycott said that would be you. And I haven't seen or heard anything from you to cause me to doubt his opinion." He gestured at the paper. "An oval face, as I recall."

"So Rycott simply told you I worked for Wellington?" Nate said, setting down the pencil and using every bit of willpower he owned to keep from dropping the marquis and permanently silencing the man before he could go about wagging his tongue to anyone else. "I doubt that."

"Very well, he didn't say it directly. In fact, he said he'd heard that the new Earl of Westfall liked to find lost cats. And then he said, 'Why a man would go from lions to cats I have no idea, but there you have it. He'll do you for the job. And then some.' When I deduced the rest, he didn't deny it."

Now *that* sounded like Jack Rycott. "I won't deny it either, then," Nate said aloud, "though I will clarify that I *consulted* with Wellington during the war. There's a large difference between tracking down a lion and going into a cage with one." It sounded believable, anyway. "Cats—and females—are in my experience much more manageable."

And given what the Marquis of Ebberling thought he knew, the sooner Nate could find this particular female and be done with it, the better. Then he could drive himself to Brighton and have a little chat with his former comrade and remind Colonel Rycott just how little he appreciated being gossiped about. Or mentioned at all, for that matter. He'd found and trapped and killed his share of lions. More than his share, according to the French. And now cats and females and the occasional piece of lost jewelry suited him just fine, thank you very much.

Once Ebberling was satisfied that the drawing accurately depicted Miss Rachel Newbury—or her image as of three years previously, anyway—the marquis handed over a hefty stack of blunt along with his address both in London and in Shropshire's Ebberling Manor. Nate sat back and studied the pencil sketch. She was pretty, with that lifted-chin haughtiness Ebberling had described. In truth she could be anyone, residing anywhere in England. Given the supposition that she wouldn't want to be found, however, he'd never encountered a better place to lose oneself than in the crowded streets of London.

A stranger in a small village would be noticed. People would ask questions. Rachel Newbury wouldn't want to answer questions, and she wouldn't want to be remembered. She would likely be employed in some quiet, nondescript occupation where she was unlikely to encounter anyone from her prior life—as a seamstress or a baker's helper, a shopkeeper's assistant or even an old lady's companion.

Yellow-blond hair, brown eyes, haughty, and highly intelligent. Not much to begin with. But he'd found people in Europe in the middle of a war. That had been a matter of life and death, of security for England. *This* would be fun.

The moment Lord Ebberling left the house, Nathaniel summoned his valet. "Franks, retrieve my saddlebag from the attic, will you? I've a bit of traveling to do."

The valet wrinkled his long nose. "My lord? How long will you be gone? I can't possibly pack such a small bag with adequate garb and your toiletries. Allow me to fetch you a proper valise."

"A valise won't fit on my saddle," Nathaniel returned, the stifling robes of earldom beginning to close on him again, not that they'd ever fit well. For Christ's sake, until two years ago he'd practically lived out of a saddlebag, acquiring additional things as necessary and discarding them once they were no longer needed. Evidently an aristocrat didn't pilfer shirts from clotheslines, however.

"Please reconsider, my lord. Wherever it is you're going, you will have need of pressed shirts and starched cravats. You—"

"Very well." Cursing under his breath, Nathaniel motioned the servant toward the door. "One small valise. And tell Garvey I'll be taking the phaeton. To Shropshire and its environs, since I'm evidently to inform people of my comings and goings now."

From his expression, Franks didn't quite know how to respond to that, but Nate wasn't in the mood to explain himself. He'd done his duty by the Crown, and now he did his duty to his family by taking the title his cousin Gerard had vacated after falling from a boat in the Lake District. What grated was the remaining wish to do something for himself, something that he wished to do for his own curiosity and interest. At the moment, that was riding—no, driving now—to Shropshire and the neighboring villages to look for a trace of Miss Rachel Newbury. And by God, he meant to find her.

Chapter Two

The washroom was the plainest room in The Tantalus Club. Even the kitchen had a selection of antique pots and pans lining the walls. The washroom, however, featured only a wooden chair, a small cabinet for towels and soaps, and a large brass tub in the middle. A small window did look out over the carriage drive, but after several men were caught trying to look inside, the window was actually raised so high on the wall that it now looked out into the sky.

Considering the reputation of The Tantalus Club for hiring beautiful, unavailable women, Emily Portsman was somewhat surprised the window hadn't been boarded over entirely. The fascination of the unobtainable, she supposed it was. But as she'd been obtained several times over the past three years, that explanation didn't quite serve.

As usual on Sundays and Thursdays, Emily was the last to use the bath for the day. With her making the schedules, that feat was particularly easy to arrange. By now the water had moved past tepid and into cool and unpleasant, but it served its purpose. And she needed the extra time that being at the end of the line provided. It wasn't that she felt a particular need to scrub herself clean; in fact she had stepped from the tub nearly an hour ago.

She currently sat in the simple wooden chair beside the bathtub, a warm woolen robe wrapped around her, and her latest gothic horror novel open in her lap. *The Scottish Cousin* featured a plot so convoluted she had no idea what was truly going on. It had passed the border of impossible five chapters ago, but it kept her entertained. And that was the point of it.

Finally the small, secondhand clock sitting on the cabinet ticked past three o'clock, and she set the book aside and stood. Making her way back to the cold bath, she knelt beside the brass tub and unceremoniously dunked her head. Immediately the water turned a reddish brown, spreading out from the long strands of her hair until the entire bath was the color of weak tea. Emily drew her fingers through the mess, shaking it out vigorously, then grabbed for the stained brown towel she always used and wrapped it tightly around the dripping cascade.

Immediately she went to the bowl of clean water she'd set aside and thoroughly washed her hands in the most abrasive soap she'd been able to find. No sense going through all this twice a week and then having stained brown fingers giving her away. Sitting on the chair again, she toweled off her hair, then combed through it until it was smooth and glossy. She would have to wait until it dried before she could take the straightening iron to it—only once had she made the mistake of putting metal to her hair while it was still wet, and she'd had to wear a matron's turban for a week until the green tint faded.

Now, once the thick paste of henna and tea and lemon juice had been rinsed away, she would have a head of pretty, if utterly unremarkable, dark chestnut hair. The color of a bay horse, one of her intimate companions had once said. Nothing to write a poem about, certainly, and that was precisely what she wanted.

The door rattled, and she started. "Nearly finished," she called, reaching over to collect her shift and pull it on over her head.

"It's Jenny," a feminine voice in a light French accent called. "I have the new gown you ordered from Gaston's."

Emily sent a glance at the tea-colored bath, then padded over in her bare feet to unlock the door and pull it open. "You know I didn't order a gown from Gaston's," she said in a low voice, allowing the club's majordomo into the bathroom before she closed the door again.

Genevieve Martine, her blond hair pulled tightly into a bun that bespoke a governess rather than the second-in-command of an exclusive and decidedly unconventional gentlemen's club, shrugged her shoulders. "It sounded plausible, no? Not that I think anyone cares to hear that you color your hair, Emily."

"It's a matter of pride," Emily lied with a short smile. "Not all of us have ravishingly lovely golden hair." She fingered the mostly dry ends.

"Mm-hm."

She would've preferred an even plainer brown color, actually, but the henna tended to turn everything red before it deepened to brown. The tea and the lemon juice helped, but to keep her hair from changing color every other day she had to apply the dye twice each week. "Was there a reason you wanted in here, then? The bathwater cooled past tepid an hour ago."

"I thought I might assist you with carrying buckets to empty," Jenny replied, "since you'll be overseeing the dinner service in an hour."

Emily blinked. "I did the schedule. *You're* overseeing dinner service tonight."

"I was," Jenny countered. "Now I've been volunteered to speak at a meeting for women who wish to
own their own businesses."

"But—"

"Yes, I know. I don't own The Tantalus Club. Diane
does. She also asked me to attend, as she refuses." Jenny
grimaced. "I would decline also, but women who can
envision owning their own businesses are also ones
who can afford to wager here on ladies' nights. In order
to serve our own interests, I can be politic for an evening."

"You're always politic, Jenny. It's a talent of yours."

This time Miss Martine grinned. "One among many."
Walking over, she picked up a bucket, dipped it into the
bathwater, and headed for the door. "You dispose of
this in the back garden, do you not?"

"The roses seem to like the henna. Or the tea. Or the
lemon juice. I don't know which one it is." She frowned
as she pulled on the simple blue muslin she'd brought
into the bathing room with her. If she was to oversee
dinner, she would need to change into something more
enticing. Being noticed intentionally seemed mad to
her, but on the other hand this was a house of beautiful
women. A plain one would stand out like a crow amid
peacocks. "You don't need to help me, Jenny. I'll manage."

"Nonsense. And if you're worried about my discretion, consider that I've known for the past two years
that you color your hair, my dear. And this is the first
word I've spoken on the topic. If you wish, it will also
be the last."

Clearly Genevieve Martine didn't believe that Emily

altered her hair color because of vanity, just as both Jenny and Lady Haybury knew that she had a past of which she refused to speak. "I would prefer that the topic be closed," she said slowly, reflecting that while it might have been nice to have someone with whom to discuss whatever she wished, the counter to that would be that someone else would have information she'd worked for the past three years to bury.

"Then it is closed." Jenny waited until Emily had finished buttoning up her muslin, then pulled open the door. "And I will still help you carry water to the roses."

Emily cracked a smile. "Perhaps one day we can chat about henna," she said in a low voice, "but for the moment I prefer to keep my secrets."

"I have several of my own, as well. I do understand."

Considering what she did know of Jenny Martine, of her mastery of several languages and the occasional references Diane made to her dearest friend's "adventures" in Europe during the Peninsular War, Emily didn't doubt that for a moment. She did wonder, however, if any of Jenny's secrets involved murder. But that was one conversation she meant never to have.

A week roving across Shropshire had made one thing very clear to Nathaniel Stokes: Rachel Newbury knew how not to be found.

None of the Marquis of Ebberling's servants knew where she might have gone. None of them even knew who or where her parents might be. The letter of recommendation she'd produced upon applying for employment at Ebberling Manor proved to be false; at the least *Debrett's Peerage* had no listing for a Lady Sebret. The fact that altering one letter of this mysterious previous employer's name made it read as *Secret* didn't escape him, either.

"Was your trip successful, my lord?" his valet asked, as Nate took a seat on the edge of his bed to pull off his boots. The button fell to the floor, spinning on its end, and he stepped on the damned thing to silence it.

"No, Franks, it was not," he stated, flexing his tired feet. However necessary he'd come to think of his assumed frailties, another day or two without resting his foot and his limp would have become real. "You servants chat with each other, do you not?"

"We do all dine together, generally."

"You know about each other's families, relatives, places of birth, yes?"

The valet continued emptying out Nate's travel valise. "For the most part, yes. Some are more reticent than others, and I can't say I know—or remember— every detail, but we do talk."

"And what would you say if one of your fellows never divulged anything of her past? Never said a word about anything that occurred before the moment she took the position?"

"I would say that perhaps she was fleeing from something unpleasant, or sad." Franks scowled briefly. "Or illegal. In that instance it would be the butler's duty to discover if a crime had been committed, because that would reflect badly on the entire household."

"That's what I thought." Ebberling's butler hadn't known anything useful about Miss Newbury other than to second the marquis's statements that the woman had been quite young, pretty, well educated, and rather haughty. *High in the instep,* as the butler had declared.

"Will you be staying in this evening, my lord?"

He shook himself, belatedly removing his spectacles

and tossing them onto the bed. "Yes, I believe I will. Inform Mrs. Blanchard, will you?"

"Certainly, my l—"

"There you are." A warm male voice came from the doorway.

Nate turned his head, pushing back against the instinct to reach for the pistol in his bedstand. "Laurie." *Damnation.* He'd completely forgotten about his brother's impending arrival. It wouldn't do if he actually became as absentminded as he pretended.

"I expected a dressing-down when I arrived," the nineteen-year-old drawled, strolling into the room. "Had a defiant speech memorized and everything. Didn't expect you wouldn't even be in London to hear it."

Clenching his jaw, Nate sent a glance at the valet. "That will be all, Franks."

"Very good, my lord."

"You were on one of your hunts, weren't you?" Laurence Stokes asked, shutting the door behind the servant. "What is it this time? A missing ring? Some lordling's stray dog? You're an earl now, you know. Your new peers will only look down their noses at you if you allow them to hire you to find their bits and baubles."

"Are you certain now is the best time for you to be criticizing how I choose to occupy myself?" Nate countered. "Unless you're hoping I'll be so busy with defending my honor that I'll forget why you're here."

Laurence waved a dismissive hand at him and flopped into one of the chairs placed before the empty fireplace. "I learned a long time ago that you never forget anything, Nate. You've a library for a brain, with every topic neatly indexed for later reference."

"And you have a sieve for a brain, retaining nothing

but absolute nonsense." Nate stood, but with his tired foot he didn't feel much like pacing. Instead he sank into the chair placed at right angles to his brother's. "In your letter you said you had a disagreement with one of your professors. At least tell me it was something academic and not a moral clash over whether you should be allowed to have a whore in your rooms or not."

Laurie wrinkled his nose. "Do you have any idea how tiresome it is to have you for a brother?" he finally said, a sigh in his voice. "However clever I may think I'm being, you simply cut a swath through all the cobwebs of deceit, put your hands on your hips, and bellow out the facts."

Ignoring the fact that he hadn't bellowed anything, and that evidently his brother *had* been caught with a chit in his rooms, Nate cocked his head. " 'Cobwebs of deceit'?" he repeated.

"I was going to say *clever cobwebs,* but I'd already used *clever,* and you would have said I was repeating myself." Laurence thudded a fist into his thigh. "I know you don't want me here, and honestly I'd rather be back at Oxford with my friends, but I made a mistake. I'm sorry."

"How long is this punishment?"

"Yours, or mine?" Laurence shrugged. "The term's nearly over. I'll miss a fortnight, and the final exams."

For a long moment Nathaniel gazed at his brother. People said they looked a great deal alike, but other than having the same green eyes, he didn't see it. Laurie's hair was darker, more of a solid brown than his own. Nate was taller by two or three inches, but he remained uncertain how long that might be so. No one, however, had ever said they behaved alike. And for that, he was generally grateful. "Being excluded from final exams isn't a first offense, Laurence," he finally said. Ten years separated them, but most of the time it felt more like a hundred.

"I—"

"I hope you realize this isn't a holiday. You're not going to spend your days at Gentleman Jackson's or Haymarket or Tattersall's, and you damned well aren't going to any clubs or soirees."

"So you mean to keep me locked up here? In the cellar, I presume?"

"You're heir to an earldom now, and you're going to be more prepared for it than I was."

"Prepared how?" his brother asked, green eyes narrowing suspiciously.

"To begin with, I'm going to show you all of the accounts and ledgers. And then you can balance them."

"On my head?"

"Very amusing. And yet I'm not at all moved toward sympathy."

"Nate, that isn't—don't you have people who do that? Cousin Gerard must have, because he couldn't do a sum to save his life."

"I do hope that wasn't a jest aimed at our dear late cousin's unfortunate and untimely demise, Laurence."

His brother flushed. "No, of course not. He drowned, anyway. That had nothing to do with ledgers. Unless he threw himself into the lake to avoid balancing them."

Nathaniel stood. "And now I'm even less sympathetic toward you. I've been the Earl of Westfall for two years. It's time you learned something useful. Let's begin with the accounts of three years ago, shall we?"

"Nate, I was only attempting to keep you from yelling at me for the chit in my rooms. Don't be a bloody axeman."

Hm. That actually seemed a rather apt description. But no one had ever asked him how he meant to deal with inheriting either an earldom or a younger brother, and he was expected to manage both. "It'll be good for you. You shouldn't have to rely on someone in your employ to tell you your own finances. Now come along. We might as well get started."

With a curse, Laurie clomped to his feet. "You know, suddenly I'm not so grateful that Gerard's inheritance got you this position, or that it paid for me to be at Oxford in the first place." He sidestepped on the way to the door and snatched up Nate's spectacles. "And I don't think you are, either," he said, putting them on. "Hah. Glass, just as I thought. Why are you pretending to be addlepated again? You resigned from the service, you said."

"I'm not being addlepated; I'm being absentminded. And I did resign from the service. I wouldn't lie to you about that."

And whatever duties had pushed him to leave Wellington, part of him had been relieved to finally set all the lies and deceits and disguises aside. In truth, he'd never expected to live long enough to retire from that particular service. At the same time, there were bits of it that he missed—the thrill of knowing more about everyone else in the room than they would ever know about him, the satisfaction he found in weeding through piles of nonsense and distractions to find one true thread of information.

But it had also meant other things: pretending friendships with people he despised, or worse, with people he might otherwise have liked. Lying about who and what he was in so many different ways that on occasion he'd been hard-pressed to remember the truth. Distancing himself from his emotions as well as from his brother, even after their mother's unexpected passing, in order to protect both of them. "You do remember that you're not to discuss my service," he said belatedly.

"Oh, you made that very clear."

"Laurie, there are lives I took, and others I destroyed. And those people still have families and friends. If they ever learned that I had anything to do with it, that I was anything other than a fool seeking to preserve antique tomes in the middle of a war, I—"

"I know, I know." His brother's shoulders sagged. "I've never said anything, and I never will."

"Good."

For a moment they walked down the hallway toward his office in silence. "Nate?"

"What is it?"

"Could I perhaps help you find whatever it is you're hunting for?"

A shudder ran through Nate before he could suppress it. The idea of setting his brother toward that life . . . "No. Discretion is required, and it's *my* hobby, as you call it."

The expression he glimpsed on Laurence's face wasn't the annoyed, thwarted one he'd expected, however. For that bare moment his brother had looked hurt. Truly disappointed. Nate took a slow breath. "Why do you want to help? I've heard you several times say I shouldn't be stooping to fetch and carry for my fellows."

"I don't know. I just thought . . ." Laurie trailed off. "Never mind. Where are the damned ledgers?"

Nate stopped. "You just thought what, Laurie?"

"I just thought nothing. That's what I do, isn't it?"

Whether he'd spent much time around his brother lately or not, Nathaniel did recognize a plea for sympathy when he heard one. "If you want me to trust you with anything," he said, shoving open his office door and gesturing for his brother to precede him into the room, "it's not going to be out of pity. You tied your own noose and stuck your own head into it. People always do."

And that would be how he'd find Rachel Newbury, as well. Everyone made errors. He merely happened to be very good at spotting them.

"Well, you're people," Laurie countered, sitting behind the desk when Nate pulled out the chair for him. "At least I think you are. What noose have you stuck your head into?"

"If you think for a moment that I mean to lay out all my mistakes for you to use against me later, you're even more daft than I thought previously. Top drawer, bottom ledger."

"Then it would seem that the trick is to keep your mistakes private."

"That would be a beginning, I suppose. Open it up, Laurie. For God's sake."

His brother, though, wasn't looking at the ledger on the desk. His attention was on something else in the desk's top drawer. Swiftly Nathaniel ran through what he'd left in there: pen nubs, paper, a ruler, pencils, a knife for sharpen—

"What the devil is this?" Laurence exclaimed, pulling out a card. " 'As a member in good standing of The Tantalus Club, you are cordially invited to our annual wine-tasting event on . . .' " His brother looked up. "You belong to the bloody Tantalus Club?"

Damnation. "Yes. It's a—"

"I want to go."

"No."

"Marty Gayle's uncle took him there last semester, and he still hasn't stopped talking about it. I'm a year older than Gayle. Is it true none of the ladies wear anything?"

"What? No. It's not a bawdy house, Laurie. It's a gentlemen's club."

"Run by the prettiest chits in London! And Marty says they choose men they like and invite them upstairs. Have you been upstairs?"

Nate cleared his throat. Upstairs. Sex meant intimacy and secrets, neither of which he felt comfortable sharing. The last woman he'd slept with—God, had it been two years ago, now?—he'd handed over to the army for attempting to sell the pillow-talk confidences she coaxed over to Bonaparte. "Stop yammering, will you?" he said, when he realized Laurie was staring at him. "You sound like a donkey. You're being punished, and you're learning how to do household accounts. Open the ledger."

Laurence planted his elbows on said account book to lean forward over the desk. "You have been upstairs, then! Was it glorious? Bedouin draperies and pillows? Who was she? They say that every female there is scandalous and highborn and beautiful."

"No, I have not been upstairs at the Tantalus, for God's sake. I've visited twice. And they aren't all highborn. They are all well educated and attractive. And you're still not going."

With a scowl Laurie sat back in the chair again and flung open the ledger. "Well, I wish that men had a club where they could go work, so I wouldn't have to put up with being bullied by you."

"They do. It's called the army."

Nate sat in the deep windowsill. Hm. The Tantalus Club did have a reputation for accepting well-educated women who'd been forced for one reason or another to leave more acceptable circumstances. He doubted

Rachel Newbury would settle in a place so public after committing a robbery and a murder, but it provided more of a starting place than he'd had five minutes ago—and he'd certainly had no luck tracking her in Shropshire. Someone might know something, anyway.

It actually had a certain poetical logic to it. As a pretty and well-educated chit, she'd fit in well there. As a haughty female, however, she'd likely turn up her nose at finding employment by flirting with men. Still, he'd on occasion found information at the least likely of places. And The Tantalus Club might be *un*likely, but it certainly wasn't the *least* likely lead he'd ever had.

"I've changed my mind," he said, pushing upright again. "Go dress for luncheon."

Laurie shot to his feet. "At the Tantalus?"

"Yes, at the Tantalus. If I see one instance of you drooling or leering or doing anything unseemly, I'll drag you out of there by your ear. Is that clear?"

"Absolutely." Laurie paused halfway through the doorway. "Is this about your hobby?"

"Possibly. If you can behave yourself today, perhaps I'll tell you something about it."

Ah, he would likely regret giving in, but he'd learned a very long time ago to accept inspiration from any source available. And that now included his brother, evidently.

Chapter Three

H e's here," Lucille Hampton said, bending down to whisper in Emily's ear.

Emily looked up, abrupt uneasiness filtering down her spine. "Who's here?"

"My beau."

Stifling an annoyed sigh and at the same time immensely relieved, Emily returned to next week's work schedule. "Who is it this week?"

"The Earl of Westfall. I daresay he's as handsome as Lord Haverly."

"Is he the one with the spectacles?" the other lady at the table, the unlikely named Miss April March, asked, smiling. "He asked for tea the other day, took a drink, and said, 'Blast it, I meant coffee.'"

"I never said he was brilliant," Lucille countered. "Only handsome. And wealthy."

"Have a care about how you refer to the club's members, both of you," Emily commented. "If Diane hears you swooning over any of our guests while you're working, she'll have you scrubbing pots in the kitchen."

As if on cue, Diane, Lady Haybury, walked into the upstairs common room all the Tantalus ladies and the large, formidable Helpful Men shared. The marchioness, in a gown so black it shimmered, strolled toward the table Emily had commandeered. "Good afternoon, Emily."

"Diane. Lady H." The other ladies scattered with such speed that the marchioness lifted an eyebrow.

"That was . . . interesting."

Emily grinned. "Lucille's after a new beau, and doesn't want you forbidding her to pursue anyone."

"I have no objection at all, as long as she treats all our members equally while inside the club proper." She sank onto the bench across the luncheon table from Emily. "Who is it, anyway?"

"This time? Lord Westfall. Evidently she thinks he's dim enough to fall for her charms and sweep her into a life of luxury."

Diane shrugged. "It's happened before. More often than I would have expected, actually." She smiled. "I can't imagine that I've been too cynical in my life, but there you have it. Some fairy tales do come true."

Personally Emily wouldn't wish the prattling, preening Lucille on anyone, but if Miss Hampton was after Westfall, then Emily would leave him be. Despite the fact that handsome and dim was just her type of gentleman, and that if she were ever to write a handbook on how to win a man's compliance and affections it would have one chapter, and one word in that chapter. *Sex.* "Jaded or not, your degree of cynicism seems to have served you well," she said aloud. "And I assume you're here to see the schedule? I thought we were meeting at two o'clock."

The marchioness waved a hand at her. "We were. I'm early. Haybury wants to take me driving this afternoon, annoying man." The slight smile she gave spoke of an entirely different emotion, and Emily couldn't help grinning in response.

"I thought you looked exceptionally stunning today. Perfect for an outing."

"I'll likely be miserably warm, but I'm finding that while previously I was horribly scandalous to continue wearing widow's black even after remarrying, now I'm known for the convention. Or unconvention. Who knows? I may have to begin wearing white simply to be noticed again."

With a laugh, Emily turned the book in which she'd been writing next week's work schedules around for her employer to see. "As long as you continue running The Tantalus Club, I don't think you'll have to worry about going unnoticed."

"Well, that's very kind of you to say," her employer replied. Still chuckling, Diane took the schedule and looked through it. "Are you certain you wish to pair Marianne Stuart with Lucille? I have to admit, while our members love Lucille's . . . enthusiasm, I'm not convinced she should be training anyone."

"At this moment I think Marianne would faint if anyone glanced in her direction, much less if they leered at her. And if nothing else, Lucille does enjoy being the center of attention." She hesitated, disliking this part even if it did make her more vital to her employers. "I can check in on her from time to time if you wish."

Lady Haybury eyed her for a moment with that unsettling way she had, that expression that left her seeming much older and wiser than her twenty-six years of life should have granted her. Would have granted her, under better circumstances. Emily might have been the same age as her employer, but there were times she felt decades younger—and more when she felt centuries older.

"That would be helpful," the marchioness finally

said, lowering her gaze to the schedule again. "Most of the peerage is supposedly at Tattersall's today for the horse sales, so we're evidently going to be a bit light on membership. Jenny will be supervising tonight, and I won't be back until later."

With a nod, attempting to hide her reluctance, Emily handed over a second sheet of paper. "According to Charity, she cannot continue purchasing peaches piecemeal if everyone is going to insist on recommending the peach tarts. This is a list of the three farms nearest London where we might make a contract for the fruits."

"Ah, contracts for peaches. Another of the things I never foresaw when I began all this." She looked at the paper. "Was this Miss Green's idea?"

"Yes. I've never seen a cook—chef, rather—who has such a head for numbers." Diane had hired Charity Green only a month ago, but the menu and meals had never been more praised, and the Tantalus was already nearly as famous for its food as it was for its employees. "Shall I give the task to Jenny? She does seem to have a talent for convincing merchants of the true definition of fair pricing."

This time Diane laughed. "The penalty for attempting to overcharge a gaggle of females—a visit from Genevieve Martine. But actually I think Oliver and I will go. It will keep him from whatever deviousness he had planned for the afternoon, anyway."

"Nothing can keep me from that." The Marquis of Haybury walked up to the table and took the seat beside his wife. "And where are we going?" Diane might claim to speak for Oliver Warren, but there was nothing in his steely gray eyes or lean, hard frame that spoke of any kind of subservience. Whatever had passed between the two of them had been resolved to their mutual satisfaction, but the path there had been littered with everything from blackmail to pistols—and Emily was quite aware that she didn't know the half of it.

"To negotiate for peaches, out in the country," Diane answered.

"So this is what my life has become. Peach treaties." He sent his wife a sardonic grin. "Could be worse, I suppose, though I had a thoroughly devious afternoon of naked swimming planned. Carriage, or horseback?"

"Horseback, definitely."

The marquis stood again, putting his hands on his wife's shoulders and leaning in to kiss her. The marquis and marchioness weren't precisely known for avoiding public displays of affection, but Emily looked away, anyway. She'd had a handful of lovers over the past few years, but she didn't kiss them—and that was why. A kiss wasn't about sex; a kiss was about affection. And Lord and Lady Haybury fiercely adored each other.

"Emily, don't forget that you're to oversee luncheon today," Diane continued, rising and lightly shoving her husband toward the door. "I apologize that we've been asking you to supervise so much lately."

A responding chill swept down Emily's spine at hearing her duties spoken aloud. "It's no problem. I'm happy to do my share." It wasn't anything new; she went into the public areas of the Tantalus at least once a week. That didn't mean, however, that she enjoyed it.

"Let's be off, then. Negotiating peach treaties is a delicate matter, I'm certain," Haybury said.

Diane made a face as they walked toward the door. "Are you going to say that all afternoon?"

"Very likely."

As they left, Emily glanced at the clock. She needed to go downstairs. Thankfully the luncheon rush only lasted a few hours, and then Jenny would step in before the evening setting with its presoiree and posttheater rushes that would last until well after midnight.

Once she'd pinned the Thursday-through-Monday schedule onto the cork-covered wall in the common room, she descended the stairs to the main floor. A narrow, private corridor ran down the east side of the gaming and dining rooms, with doors leading into each of them. They allowed the female employees to come and go with an added air of mystery, and they also provided a swift escape should any of the myriad male members become . . . unpleasant. She lingered for a moment behind the door opening into Demeter, the largest dining room.

Emily shook herself. Over the past few years she'd learned just how little attention people paid to one another, and precisely how little she had to gain by worrying over what other people did or thought. She'd survived, managed to find employment at The Tantalus Club, because of no one but herself. And as for what had happened before then, and what happened outside these walls, she didn't care. Not an ounce, not unless it concerned her; which it wouldn't, because she never stepped through the front entryway.

She did need to step through this door and into the dining room, however. Putting the cool smile on her face that tended to keep men at a distance, she took a breath, pushed down the latch, and stepped inside.

Every other Wednesday was designated as a ladies' day at the Tantalus, because Lady Haybury had found that women enjoyed gambling as much as any man, and they had many fewer places where they could indulge themselves. This Wednesday, however, the Demeter room was stuffed to the rafters with gentlemen. So much for the distraction of Tattersall's.

Thirty tables lay spread about the room, with the most coveted seats in the middle of the mass and beneath the trio of tall windows that overlooked the club's garden. The Demeter was the largest room in the club; evidently when gentlemen dined they preferred to do so in view of their fellows. The gaming rooms—the Persephone, the Psyche, and the Ariadne—were slightly more intimate, but of course there were more of them. Back three years ago when the club had opened she'd expected the least used room to be the Athena, but these days even the library had become a well-populated place for smoking cigars and reading in relative quiet.

At the moment, however, she didn't have time to reflect on the surprising success of the Tantalus. Lucille stood half draped over one of the tables, while Marianne Stuart stood just behind Miss Hampton, a mortified expression on her pretty, pale face. *Damnation,* Emily thought, and squared her shoulders as she walked forward.

"Miss Hampton, are you well?" she asked, stopping on the far side of the table.

Lucille straightened, a deep smile on her face. "I was just examining Lord Westfall's new watch fob," she returned.

Stifling her irritation, Emily faced the seated man to her left. "I apologize, Lord Westfall. Might I offer you and your guest a complementary bottle of wine?"

Behind a pair of metal-rimmed spectacles, light green eyes met hers. The eyes, set nicely beneath a disheveled head of tawny brown hair and above a straight nose and a mouth that briefly quirked in a quick, dismissive smile, blinked. "Hm? Miss Hampton has declared that watch fobs are a hobby of hers. I collect tomes, myself, but fobs do take less space, I assume."

"I would imagine so," Emily returned, maintaining her own polite smile. He couldn't possibly be thick enough not to realize that Lucille had literally been throwing herself at him. If he was, though, then good. The Tantalus thrived in part because of its policy of hands off toward the female employees. The Tantalus girls, as they were known, were allowed to have callers upstairs, as long as it was firstly the lady's idea and secondly it didn't interfere with her duties. Flinging herself bodily across a man who simply wished to eat a meal was unacceptable.

"Don't mind him," Westfall's companion commented, standing. He held out his hand. "Laurence Stokes," he announced. "Westfall's charming younger brother."

Emily shook the offered hand. "Emily Portsman, Tantalus girl."

The two men did look a great deal alike now that she considered it, though clearly Laurence hadn't yet filled into the lean, hard frame his brother quite handsomely occupied. He did seem to have more wit and charm than his older brother, however. Mix the two of them together, the one's appearance and maturity with the other's easy smile, and the resulting creation would have been very enticing, indeed.

"This place is bl—"

"Laurie," the earl broke in, scowling.

"I mean to say it's . . . blistering marvelous," the younger Stokes said, his cheeks flushing a little. "They talk about it all the way in Oxford, you know."

With a smile, Emily retrieved her hand. "Only as far as Oxford? We shall have to work harder." She faced the earl again. "Would you prefer white or red wine?"

"Red, if you please," he returned, pushing his sliding spectacles up the bridge of his nose. "Though it isn't necessary."

"Which makes it all the more appreciated, I hope," she replied. Emily took Lucille by the hand. "Marianne will see to you for a moment, my lord. I need to borrow Miss Hampton."

Without waiting for a reply, she led the resisting Lucille to the dining room's privacy door and pulled her through. Once the door was safely shut, Lucille jerked her arm free. "What the devil was that for?" she protested. "I was near to asking him upstairs!"

"Yes, and everyone in the Demeter—if not all of Mayfair—knew it."

"You have men up to your rooms, Emily. I have as much right to do it as you do."

"Yes, you do. What you don't have is the right to throw yourself all over someone so that if he declines, you'll both look like fools. Don't be so obvious. And remember where you are. This is not a bawdy house. If you don't wish to be prodded and groped simply for walking by, pray extend the same courtesy to the men who pay for a membership here."

Lucille screwed her face into a grimace. "Sophia and Camille both netted husbands from among the membership. Why can't I do the same?"

Inwardly Emily sighed. She couldn't even imagine setting all her hopes on something so unlikely—or even assuming that someone else could possibly do better for her than she could in looking after her own interests. But that was her, and Lucille was definitely . . . Lucille.

"Perhaps the trick was that neither of them was actually looking to make a match," she said aloud. "Don't embarrass the Tantalus, Lucille. For all our sakes." To herself she could make the argument that no woman came to the Tantalus because she was looking for a husband; she came here because there was nowhere else to go but the alleyways. Lucille didn't want to hear that, though, so she didn't bother saying it.

"I'm using honey to catch flies," Lucille said stubbornly.

"A little less honey, and in more moderation. And less desperation."

From Miss Hampton's offended look, Emily decided she likely shouldn't have said that last bit. But it might have been worse; she might have said that the odds of Lucille finding a husband here were as poor as her own. Now that would have been cruel.

"And Marianne will be seeing to Westfall's table for the duration of luncheon," she finished.

"Oh, you can't do that! Marianne will faint or spill something. She can't even set down a plate without blushing."

Lucille did make a valid point. "Then *I* will see to the earl's table," Emily countered, sighing. Little as she liked the idea, it was better than allowing either bosoms or someone else's luncheon to end up in the earl's lap. "Let's get back to work now, shall we?"

"Close your mouth, Laurie. You look like a drowning trout."

Nathaniel's brother leaned forward across the small table. "But that chit was throwing herself at you," he whispered. "Nearly fell into your lap. I've dreamed about that sort of thing, you know."

Yes, she had, and no, he hadn't entirely appreciated it. It wasn't that he didn't think her attractive—all the ladies of The Tantalus Club were more than passing pretty—but in his life he'd become accustomed to a bit more subtlety than that. The fewer people who knew what he was about, the better, and having a woman drape herself across him left little to anyone's imagination including, clearly, his brother's. "That's generally frowned upon here," he said aloud, returning to his mutton pie. "As you saw by the way the other lady swooped down upon us."

"But Marty Gayle said the ladies could ask you upstairs!"

Laurence sounded so disappointed it was almost amusing. And this little tête-à-tête with Lucille Hampton would have been more interesting if Miss Portsman hadn't swooped in to put an end to what was becoming a very telling line of questions about the club's female employees. "They can, Laurie. But as I'm not going anywhere during luncheon and while I'm accompanied by my younger brother, it's just as well, don't you think?"

"That's because you treat everything like it's some sort of strategy in a chess game," his brother returned. "Sometimes it's only about wanting something and taking it."

To give himself a moment, Nathaniel lifted his glass of wine and examined the deep red color. "You're a bit young to be so mercenary, aren't you?" he finally asked, nodding as Miss Portsman returned with his complementary bottle.

"*I'm* mercenary?" Laurie shot back, giving an exasperated scowl. "You're the one who only brought me here to figure out which of these chits stole some bauble or other, aren't you?"

Bloody hell. He could have done without any of the chits knowing he was here for anything other than luncheon with his idiot brother. Nathaniel glanced up at Miss Portsman, to find her oval-shaped brown eyes a touch wider than they had been a moment earlier. Her lips closed, then curved in a soft smile. "Shall I pour for you, Lord Westfall, or do you wish me to keep the bottle here for your next visit?"

She was exceptionally pretty, he decided. More worth a trip upstairs than that obvious Lucille chit. Belatedly Nate remembered to push his spectacles up his nose. "Hm? Oh. My next visit, I think. We're nearly finished here, aren't we, Laurie?"

"But—"

"I do wonder if you would ask Miss Hampton back again, though," he continued over Laurence's protest. "There was truly no offense taken."

Her smile stiffened just a touch. "Certainly, my lord."

The moment she turned away, he reached across the table to tap his brother on the knuckles. "As Miss Hampton approaches, say that again," he murmured.

"Say what again?"

"The bit about me bringing you here to figure out who stole something," he said quickly, spotting Lucille Hampton's bouncing brunette hair as she practically skipped in his direction. "Be certain she hears you."

His brother frowned, but turned his gaze to his glass until Lucille was only a table away. "We're here so you can figure out which of these lovely ladies made off with a treasure, aren't you?" he uttered in a stiff, too-loud voice.

Oh, brilliant, that. If Nathaniel had had any illusions about his brother's talent for acting, say, that would have slaughtered them. "Hush," he said aloud, offering Lucille a smile. "Hello, my dear."

Her mobile brow furrowed into a deep scowl. "You aren't with Bow Street, are you?" she asked. "Because we aren't thieves, here. We're independent ladies of good education who simply had nowhere else to go."

Swiftly Nate removed his glasses and made a show of cleaning the lenses with his napkin before he replaced them again. "Nothing of the sort, Miss Hampton. People do occasionally task me with finding things, but I am here for your delightful luncheon and to give my brother here a chance at gaining a bit of Town bronze."

"Bloody snake," Laurie muttered under his breath, but Nathaniel ignored him. As he continued to chat with the mollified Lucille, his attention was on the lady halfway across the room.

Unlike the chatty Miss Hampton, Miss Portsman hadn't asked what the devil he was about, why he would be here of all places looking for thieves. There was, of course, the slight chance that she hadn't heard Laurie's comment, but he didn't think that was the case. In his experience, people didn't ask questions for two reasons: either they didn't want to attract attention to themselves, or they already knew the answers.

"How long have you worked here, Lucille?" he continued conversationally, while he urged Laurence to request one of the cook's rather famous peach tarts.

"Nearly two years now," she responded promptly. "Not since the beginning of the Tantalus, but near enough."

"Are there still any ladies here who've been employed by Lady Haybury since the very first?" he pursued, recalling that the club had opened just over three years ago—at nearly the same time Miss Newbury had fled Shropshire.

"Certainly. Emily, for one. And Madeline over there seating Lord Benwick. Half a dozen more, but the ones who've been here longer like to work in the evenings or the gaming rooms, mostly."

"Why is that?"

She favored him with a charming smile. "Because the gentlemen have had more to drink, and they're more generous with their tips. And because if a fellow were to strike their fancy, it's easier to become better acquainted."

"I think I may faint," Laurie whispered hoarsely, tugging at his cravat.

"Well, then," Nathaniel continued, "perhaps my brother and I will return here for dinner."

"And perhaps I'll trade a shift with someone so I can serve you dinner." With a very unsubtle wink, Lucille pranced away again to offer Lord Benwick a look at the luncheon menu and her own barely covered charms.

"Please tell me you weren't jesting just then," his brother hissed, leaning across the table. "Because I may have to bludgeon you if you were."

"And you think I'd have you accompany me upstairs if I went? Don't be ridiculous, Laurie. You wagged your tongue about my business, and I attempted to use your blunder to my advantage."

"Bastard."

"Mm-hm. If you want to assist me, you're going to have to be more subtle. Now shut up and eat your tart. I'm observing."

His brother might have muttered something else, but at least he was quiet about it. Miss Portsman summoned Lucille to her side and said something that had her brunette-haired companion glancing back in his direction and grinning. It was about him, then, or more likely, his conversation.

Once Emily Portsman returned to her task of overseeing the room, he settled in to watch her. With her pretty, straight-looking brown hair with its whisper of red in the chandelier light, she didn't quite match Ebberling's description of his blonde-headed former governess. Her brown eyes were a match, but as for the rest, he wasn't certain. Not yet. In the sketch he'd done according to the marquis's direction, Rachel Newbury was taller and thinner, her chin longer and her eyes narrower and more cold. But while it was too early to wager that Miss Portsman was his quarry, or even that she knew someone who might in fact be the chit he pursued, he had a hunch that she knew something about something. Or at the very least, that she possessed a secret. He loved uncovering secrets.

His gaze lowered to her hips. Secrets weren't the only thing he would be inclined to enjoy where Emily Portsman was concerned. Nate stirred, sitting forward just a little before he caught himself lusting. He blinked. Generally, uncovering secrets meant a different kind of enjoyment. A more cerebral satisfaction.

Hm. Perhaps it had been too long since he'd been truly challenged, and he was overly anticipating the chase. Or it could be that two years of celibacy had just made themselves felt. Whatever it was, at this moment it centered around her. Just how interesting this line of questions could be—well, that was up to her.

When she circled past his table, he lifted his hand. "Miss Portsman. I changed my mind. Would you fetch me that bottle, after all?"

She nodded. "Of course."

"Are we working again?" Laurence asked, wolfing down the last few bites of his peach tart. "Am I supposed to do anything?"

"Yes. Go wander the gaming rooms." Nate pulled five quid from his pocket. "Lose some blunt."

Laurie shot to his feet. "I apologize for the bastard comment."

"That's premature. You have thirty minutes."

As his brother strode off looking precisely like the

green boy he was, Miss Portsman approached again. "Here you are, my lord."

"Would you uncork it, please?"

"Cert—"

"And sit with me while it breathes. My brother's gone to try his hand at faro or something, and I'll look foolish if I sit here talking to myself."

For a moment he held his breath, wondering whether she would state that she was on duty and had other things to see to, or whether she would sit and ask him his business. Everything meant something; deciphering the whats and hows and whens was the interesting—and more difficult—bit.

She sent a glance about the room. "I can sit for a moment," she said, pulling out his brother's vacated chair and sinking into it. "Most of the rush has finished with."

So at the least she was curious. He refused to read more into the equation than yet existed; that folly had cost men their lives. Information was just that, until it became more. And it was only the need for information that made him note that she smelled of lemons. "Lucille says you've been employed at the Tantalus from the beginning."

Would she retreat, or attack, or deflect? Miss Portsman glanced down for a moment, then smiled up at him. "I have, my lord. Nearly three years now. But if you've been encouraging Lucille merely for the purpose of asking about me, well, you'll injure the poor girl's heart." She rested both elbows on the table and sank her chin onto her downturned hands. "She thinks every man who looks at her will offer marriage and sweep her away to his castle."

"And what do you think?"

"I think I'm happy to avoid sweeping of any kind."

Her smile deepened. "So why were you asking about me? Did you hope for an invitation upstairs?"

Logic and intelligence and a fair portion of good instincts mixed with luck had always served Nate Stokes quite well. At this moment, however, he knew it wasn't any of those things that make his cock jump and come to life.

She wanted to distract him. Whether it was on her own behalf or that of one of her fellow Tantalus girls, he was more interested in discovering if this was a bluff or not, and in how far she would go to protect whatever secret this was. She was likely to find that he had no difficulty with using his own skills to get answers. Especially when the package in which they were wrapped was as delicious as she was.

Circles in circles in circles. If his life had ever been as simple as seeing someone he wanted and taking her, he couldn't remember it. And it shouldn't happen today, either, however gullible she was meant to think him. Or however attractive he found her. Unless he could make his mind stop spinning its wheels for a moment and simply do what his body wanted.

"'Upstairs'? The thought might have crossed my mind," he returned. "In passing, of course."

"Oh. Has it passed away, then, or does it linger?"

"It lingers. It has a great deal of stamina, actually."

Even as he spoke, he was quite aware that his nether regions were attempting to take over the conversation. He clenched his jaw. His brain made an effort to step in again, though it unhelpfully pointed out that if she was suspicious he might be pursuing her or someone she cared about, she would either attempt to keep her distance from him, or wait for a vulnerable moment and stab him in the throat. But it wouldn't be the first time someone had attempted either of those responses, and he wanted Emily Portsman.

"Does it now?" she asked in an intimate murmur. "I happen to be off duty in twenty minutes, if you'd care to make your case." A furrow lined her brow. "Though what are you going to do with your little brother?"

How determined was she to act on her innuendos? He would follow the steps to this waltz only as long as she played the music, after all—and whatever he privately, secretly, wanted. "I'll send him home in the carriage."

"Then meet me by that door," she said, as she straightened one elegant finger to point toward one of the club's famed privacy doors, also known as "the gates to heaven," as he recalled. "In twenty minutes."

As she rose, he reached for any morsel that would make this a part of his investigation. Something to prove to himself that somewhere in the last two minutes he hadn't lost his mind. "What of Miss Hampton? We don't wish to injure her heart."

Her smile slid into something far more wicked and intimate. "Shall I ask her to join us, then?"

That answered one thing: The odds of Miss Portsman being the high-in-the-instep Miss Newbury were considerably diminished. And he was supposed to be absentminded and a bit dull, damn it all—though truthfully, *she* intrigued him far more than did the determined Miss Hampton. Why that should be, he wasn't entirely certain, because on the surface both women had suggested the same thing. None of this, though, was about the surface. "I—no. I think, ah, the two of us could make do. This time, at least."

"Good."

Business and pleasure so rarely mixed, in his experience. And if she meant to do him harm, well, it was a risk he was willing to take. He would have an answer for his investigation in that case—though if it came to a battle for survival the odds of her making it back into Lord Ebberling's hands would be considerably diminished. Finishing off his glass of wine, Nathaniel stood and went to find Laurie. His brother would more than likely call him names again, but as he had just experienced the rarest of things, he didn't much care which epithets Laurence showered him with. Because he'd just been surprised.

Chapter Four

Doing everything she could not to hurry her steps, Emily returned to her post at the lectern by the main doorway. Was the Earl of Westfall the reason for that whisper of uneasiness she'd felt curl up her spine this morning?

Of course, that was likely utter nonsense. She hadn't believed in portents or signs from above since she'd been five years old. But the younger brother had mentioned something about searching the Tantalus for thieves, and that had been enough to begin her heart pounding. If this wasn't about her, that was well and good, but clearly it was about someone, and quite possibly someone *here*. None of the Tantalus girls, as the club's members had taken to calling them, were unblemished angels. What they were, however, were her friends. Her odd little scandalous family. And no harm was allowed to come to any of them while she had any say in the matter.

If protecting them meant tricking a handsome, slightly dull earl into thinking she meant to let him bed her in order to discover what, precisely, he was after, well, she'd invited less attractive men to her room and actually slept with them. She sent a glance toward his table, but he'd already left the Demeter room, no doubt to dispose of his brother. Dull, handsome, and with poor vision. If he wasn't present to make trouble, if she was overreacting—which she desperately hoped she was—he might well have been perfect for her. She sighed, attempting to ignore the warmth spreading through her. It had been a while, but this was about discovering what he knew. Suspicion and sex made poor bedfellows.

As she finished totaling up the number of luncheon guests and the amount of alcohol consumed, she caught sight of Lucille looking hopefully in the direction of the Persephone, the nearest gaming room. She'd never made a habit of poaching men from her companions— heaven knew there were more than enough to go around—and this wasn't poaching, precisely. It would certainly appear like it to Lucille, though.

If she'd discovered one thing in the past few years, it was that men enjoyed talking about themselves, par- ticularly when they were relaxed, well complimented, and distracted. That had been a happy coincidence, though, as mostly what she'd been after with her bed companions was—well, she wasn't certain what it was, but she did enjoy men and their companionship. Gener- ally, and under a very narrow set of conditions.

Taking a breath, Emily walked up to Lucille for the third time that afternoon. "I need a word with you," she muttered, taking Miss Hampton's arm.

"What now? I've barely spoken to anyone. Except for Westfall, but he invited me back to chat with him."

"Yes, I know. I . . . Lord Westfall is going upstairs. With me."

Lucille scowled, her face darkening. "That is not fair, Emily. I told you I meant to pursue him. How could you?"

"He asked," she returned, though at best he'd intimated, and after she'd directly invited. "You said he mentioned looking into a theft. I need to know if one of our friends is in trouble."

"Then just ask whom he's after."

"I can't do that, and you know it. I need to be a little subtle, for heaven's sake." Even if it didn't concern her, but especially if it did.

"I don't like it. You're stealing him."

"I am not. You may have him back tomorrow, unless I discover that we need to keep him away from the club." She paused. "Would you wish to be the one to go up to Lady H and say you've been intimate with a man and now you need him to be banned?"

"No, I'd rather have that be you," Lucille returned grudgingly. "But if he ends up offering for you, I'm going to be very cross."

"I don't think that'll be a worry, Lucille. I'm not going to actually be with him, anyway. He merely needs to *believe* we'll be together."

"That's deceitful."

For heaven's sake, she wasn't going to spend the afternoon discussing her motivations and methods with Lucille Hampton. Particularly when she was fairly certain there was a ready alternative to asking him upstairs. But getting him drunk would take too much time, she decided. And they wouldn't be doing anything—or she wouldn't be, anyway. A man could become quite distracted with a strategic use of compliments and hands, after all. If it came to that.

She just resisted glancing over her shoulder after him. The poor fellow might not even require more than a seductive glance and a whisper—which would be beneficial for asking questions, of course, but as for her . . . Well, if he turned out to be merely pretending to know something in order to make himself more interesting, she could always invite him back for an actual liaison.

Emily drew a breath. She could invite him back, that was, depending on whether she could turn Lucille's attention elsewhere. "Look," she said aloud, inclining her chin. "Lord Burkiston is gazing at you."

That wasn't strictly true, either, but it served both to mollify Miss Hampton and to send her swirling off in the opposite direction. Lucille might have been a better bed companion for Lord Westfall than Emily would turn out to be, but he could mean to murder them all in the night and the bouncy brunette would never notice as long as he told her she had pretty eyes. Emily knew herself to be more cautious than that. And more alert for trouble, certainly.

As the clock hands tipped toward the hour, she handed her ledger over to Jenny Martine and made her way to the dining room's privacy door. For a moment she thought Westfall might have changed his mind, because the space around the entry stood empty. That could be a complication—especially if he'd actually learned something. Lucille did like to prattle on, after all. And the tingle in her fingertips was merely nerves over how easily she would be able to sway him to talk.

On the positive side, even with the sliding spectacles he wore, Lord Westfall was not at all hard on her eyesight. She lowered her gaze for a moment. Lucille could easily find another wealthy aristocrat over which to hover and dream. By necessity Emily had to be more particular. And even if easily manipulated men were dull, they did help dispel the night's shadows. Just not tonight. Not until she was certain this rather comely gentleman was of no further use than that.

"Are we to look as though we're meeting coincidentally, or may I acknowledge your presence?"

Emily started at the low voice directly behind her. Heaven's sake, he was quiet, especially for a man who walked with a limp and a cane. "Just follow me," she intoned, and pushed open the door.

She nearly ran into Pansy in the narrow hallway, but other than sending her companion a suspicious look, Miss Bridger paid them no mind. And as Pansy had a distinct dislike for the male of the species in general, no one Emily brought into the club's private area would have earned her scowling friend's approval.

With Westfall on her heels, she climbed the stairs, then skirted the bustling common room for her bedchamber at the end of the hallway. Her roommate, Lily Banks, was still working at one of the roulette tables, but as she slipped into the small room, she reached around to pull the scarf from the inside handle and loop it around the outside one.

"You've done this before," Westfall commented, following her actions with his eyes.

"If you were expecting virginity, you'll need to visit a bawdy house and pay extra for it," she returned.

For just a moment his expression became surprised. Then the amused, befuddled look returned to his lean, attractive countenance as he set his cane down against the back of the room's one, plain chair. "You're quite cynical," he announced unnecessarily. "Now, how do we go about this?"

She eyed him for a moment, taking him in from his longish mahogany hair to his spectacles to the pleasant curve of his mouth and the way she had to look up to see all of that. He must be two inches over six feet, at least, exceptional for one of the inbred gentry. But then he looked more like a professor than an earl, any-way—a very fit, lean professor. "*You're* not a virgin, are you?" she queried. It would certainly make things easier if he was.

Westfall grimaced. "No, I am not. I only meant that this seems very . . . well ordered. Do we kiss passion-ately? Do I undress you, or merely myself? Do we fall onto your rather narrow bed or sink bonelessly to the floor?"

Emily laughed, then stifled the sound with a cough. There were times—admittedly brief ones—when she wished she could invite someone interesting upstairs. Handsome and fit-looking were enough to warm her bed, but a strong jaw didn't necessarily translate to good conversation. But then, good conversation could only lead to trouble. And this encounter was about getting him to talk; her own pleasure could wait for someone who wasn't possibly looking for trouble.

Stepping up to him, she pushed the jacket from his shoulders. *Hm.* No additional padding there; the mus-cle was all him. Before she could begin kneading his shoulders or something, she turned her attention to his cravat, untying the rather simple knot and drawing it from around his neck. "How did your brother react when you packed him off in your carriage?" she asked, low-ering her fingers to the buttons of his dark blue waist-coat.

"With offended outrage," he returned, his gaze on her hands. "But that's nothing new, so I was unmoved."

"And are you unmoved now?" she continued, pull-ing open the waistcoat and pushing it down his arms. In another moment or two she would have him answer-ing any question she asked.

"What do you think?" Stirring into motion after several moments of stillness, Westfall reached out and tugged on one of her sleeves, lowering it down her shoulder and exposing her right breast. Before she could react, his long, elegant fingers brushed across her nipple, then pinched it lightly.

Unexpected arousal shivered down her spine. That wasn't supposed to happen. Lord Westfall was supposed to be befuddled and easily manipulated. Trying to slow her breathing, Emily mentally shook herself. She could manage a pleasurable pinch or two in exchange for the information she needed. "Why don't you remove your spectacles?" she suggested aloud. Being unable to see should—would—leave him more off balance. "We don't want them broken, do we?"

His light green eyes narrowed for the briefest of heartbeats, and then he pulled the metal-rimmed things free and set them on Lily's dresser by the door. As she studied his face again, she decided she preferred him with the spectacles on. Without them, he seemed less harmless. More . . . sharp. More predatory. She drew a breath, taking a half step back as those light eyes met her gaze. The sensation running down her spine, though, wasn't fear or trepidation. It was far headier than that.

Abruptly he blinked and reached up to rub the bridge of his nose. "Damned things," he murmured. "I can't tell a button from a beetle without them, but they are tiresome, all the same."

"Oh. No doubt," she returned. "You—"

"I have to feel my way," he interrupted. Sliding a finger around the ribbon that belted her waist, Westfall tugged her up against him. Before she could announce that she preferred to avoid kissing, he bent his head, capturing her mouth. Heat speared through her. That was not a kiss of sentiment; as his tongue tangled with hers, hot and insistent and very capable, what she felt from him was pure, forceful lust. *Good God.*

He slid his hands down to her hips, pulling her up against his lean body. The hard bulge pressing against her abdomen made her catch her breath. When he lowered his head, shifting his attention from her mouth to flick his tongue across the sensitive nipple of her exposed breast, she gasped.

Clearly he was no fumbling virgin. That realization should have had her scrambling to compose another strategy to get him talking to her. In a moment. First, she pulled the hem of his shirt from his trousers. When he lifted his arms, she tugged the white superfine over his head and then dropped it to the floor. She couldn't seduce him when he had on more clothes than she did, after all.

Even fully dressed he'd looked lean and fit, and she saw nothing—nothing—to dispute that assessment. Emily ran her palms from his shoulder across his chest, and down to his waist. Hard muscles flexed beneath his skin, sending her own body humming. *Mm.* As bookish as he appeared, he clearly used his body as well as his mind. She drew another quick breath. What she needed to do was gather her thoughts back in and decide how best to get the questions she had, answered. She needed to back away, to—

"Turn around," he ordered, his voice low and rough.

Before she could consider objecting to being dictated to, Emily found herself facing away from Lord Westfall. With swift fingers he untied the ribbon that gathered her deep green gown beneath her breasts, and then pulled the soft silk down her shoulders and over her arms and past her hips.

Her gown puddled to the floor. Somewhere in the back of her mind she knew that she was supposed to be seducing him, and that he should have been the one having difficulty thinking coherently. It was only because of the kiss, because she wasn't accustomed to kissing. That had to be the reason she shivered as his hands wove into her hair, sending pins and clips clicking to the wooden floor. Her long red-brown hair, carefully ironed straight, fell past her shoulders nearly to her waist.

Westfall spun her to face him again, back her into the door, and nearly lift her off the floor with the force of his kiss. His hands teased at her nipples, pinching and tugging until she moaned. *Oh, this was too much.* Too unexpected. Too heated.

She grabbed his waistband, unbuttoning his trousers frantically, shivering again when he licked her ear and his wandering fingers slipped down her stomach, past her curls, and touched her between her thighs. The tent at his crotch made unfastening him difficult, and when he closed his mouth over one breast, she jerked and nearly tore the last button off.

Finally she shoved his trousers down to his thighs. *Steady, Emily,* she practically screamed at herself, trying for calm and logic and reason even with his fingers dipping inside her. "Very nice," she managed, running a shaking finger along the hard, jutting length of him.

"Likewise," he murmured, turning them so he could push her backward onto her bed. Or was it Lily's bed? Blast it, she didn't care.

With his boots still on and his trousers around his thighs, he followed her down, kissing her again until she could barely breathe. When he sank lower along her body, licking first one breast and then the other, Emily tangled her fingers into his dark, disheveled hair and made a whimpering sound that came unbidden from her chest. More. She wanted more.

Shifting down further, Westfall gripped her knees, lifting and parting them before he moved forward and licked where his fingers had danced. Emily jumped, sensation and heat and lightning shooting down her spine and up again. Writhing, digging her fingers into his hair, she wondered how a man who looked like a scholar could have more than ten fingers and one tongue, and where he'd learned to use them so well.

Finally he straightened again, wiping his mouth with the back of his hand as he moved up the length of her again. His eyes had that predatory look to them again, but this time it made her damp. Fumbling, Emily reached into her night table and produced a goat intestine with a black ribbon tied at one end and open at the other. "If you please," she managed, still shaking.

Wordlessly he fixed it over his manhood, tying the other ribbon to hold it in place, then placed his hands on either side of her shoulders. Emily took a shallow breath as his impressive cock brushed the inside of her thighs. Westfall settled over her, lowering his head to nip at her shoulder as he canted his hips forward and slid deeply inside her.

With another helpless moan, Emily dug her fingers into his shoulders and arched her back. She loved that sensation, the heated fullness of an aroused male, his weight across her hips, the warm push of his breath in her ear. She drew tighter and tighter as he plunged into her, the rhythmic creaking of her bed and their labored breathing, the slap of flesh against flesh, adding to her arousal.

Finally she burst, burying her cry in his hard shoulder. Westfall slowed his pace, then sat up, his knees bent, and pulled her legs around his hips as he continued his assault. She looked up at him, at his heated expression with his gaze focused on where they met, and she came hard and suddenly all over again. His hands closed on her breasts as he rocked into her deeply. With a low groan he emptied himself, shuddering.

Almost immediately he pulled out of her and rolled onto his back next to her. For a long moment Emily listened to the sound of his panting and felt the hard, fast pounding of her heart. That had been . . . shattering. She blinked. There was— She needed to— There was something— She needed to discover. *Think*. She needed to think.

"I nearly went to White's for luncheon today," he said, his eyes closed and his breathing still heavy.

Questions. She had questions. Managing a chuckle, she stroked her hand across his chest, running her fingers through the light dusting of hair there before she began a series of hopefully languid circles around his nipples in a slow figure eight. "That would have been a tragedy," she breathed, attempting not to note the responding tingle down her spine as she felt his muscles flex and relax again. Oh, she hoped his mind was as muddled as hers was. "You wanted to show your brother the Tantalus, I presume?"

"Once he discovered I'd inherited my cousin's membership, he nearly began weeping."

Now she remembered. The former Earl of Westfall had drowned up in the Lake District a year or so ago. He'd been a young, attractive fellow, as well, though not quite as exceptional a physical specimen as his cousin. "Your kindness toward your brother worked out well for me," she returned, trying to keep her voice soft and silky. A relaxed man, and a well-complimented one, was so very easy to chat with, she'd discovered. And this one had earned every accolade. "And you're looking for someone. Do I know her? I could help you."

"Oh, it's nothing, really. Someone lost a necklace, and asked me to look for it. I like to look for things."

His eyes remained closed, his face relaxed. Was that all it had been? Someone with a lost trinket? Well, she'd perhaps done more than necessary to discover that, and more than she'd intended, certainly, but the inquiring had been delightful. "Do you often look for other people's things, then?" she asked, trying to regain control of the conversation. "That's an interesting hobby, my lord. Much more so than chasing foxes or shooting at birds—unless you do those things, as well, in which case I shall call you adventurous."

One green eye opened, then the other. *Damnation.* Had she stumbled and pushed too hard? Then he blinked fuzzily and rubbed the bridge of his nose. "Where did I put my spectacles?" he asked, sitting up.

"On the chest of drawers. I'll get them." Relieved to have a moment, she swung her feet over the side of the bed and stood, in the same motion pulling a cloth from the folded clothes on her bed stand and handing it to him.

While he cleaned himself, she padded over to the chest and retrieved his spectacles. He hadn't answered her last question, but he didn't seem to have realized that he was being interrogated, either. If she trod carefully, then, she still had a chance to learn whether there was anything to discover. If she could stop thinking about how much she wanted to have him again.

Nathaniel watched the lovely, swaying backside of Emily Portsman as she went across the room to fetch his spectacles. The chit asked interesting questions, though he remained undecided whether they were pillow talk or if she was attempting to discover what he was after. Experience made him suspicious, but it had also taught him that suspicion was not the same thing as proof.

She faced him again, so he blinked and smiled. "Thank you, Miss Portsman."

"You should likely call me Emily," she said easily, handing the damned things over.

He dropped the cloth onto the floor and slung the spectacles over his ears. "That's right, we haven't actually been introduced, have we? Westfall." Even after two years the word still sounded foreign on his tongue. "Or Nathaniel. Or Stokes. Whichever of the three you prefer."

"So many names," she mused, swinging her hair over one shoulder as she sat beside him on the bed again. "Westfall, I think."

The least personal of the three. Everything meant something, and so did her choice of moniker for him. "Westfall it is, then," he returned, forcing his gaze to remain on her face, though this body was more interested in having her again. Now. And repeatedly. "In which case I believe I'll address you as Portsman," he continued. "You were asking me about my hobbies, yes? What are yours? What does a Tantalus girl do when she's not tantalizing Tantalus guests?"

She grinned. "Very good, my lord."

Ah, it had been rather pitiful, actually, but he'd pushed his bumbling disguise to the limit already with the way he'd mauled her lovely, naked, smooth body. Nate swallowed. "Thank you."

She nodded. "Since you asked, I like to read."

In a bawdy house her answer would have been surprising, but the Tantalus girls were all said to be well educated as well as lovely. But according to his interviews, Rachel Newbury was a reader, as well. "Ah," he said aloud. "Shakespeare? Johnson? Richardson? Smollett?" She didn't resemble the description Ebberling had given for Miss Newbury all that closely either in appearance or with her enthusiasm in bed, but he wasn't about to call her innocent yet, either. And considering that the governess was reputed to be high in the instep, she would read at least one of the authors he'd mentioned. Probably.

With a chuckle, Emily shook her head. "Radcliffe and Lewis, more like. At the moment I'm reading *The Scottish Cousin*." She pulled the book from the bedstand and handed it to him.

"You are?" he returned dubiously, flipping through the pages.

"Oh, yes. You see, it's very romantic," she continued with a grin. "The cousin, Bartholomew Pinkerton, attempts to seize control of Lord MacKenzie's estate, and MacKenzie must marry a duke's daughter to end a family curse and thwart the evil Bartholomew's plans. His grandfather's ghost is determined that only a true Scotsman live on the grounds of MacKenzie Mew."

"But isn't the cousin Scottish, as per the title?"

"Well, it's very complicated, but evidently he's actually the illegitimate son of a Spanish troubadour." She took the book back and set it aside. "I haven't actually finished it yet, but there's been something about a mermaid, as well. And smugglers."

"You know that's drivel, don't you?" he countered. Logic and torrid, sentiment-filled romance certainly had very little to do with each other, and logic served him much better.

"So is Anderfel's treatise on the poor," she returned. "At least *The Scottish Cousin* is amusing, and doesn't make me wish to hit someone."

He pounced on that. "You've read Anderfel's treatise?" Nathaniel pushed his spectacles up.

"Haven't you? It was serialized in the *Times*." Emily

stretched, the bounce of her round breasts making his cock sit up and take notice all over again.

Other than discovering that Emily Portsman wasn't quite what he'd expected of any Tantalus girl, this particular interrogation was netting him nothing. Well, a very diverting afternoon, certainly, but nothing of use to his investigation. Even so, he was loath to pull his trousers back on and leave. At home he would have Laurie complaining about being sent away from the Tantalus, and he would have to review all the notes he'd taken about Rachel Newbury in order to attempt a different strategy for hunting her down—all of it much less arousing than having Portsman again.

The idea that his quarry might have been—might still be—at The Tantalus Club was an intriguing one, and it remained a possibility. Short of directly asking his bed partner if she knew a Rachel Newbury, however, he needed to retreat and reconsider his plan of attack. The last thing he wanted to do was warn Miss Newbury before he'd identified her, because then she would likely flee—or decide that removing him from the equation would be the best solution to her difficulties. Aside from that, it would remove an excuse for a second visit to Portsman's bedchamber.

At that moment she stood again. "Well, that was much more pleasant than the way I'd intended to spend the afternoon," she commented, smiling at him, her gaze lowering to his waist, as she bent down enticingly to retrieve her gown.

Evidently the interlude was over. Since he'd practically assaulted her, he supposed it was only fair that she dictate the end of the encounter. He could use some damned space to think for a moment, anyway. Nate climbed to his feet and yanked up his trousers. "And how had you intended to spend the afternoon?" he asked. This was supposed to be an interrogation, after all.

"Finishing the work schedule for next week. Which I still need to do." Rather than pull on her sumptuous dark green, gown again, she folded it over a chair and went to her wardrobe for a modest shift and a much plainer yellow muslin.

Nate took a swift glance past her shoulder, but there was no governess's multipocketed pelisse inside that he could spot. If Rachel Newbury had ever even worn such a thing it would have been long gone by now anyway, but he refused ever to discount luck. "May I say I'm disappointed that you dress so sensibly when you aren't out among the club's membership, Portsman?"

"You aren't the first to say so, Westfall. Apparently half the membership believes we wear nothing at all back here." She grinned, tying her red-brown hair back with a simple ribbon.

Pointless to his investigation or not, there were a great many less pleasant ways he might have otherwise spent the afternoon himself. Nate smiled back at her as he fastened his trousers and sat again to pull on his shirt and waistcoat. Somewhere in the past thirty minutes the button in his left boot had slipped down to his toe, but he merely scowled and tolerated it. A limp was a limp. "Forgive my ignorance," he began, not entirely convinced himself that he was proceeding merely because of his inquiries, "but do we simply part company? Do I suggest we repeat the enterprise, or ask if you'd care to join me on a ride through Hyde Park or some such thing?"

"I don't leave the premises," Emily returned, color briefly touching her cheeks and her gaze darting toward the window and back again. "Scandal is well and good for business in here, but outside these walls the world is much less tolerant of Tantalus girls. We're not courting, Westfall."

That made sense, whether it fit nicely into his suspicions or not. Had she protested just a hair too quickly or too vehemently, though? Or was he merely too cynical? Reaching for his cane and limping a bit to look less threatening, he supposed it was, he put a frown on his face. "You never leave? Doesn't that get frightfully dull? How long have you been here?"

"Three years or so. And no, I don't find it dull at all." She flashed a bright smile at him. "I have *The Scottish Cousin* and all its relatives to keep me occupied, and truer friends beneath this roof than I've ever had elsewhere. As for the other part of your question, I would enjoy repeating this interlude, I think. If you would, that is."

"Oh, I definitely would." Whether she was a suspect or had knowledge of his quarry or not, a fellow with his background could hardly ask for more than a pretty girl who disliked emotional entanglements. He'd had and avoided enough of those to last a lifetime. "Perhaps tomorrow?" Or did that sound too eager even for a bookish earl? "Or the day after," he added.

"You may ask for me at the front door most afternoons," she said, handing him his waistcoat. "I'll show you out the back way; we can't have gentlemen wandering about our sanctuary willy-nilly."

"What about those large fellows Haybury has lurking about?"

"The Helpful Men? They're our protectors. Older brothers with large muscles."

Hm. Older brothers frequently knew more about their younger sisters than they even realized. Perhaps one of them might be worth a chat. Later, though; he didn't know what Miss Hampton might have said about his search for a necklace, and the last thing he wanted was to have to drop one of Haybury's employees if they went after him. It would be difficult to put on his help-less mask again once he'd broken some former boxer's nose.

"They're quite effective, I imagine," he said aloud, tucking his shirt into his trousers and buttoning up his waistcoat. "I'd had no idea The Tantalus Club's inner workings were so intriguing."

She laughed. "You have an interesting idea of in-trigue."

Oh, she had no idea. "Do I? My brother says so. I love puzzles and such. And finding baubles people have lost." It made sense to confess it, and to make it sound less threatening than he certainly knew it to be.

"So if I'd lost a ring or something you would be able to find it for me?"

"That depends if it fell off while you were walking, or if someone stole it from you. In the former case, no, I likely couldn't locate it. In the latter instance, every-one leaves a trail, whether they realize it or not. They boast about it or sell to someone who's willing to share the information for a few shillings. Things like that." As he spoke, he watched her carefully, looking for a reac-tion.

She stepped into her shoes, her expression unchanged. "Goodness, that sounds fascinating. How did you come to realize you enjoyed finding things for people?"

Another innocent question? Or something more? He was beginning to think that Emily Portsman did know something, and that she was very good at disguising her questions as casual conversation. And very good at distracting him with her exceptional physical charms. "I suppose in the way some men are good at shooting or riding or sheep shearing," he responded, attempting not to sound as though he'd made this same speech a thousand times, "I've been finding bits and bobs for people since I can remember, Portsman. It's my hobby."

"I shall remember that, the next time one of my friends has something stolen." Emily gestured him toward the door, touching his arm—whether accidentally or intentionally—in the process. "Shall we exit? I do have some duties to attend to."

"Certainly." He had some duties to attend to, himself. The first one of which was to obtain the names of everyone presently and previously employed at The Tantalus Club.

Chapter Five

This was not good.

Emily closed the servants' rear door on Lord Westfall's backside, then stood for a long moment staring at the heavy oak barrier. She could lock it, of course, but the front door stood open and welcoming to anyone with a membership or a friend with a membership, and for every hour of every day save Christmas.

She shook out her hands. It could be nothing. He enjoyed finding baubles, he'd said, and that was precisely what she'd overheard. A bauble meant a necklace, or a ring, or a teacup. And she was no teacup.

Neither, though, was she a fool. He'd set her off balance. She didn't think she'd said anything incriminating, but for a few moments there she couldn't remember precisely what she *had* said. Scholarly men weren't supposed to be so adept at sex. If he meant her trouble, she needed to deal with it. With him. And she needed to stop wondering if he would call on her tomorrow and if a second meeting would be as satisfying as the first one had been.

No. First things first. Ignoring the pounding of her heart, Emily returned to the dining room to find Jenny Martine seating the Marquis of Brundy with his sons

Lord Allenglen and Lord William Brundy. Emily took a breath, pasting the usual calm smile on her face as she stood well back and waited.

"What is it?" Jenny murmured as she returned to the postern at the fore of the main dining room. "You're dressed most unsuitably."

Damnation. She'd forgotten her attire, and that wasn't like her at all. "Has Lord Haybury returned yet? Or Diane?"

"No. Is something amiss?"

"No. I just wanted a word with one of them. Nothing urgent. I'll retreat before I cause anyone to become disillusioned."

A swift smile cracked Genevieve's solemn expression. "Yes, do. We don't have enough smelling salts to revive all these gentlemen."

In the past, Emily would have gone to chat with Sophia White, because if nothing else Sophia's warm heart and quick wit would have distracted her from her own worries. But her friend was now Sophia Baswich, the most unlikely Duchess of Greaves and no longer a Tantalus girl. They could still have a coze, of course, but only if Sophia came calling here. Which she wasn't likely to do, considering that she and the duke hadn't yet arrived in London for the Season. Of course, even if Sophia had been residing across the street from the Tantalus instead of in Yorkshire, Emily still couldn't—wouldn't—have ventured out to find her.

Swallowing her nerves, Emily climbed the back staircase and retrieved her book. If *The Scottish Cousin* couldn't distract her, nothing could. She took it with her into the common room, though, disliking the idea of sitting alone in the silence of her rumpled bedchamber. With the bustle around her she could at least pretend that Lord Westfall didn't make her exceedingly uneasy and nervous and aroused all at the same time. She didn't like the sensation. All she required was safety and orderliness, and the earl had brought neither.

"Well?"

She started, looking up from the book. "Beg pardon?"

Lucille Hampton plunked herself down onto the couch beside Emily. "Westfall. Is he sinister, or are you going to leave him for someone who wants more from him than a naked frolic?"

"A what?" Emily stifled what was likely an inappropriate grin, despite the fact that she'd experienced just that. Under the circumstances, she supposed that Lucille might have distracted Westfall as well as she could, but despite the accompanying unsettled sensation, she was abruptly glad that it had been her invitation the earl had accepted. She closed her mouth against a satisfied sigh.

"You heard me. I mean to marry the earl, and you know it. I said so just this morning. You said he might be dangerous. So what is it, then?"

"I don't know yet, Lucille."

Her companion frowned, looking far younger than the twenty-one years of age Emily knew her to be. "You're only saying that so you can have another go at him. Why not simply confess that you're attempting to steal him from me?"

"Because I'm not attempting to steal him from you. You have to have possession of him before anyone could steal him. A daydream is well and good, but—"

"Don't you even finish that sentence, Emily Portsman. If you wish this to be a fight, then so be it." With a flounce of her skirts Lucille stood again and stomped out of the room.

Oh, dear. If Westfall was merely a befuddled aristocrat with a peculiar hobby, then she'd hurt Lucille for no reason other than her own paranoia and lust. But the fact was, she didn't know yet if he was a threat. Her hesitation, she could tell herself, had nothing to do with the fact that he was a very fine lover and a very attractive man, or the thought that he was too sensible and too skilled for Lucille's heavy-handed antics. Or that lately she'd been lonely and that the conversation—or fencing match, depending on what she still needed to discover about him—with Lord Westfall had been nearly as diverting as the sex.

Whatever Emily said, Lucille would never understand how vital it was that Emily discover what had motivated Lord Westfall to attend the club today, and whether the bauble he was after had brought him here, specifically. Sighing, Emily set aside her novel and returned to her scheduling. The pages could wait until tomorrow, but the numbers, the finesse of making certain all positions were covered without injuring anyone's feelings or overstaffing or understaffing, taking into account who had a holiday and who needed an extra few hours—all that engaged her mind and thereby gave her a measure of peace.

An hour later she felt someone looking at her and glanced up to see Diane, Lady Haybury, leaning into the doorway. The marchioness angled her chin toward the hall, and with a half relieved and half nervous breath, Emily rose.

Out in the hallway she faced her rescuer, employer, and friend. "How was the peach treaty?" she asked, forcing a smile.

Diane rolled her eyes. "Oh, not you, too. Oliver's been punning all afternoon."

"It's a good pun."

"So it is. Just don't let him hear you say that." Finally smiling, the marchioness took Emily's arm and guided her toward the rear of the large building, where the club ended and Adam House, the private residence of Lord and Lady Haybury, began. "Farmer Milkin and the two neighboring farms have agreed to provide us with two bushels of peaches daily for as long as the trees are producing. We've also arranged for strawberries and apples during their seasons, and at a rather substantial savings. That was a very good idea, Emily."

"Thank you. Is Lord H about, by chance?"

"Jenny said you'd asked for him first. Does this have anything to do with your tryst with Lord Westfall? He didn't hurt you, did he?"

"Heavens, no." Of course Diane would know about her intimate interlude, because Jenny Martine knew.

Some of the other girls said Jenny had been a spy for Wellington during the war. However she'd come by her skill for discovering everything, Emily was only very thankful that Jenny had proven herself a friend several times over. A thought occurred to her, and she frowned. Hopefully that friendship would continue, regardless of who was looking for, or had discovered, what.

"I only wanted to know if a certain gentleman might be in Town this Season, and I thought Lord H would be the most likely person to ask," she continued aloud.

"And so he would be." Diane sent her a sideways look as she unlocked the door leading to Adam House's upstairs hallways and then motioned her through it. "Shall I ask outright, then? Is something amiss?"

Certainly Emily had invited men to join her upstairs before, and she'd never felt the need to go question her employers afterward. There was likely no reason for it this time. "Just a . . . a niggling feeling," she said. "Once I know the answer to my question I can laugh and return to my duties."

"I do hope so, my dear." Diane knocked on the half-open office door and then pushed it open. "Take a moment from your peach—oh, no, now you've got me saying it. Damn your hide, Haybury."

The Marquis of Haybury looked up from a spread of paperwork and grinned. It was the sort of grin that, rumor had it, had spontaneously caused several ladies to lose their virginity. Emily was glad it was aimed at Diane rather than her, because it would have signaled a trouble from which there would be no escape. Not if she wished to remain at The Tantalus Club.

"What was that, darling? More compliments? You'll put me to the blush." Oliver Warren stood, motioning Emily to one of the seats that faced the desk.

Emily, however, remained standing. Now that she'd arrived, she faced another difficulty—saying a name aloud that she hadn't uttered in three years. Likely she was just being stupid, worrying over something because it hadn't troubled her lately. Questioning sunshine because it hadn't rained often enough.

"I'll be down the hall if you should require anything," Diane said into the silence, evidently reading her discomfort.

"That's not necessary," Emily returned. "Perhaps if I might just . . . whisper a name to you, Lord Haybury? And if you happen to know that the person to whom this name belongs is in London, you could nod? Or shake your head if this person is not in Town?"

The humor in Haybury's green-eyed gaze had faded, the curved line of his mouth flattening. "I could do that, Emily," he said aloud, and walked up to lean one hip on the arm of the chair in front of her.

While Diane watched, clearly curious, Emily took a deep breath, swallowed, and leaned close to the ear the marquis presented her. Even so it still took her a moment to form her mouth into breathing the word. "Ebberling," she finally murmured, so quietly she wasn't entirely certain he'd heard her.

For the space of several very hard beats of her heart the marquis stayed motionless. *You see, you ninny,* she told herself, *he's going to shake his head and you'll feel foolish, and then you'll worry that someone knows the name for no damned good reason. Idiot.*

Just as she'd begun to think that she would have to say the name a second time, Haybury straightened to look at her, though she wasn't certain for what his keen, cynical gaze might be searching. Then, very slowly, he nodded.

The world went white around her. Her blood turned to ice. She must have fainted, because the next thing she could recall was Lord Haybury straightening from seating her in a chair, and Diane bringing her a glass of whisky. "Oh," she stammered. "Oh."

"What the devil?" the marchioness asked, her expression concerned. "What name did she ask you, Oliver?"

He folded his arms across his chest. "Well, I'm not going to tell you that, now am I?"

That answer calmed Emily more than anything else could possibly have done. Logically she'd known that Haybury would keep her secret; otherwise she never would have risked speaking the name. But knowing and hearing the proof of her trust being justified were two very different things. Even so, she couldn't remain utterly silent. Three years ago she'd given her word.

"Diane, when you hired me," she said slowly, taking a grateful sip of the whisky, "you asked me to promise you something."

"I recall," the marchioness returned.

"I don't," Haybury put in.

"You weren't to be trusted back then," his wife returned without heat. She lifted a gracefully curved eyebrow at Emily. "Shall I?"

Emily nodded. "If you please."

"I promised Emily that I would never ask her about her past if she would promise to come to me if her past became her present."

"Ah. And this person is of your past?" the marquis asked.

"Yes. I don't know that he has any notion of making trouble for me at all, really," Emily said, every word wrenching at her insides, "but if he were to . . . see me, or suspect I was anywhere about, I—it would not go well." That was as nebulous as she could make it without outright lying to the woman who'd likely saved her life.

"Then he shall be banned from the club," Diane stated without hesitating.

"I think that might make him suspicious." Emily *knew* it would make him suspicious, in fact. Another stab of ice slid down her spine. She would have to leave the club, and then he would surely be able to find her.

"Do you think this person has an inkling that you're here?" Haybury queried, walking to the open liquor tantalus by the door and pouring himself a glass.

"I'm not certain." That answer depended on discovering whether Ebberling had hired Westfall, and whether she was the bauble he sought. "I don't think he possibly could. I've taken steps to not be found."

"Then we'll keep you out of the public areas of the club for as long as this person is in Town. We will tell the other girls and the Helpful Men that they are not to speak your name, and that they are never to have heard of you."

Emily twisted in the chair to face Diane. "As long as

you'll allow me to remain hidden, the rest won't be necessary."

Now Haybury was eyeing her again. "Emily Portsman isn't your true name."

"No." She glanced at Diane again. "I told you that when you hired me, did I not?"

"You did. I'd forgotten. Might he ask after the actual you?"

"Very likely. But other than Sophia and Jenny, I don't think anyone knows I'm not brown-haired Emily Portsman."

The marchioness nodded. "Jenny is safe." She grimaced. "I won't demand it, but it would be easier if I had this man's name for myself, and to give to her."

For the first time in over three years, tears gathered in Emily's eyes. Kindness. She'd known of it, but had rarely experienced it. And to hear it now . . . "Ebberling," she said as clearly as she could, the word tasting foul in her mouth. "The Marquis of Ebberling." And since she'd said it aloud, she needed to continue. "It would likely be better for everyone if I simply left. Then no subterfuge would be required."

"My dear," Haybury said, glancing at his wife and then leaning down to plant a kiss on Emily's forehead, "if there's one thing we do better than running a gentlemen's club, it's subterfuge. You will remain here."

"But you don't even know why he's looking for me. If he's looking for me."

"But I know you," Diane countered. "Not Emily or Jane or whatever your given name is. *You.* And that is sufficient for me." She clapped her hands together. "Now. This began after you . . . conversed with Lord Westfall. Is he involved?"

"Do we get to ban him, at least?" Haybury seconded, obviously attempting to lighten the mood. "I haven't banned anyone since Fenton and Greaves, and we had to let Greaves back in."

"I don't know for certain if Westfall is involved," Emily replied. "I do think that if he is, banning him now would make him look directly at me." She squared her shoulders. What in the world had she done, sleeping with him? And why did she still wish to do so again? "I would prefer to discover a bit more about him before any further action is taken," she said, half to herself.

"You don't wish to avoid him, then?" Diane sounded dubious.

"Just the opposite, actually," she returned, something electric traveling down her spine. "If he does know something, and if he is working with Ebberling, I mean to discover it. Without him discovering anything at all about me."

"That's a dangerous path, Emily," Haybury warned her quietly.

"My life has been a dangerous path. If I'm not to run, then I need to know where the pitfalls and traps lie." And that, at least, was the absolute truth.

"I don't like it," the marchioness said, finally giving in and pouring herself a glass of whisky, as well, "but I do understand. Go carefully. And while I hate to add to your troubles, there is one rule at The Tantalus Club."

Emily nodded again as she drained her glass. "Don't injure the club. I know. And I won't. If that should become likely, I will leave. I swear it. But if I retreat from Westfall now without knowing precisely what he might be up to, I will *have* to leave."

Once her employers had assured themselves that she was completely recovered, they allowed her to return to the employees' private part of the Tantalus. She hadn't told them everything, and it meant a great deal to her that they hadn't asked. They trusted her, and she would not betray them. No matter what.

That decision didn't explain, however, why, despite the worry and the dread over Ebberling's abrupt arrival in London after three years away, she was looking forward to her next meeting with the Earl of Westfall. And not because of the sex. Well, not entirely because of the sex. If she was to be destroyed, she meant to learn all the facts first. Westfall might be innocent in this, or he might only be playing at innocence while he sought Rachel Newbury. He wouldn't find her. What he would find, however, was a great deal more than he had likely bargained for.

"You're a hypocrite," Laurence announced from the balcony overlooking Teryl House's foyer.

Nathaniel continued shedding his gloves and hat, handing them over to Franks. "And why is that?" he asked, the rather pleasant mood he'd been in beginning to dissolve.

"You had sex with that Emily chit, after you bellowed at me for doing the same thing at university."

"I didn't break any rules," Nate returned, shrugging out of his caped greatcoat and retrieving his cane from the butler. "And you are nineteen. So shut up."

"Well, that's not your usual brilliant argument."

"Isn't it? Perhaps because I'm tired and my foot hurts."

" 'My foot hurts?' " Laurie snapped back at him. "Of course your foot hurts. You—"

"Had a horse step on it," he cut in before his brother could announce to the entire household that he put a button in his boot to make himself limp. Half-wit.

"Yes, a horse. A stupid horse stepped on it. Which isn't my fault, I'd like to point out."

As Nathaniel climbed the stairs, Laurie retreated in

the direction of the library, though Nate doubted his brother meant to go read a book. No, he wanted a chance to yell in private. Very well. "In the library. Now," he said aloud, to be certain Laurence would keep his mouth closed until then.

Once they were ensconced behind the thick oak doors of the large Teryl House library, Nathaniel walked to the fireplace and sat in one of the comfortable chairs there. Those in his business did not share information lightly; the ones who did were generally not alive long enough to learn from the mistake. But, as he kept telling himself, he wasn't in that business any longer. It still trailed him, and would for the remainder of his life, but he was now an earl, a respectable and very visible member of the aristocracy, and an older brother who had neglected his sibling for a great deal too long. The fact that it was for Laurie's own safety didn't signify—the deed had been done.

"Sit down," he said, when his brother seemed determined to stomp up and down the library floor until the shelves came tumbling down.

"I'm not going to be yelled at by you when I've done nothing wrong," Laurence returned, though he did alter his course and drop into the chair on the far side of the hearth.

"Do you truly wish to help me with my latest bauble hunt?" Nate asked. "If you do, I have to know that I can trust in your discretion. That you won't go shouting secrets down the stairs if I ask you to do something you don't like."

Laurie's cheeks reddened. "I wouldn't have said anything."

"Yes you would have. My question to you, however, is whether I can trust you now?"

Sitting forward, Laurie put his elbows on his knees.

"You may trust me with anything, Nate," he said earnestly. "I swear it."

This was not going to end well, Nathaniel decided, but at some point he would need to entrust certain information to his brother for the good of both of them. And since Laurie had already stumbled and given away information at The Tantalus Club, the lad needed to be included anyway. This could be a good test of how much Laurence could be allowed to know later. He took a breath.

"Very well," he said aloud. "I was hired to find a necklace."

"A . . . well, that's dull," his brother exclaimed, sitting back again. "You embarrassed me in front of that pretty faro dealer and Lord Cleves—when I was ahead by thirty quid, I might add—for a necklace?"

Stifling his urge to snap back, Nathaniel picked up a small carved elephant—his late cousin seemed to have collected the things from everywhere, and he'd taken something of a liking to them himself—and turned it over in his hands. "That would have been shoddy of me," he conceded, "if that was all I was after."

"There's more?"

"There would be, if you would shut up for a moment and let me finish."

"Oh. Right. Shutting up, then."

Nathaniel shook his head, but set the elephant aside. By age nineteen he'd done some things that still gave him nightmares, but those same things were what allowed Laurie to be . . . well, to be a lad of nineteen. And on his way to becoming a better man than his brother, if he could learn to manage some discretion and better timing.

"The necklace was taken by a woman who is also suspected in a murder. In fact, the necklace is secondary;

a means by which I may find the murderess." He paused, but to his credit Laurie kept his mouth closed. "Now. I'm prepared to tell you what I know and to enlist your assistance, since you so kindly blabbed about my bauble search in the Tantalus, but only if you give me your word that this stays between us. Completely."

"I sw—"

"No. Think about it for a moment. No mentioning what you've been up to in letters to your friends, or bragging about any of it when you return to Oxford. No pillow talk about missing gems or how important your work has been. Not now, and not in ten years. Never."

For a long moment Laurence looked at him, his light green eyes for once solemn. "That's how it is for you, isn't it?" he finally said. "You've done some heroic things for England, but you can never whisper a word about them. Instead you walk about with a false limp and false spectacles and rumpled clothes, because that's all you know how to do any longer."

Shifting, Nathaniel sent his brother a brief scowl. "I don't think that's *all* I know how to do, but yes, I'm accustomed to being other than who I am." And who he actually was, was a question he couldn't quite seem to answer any longer. But that was neither here nor there. "But the point of this is, can you do what I ask? Are you willing to do what I ask? And consider it carefully, Laurie."

"I—"

"Carefully," he repeated. "I'll ask for your answer after dinner tonight. Now go away and let me think."

His brother stood again. "I don't need to think about it, because you're my brother and I'd do anything for you, but have it your way. If you want me to think this vow is difficult or distasteful, so be it. I'll tell you yes after dinner."

With that he left the library, closing the door quietly behind him. Nathaniel sat where he was, turning his gaze to the orange and yellow crackling blaze in the fireplace. He couldn't say that he and Laurie had never dealt well together—or that they had—for the simple reason that he barely knew his brother. Yes, back when he'd been fifteen and Laurence had been six they'd played. Or rather, Laurie had played, and Nate had tolerated being stuck with wooden swords and having pebbles catapulted at him. When their father, George Stokes, had died two years later after doing something as dangerous as walking through his garden in the summer sun, they'd been left with very little income and with Nathaniel as the one to support the household.

Evidently someone had been watching over him, though, because when he'd used what blunt he could scrape together to purchase a commission in the army, he'd been asked whether he would be willing to put his grasp of languages and puzzles and cartography to good use. And so he'd become a spy for king and country. He'd spent the ensuing eight years in fourteen different countries, three continents, and a multitude of guises, before, during, and after the Peninsular War. When his mother had died he'd been in Spain posing as a former freedom fighter willing to spill secrets to Bonaparte for the right coin, and he hadn't even received word of her death for three months.

And then, two years ago, he'd received word that his cousin Gerard Teryl, the Earl of Westfall, had drowned on a fishing expedition. That had changed everything. Gerard had had no offspring—hell, he hadn't even been married—and so the title, lands, responsibilities, and income had gone to his closest surviving male relation. Nate Stokes, Wellington's favorite spy.

Absently he picked up the ebony wood elephant

again. He'd seen the things in person, both the African and the Indian varieties. Had his cousin? At the Tower menagerie, perhaps, or when envoys from India arrived to impress the House of Lords. Was he being a fool, to bring Laurie into his world instead of leaving that life behind, himself?

"Yes," he muttered aloud, and stood. But it had been too long. He'd been too many people, learned too many things, seen too many things, to be able to simply be Nathaniel Stokes, Earl of Westfall. Sometimes it seemed as though being that bumbling, absentminded, finder of lost baubles was the only thing keeping him sane. And at the same time it was slowly driving him mad.

And he'd certainly done nothing to earn Laurie's loyalty. Nothing but be his older brother, which was evidently enough. Or so he would have to discover. Because if he didn't find a way to allow Laurence into his life, neither of them would have anyone but himself.

Blowing out his breath, he set the elephant down again and stood to pace. Contemplating things over which he had no control was a waste of time. And he had a chit to find. So, what did he know?

Slowly he ticked the points off on his fingers. Rachel Newbury. Female. Aged between twenty-two and twenty-five. Brown eyes, blond hair, intelligent and clever, with either an unfortunate or a criminal past, given her false papers when she'd taken employment with Ebberling.

Of all those things, the only two she wouldn't be able to alter were her eye color and her wits. She could pretend to be a man, cut or color her hair, change her name, act as a fool or anything else she could conjure, but she would still be intelligent. And she would still have brown eyes. And she could be anywhere, including Europe or the Americas.

He didn't think she was anywhere, though. He thought she was still in England. When he'd talked to her fellow servants at Ebberling, one thing had been made clear: She was a fine governess. The boy had adored her, and he'd been happy to display his knowledge of French and arithmetic. Governess to a future marquis was a privileged position, and if she couldn't be a governess again anywhere (which he assumed she wouldn't dare to be, either here or abroad), she would want to be somewhere she could utilize her skills.

That pointed him once again to The Tantalus Club. After being open for three years now, the Tantalus was becoming *the* place for pretty young girls of good education and poor reputation to go for employment. There Rachel Newbury could call herself anything she chose, make up a past that hid her from searching eyes, and earn an income that—from what he'd heard—would see her comfortable in her later life. Because even selling a stolen diamond necklace, if she'd risked parting with it, wouldn't see her with an income to last more than a year or two.

He stopped before the window that looked down at his large, well-kept garden. Rachel Newbury might be intelligent and resourceful, but she wasn't a former spy. She hadn't been trained to seek out the nearly invisible signs that someone gave when they had something to hide. He had been.

And everything in him, all his training, told him that Emily Portsman knew more than she cared to say. He wasn't ready yet to say he'd already found his prey, because that would be far more fortuitous than life had ever been to him, but she knew something about someone or something.

He needed to see her again, which luckily enough was something to which she'd already agreed. That had actually surprised him, considering he was fairly certain Portsman had invited him into the club's back rooms to interrogate him. He'd struck first, so to speak, and not only because he'd wanted her off balance. Because more than that, he'd simply wanted her.

A vision of her naked beneath him, her fingers digging hard into his shoulders, the aroused delight in her eyes, touched his thoughts, but after a moment of heated consideration he brushed them away again. Yes, sex with her had been pleasurable, and he had no regrets about it or about repeating the experience. Several times, if he could manage it. He was male, after all, and intimacy so frequently was a means to betrayal that he'd been avoiding it for the past two years.

It might well be a means to betrayal yet again. But to himself he could admit that he still wanted Emily Portsman, and that he wanted to be wrong both about her involvement in his search and his suspicion that she was hiding . . . something. Nathaniel looked down into the garden one floor below him, at the late-blooming profusion of roses in their splendid reds and whites and yellows.

This wasn't the first time he'd wished to be wrong about someone. If he was indeed wrong about her, however, it would be the first time his wishes had been answered.

Chapter Six

Emily carried the last bucket of cold, tea-colored bathwater through the kitchen and out to the muddy carriage drive. Once she'd checked to be certain no one but stable boys were about, she squatted down and tipped the bucket onto the gravel.

The henna would stay in her hair for weeks, gradually losing its reddish tint in favor of a more solid brown. That would mean, however, that each time she re-dyed her hair it would change color. No, it was safer to dye it every three or four days, so that the auburn tint never altered. She could only be thankful that she'd realized strong tea darkened it as much as it did, or she would be a flaming redhead—far too noticeable even in a crowd of attractive young ladies.

Her friend Sophia was a striking redhead, anyway, with the fair skin to go with it. Her own skin was a shade or two darker, which made the brownish red she'd decided on look more natural. She might have opted to wash her hair in lemons, but that would only have made her already blond hair lighter—and still blond. No, henna was much, much better, if more difficult to procure. Thank goodness she'd read about its use in one of Ebberling Manor's many library books.

And thank goodness she'd noted that Lord Ebberling wasn't enough of a reader to go looking for clues to her appearance or whereabouts in books she'd perhaps touched.

Lord Westfall *did* seem to be a reader, but even if she happened to be the bauble he was seeking, she didn't think she'd given him much—any—reason to look in her direction. Not on Ebberling's behalf, anyway. If he was working for Ebberling. *Oh, this was maddening.* If the marquis hadn't been in Town, she would have been thoroughly enjoying the prospect of another interlude with the unexpectedly delicious Lord Westfall.

Frowning, she straightened again and set the bucket back in its place behind the stable, then returned indoors. The stable yard and the garden were as far as she ever roamed from the building, and even doing that made her uneasy. Especially over the past two days. Ebberling had been visiting her dreams again, when she thought she'd finally managed to banish him. Because he *was* in London now, when he hadn't been anywhere near it for three years. Not since . . . not since before he'd become a widower.

Her fingers had begun trembling, and she clenched them into fists as she walked back through the kitchen. No outward sign of anything but what she wished to show was ever allowed, and she'd become a damned fine actress if she said so herself. No one but those three she'd told would ever know about her connection with Ebberling, and Lord and Lady Haybury and Genevieve Martine only knew that she wished to avoid the man at all costs. Nothing more than that. And she desperately hoped that there would never be a need to tell them anything more.

"Emily," Charity Green, the head cook, said as she passed behind the round woman, "now that I have all the peaches I need, there's a shortage of hands in here."

Emily stopped her retreat to look over the half-dozen women busily stirring and chopping and rolling and slicing. Two younger girls ran hither and thither fetching plates and flour and whatever else the cooks required. "How many more hands will fit in here at one time?" she asked.

"Not enough. You tell Lady H she needs a larger kitchen if she's going to fill both dining rooms at every hour of the day and night." Charity pointed a very sharp-looking knife in the direction of the Demeter room, the main dining room at the front of the Tantalus.

With a nod and a stifled smile, Emily stepped around one of the fetching girls back toward the narrow servants' hallway. "I will tell her. Again."

"And you keep telling her until you see the workmen here to push out walls into the carriage drive."

"I will. I give you my solemn oath."

"You just remember you said that."

Saving her grin until she was safely away from the kitchen, Emily chuckled to herself. Oh, she loved this place with its ruined dukes' daughters and former high-flyers and failed opera singers and blacksmiths' sisters all of whom wanted to make a life for themselves without having to turn to other women's desperate last resort of prostitution. Yes, they could have gentlemen callers, as she did, but that was for company and pleasure, not for money. Not to survive.

It was the beginning of the dinner rush, so other serving girls and hostesses hurried from the kitchens to the dining room bringing plates of venison and pheasant and more bottles of whisky and wine and vodka and rum and whatever other spririts were in demand, while the Helpful Men manned the doors to be certain no gentlemen ventured where they were not allowed.

She nodded at Mr. Jacobs, the chief Man, as he walked through the privacy hallway toward his post by the front entry. They had a female butler, but at least one Helpful Man was always close by to see that her words were enforced. Only members and the guests of members were allowed through the front doors. And even so the dukes and sons of viscounts had to behave themselves, or they were escorted back out the doors again.

In all of England it was the safest place for her, and still she had worried. For two years after her arrival at the Tantalus she'd awoken every day convinced that Lord Ebberling would be at her door, Helpful Men or not. But over the past year or so she'd slowly begun to think that perhaps she could finally relax her vigilance a little. A few weeks ago she'd nearly been tempted into going dress shopping with Lucille and Patricia Cooper. And thank goodness she'd hadn't done so.

Stifling a shiver, Emily continued past the privacy hallway to the stairs that led to the top floor and the rooms where she and the other Tantalus girls lived and kept themselves entertained when they weren't on duty.

If she'd been out on the streets and Ebberling had seen her there—*Stop it,* she ordered herself. He hadn't, and she hadn't, so it didn't signify. Aside from that, she hardly looked like the stupid girl she'd been three years ago. Her hair had changed length and color, her dress was certainly not the high-necked, plain and proper attire of a governess, and most significantly, she didn't *feel* like the same person she'd once been.

Even so, a part of her wished Diane had put peepholes into the walls of the privacy hall so she could peer into the various gaming rooms on the other side, just to be certain Ebberling hadn't come visiting with one of his titled cronies. If he did happen to make an appearance, though, the best thing she could do was precisely what she was doing at this moment: staying away from the areas of the club where men—outsiders—were allowed.

Resisting the urge even to peer out one of the front-facing windows of the attic floor, Emily instead took a seat in the common room and opened up the ledger book where she tallied all of the club's nonoperating expenses. Since all of the employees lived on the premises, the club kept towels in the bathing room, mattresses and basic furniture in all of the bedchambers, blankets, utensils, plates, and all of the necessities that didn't go directly into the public rooms.

She generally balanced the ledger twice each month, but with her avoiding working in the rooms, she didn't feel she was pulling her weight any longer. And now, more than ever, she wanted to be . . . necessary. Because once the tipping point came where it was costing the club more to have her there than she helped to earn, she would be relying solely on the kindness of Lady Haybury. And she'd never relied on anyone's kindness.

"Juliet sent me to tell you that you have a caller, Emily," Grace Winters said, walking into the room.

Her heart stopped beating, and all she could hear was her own sharp intake of breath. "Who?" she asked the daytime butleress, when she could make her mouth work again.

"Lord Westfall. He's in the foyer."

Oh, thank goodness. Even with her abrupt relief, though, in the next moment she remembered that he wasn't simply another of her thick-skulled, occasional male companions. He had already demonstrated that he could surprise her. And that made him both desirable and dangerous. She needed to find out for certain if he was on a trail, on *her* trail, or if she'd somehow misinterpreted what both she and Lucille had overheard and what she'd sensed.

Perhaps she should never have suggested anything intimate with him at all, but whatever her actual intentions, she wanted to know if she was in any danger of being discovered. Any additional danger. Aside from that, someone different with whom she could chat, from whom she could hear about the world, was on occasion the only thing that kept her sane. And if he did have a degree of intelligence, as he clearly seemed to, that made him both more enticing—and more dangerous.

"If you aren't going out to meet him, I will," Mary Stanford said, cutting into her thoughts. "That is one fine-looking gentleman."

Emily pushed to her feet. "I'm going. Would you see him upstairs?"

"So now you won't even go into the foyer?" Grace sighed. "Very well."

"Thank you, Grace."

The butleress's comment worried her. Over the past three years most of the Tantalus girls, or at least the ones who'd been there from the beginning, had learned how diligently she avoided leaving the club's grounds. Some of them purchased and retrieved gowns and hair ribbons for her. Others knew that Emily Portsman wasn't her true name—though thankfully she was fairly certain that only Sophia White and Camille Pryce had suspected that, and they were both married and gone from the club.

Jenny knew, as well, but then Genevieve Martine knew everything. About everyone. *Hm.* Emily hesitated on the stairs, then returned to the common room where Jenny generally took her dinner when she wasn't on duty.

Her blond hair pulled into a tight bun at the back of her head and her deep blue gown conservative by Tantalus standards, Jenny sat at one of the long communal tables chatting with Sylvie Hartford and Pansy Bridger. Taking a breath, Emily walked up to face her. "Might I have a quick word with you, Jenny?" she asked, as easily as she could, considering that over the past two days she'd felt wound tighter than a clock.

"Certainly." Miss Martine excused herself and stood, leading the way to the empty corner of the room. "This man you wish to avoid is not here, is he?" she asked in her light French accent—an accent that Emily had heard vanish and alter depending on the circumstances and company.

"No. I don't think so, at least. I haven't checked with Diane this evening. And thank you for not saying the name."

Jenny nodded. "Whoever said that words cannot wound like weapons was a fool. What is it you need, my dear?"

"I had a wonder. If I asked you about another man, might you be able to tell me something about him?"

"That would depend on who he is and what it is you wish to know."

Now she had to ask herself whether she was simply looking for trouble where it didn't exist, attempting to explain to herself why she'd been so utterly unable to resist a seduction when she'd intended something else entirely, or whether she had finally learned the lessons of her life well enough to pay attention when something felt amiss. "Nathaniel Stokes," she finally said aloud. "The Earl of Westfall."

Tilting her head, for a moment Jenny looked younger than the six-and-twenty years she was reputed to be. She mothered them all, looked out for them all, and yet they were of an age. It was odd, really; Genevieve Martine seemed so much older than the rest of them. Even Diane. Perhaps her life had been even more troubled than Emily's own, though that was difficult to imagine.

"Should you not have asked this question before you invited him upstairs?"

"Yes, but I had a suspicion he was looking for something, and I thought I might be able to wheedle it out of him. But he either doesn't know anything, or he's more clever than I realized." And far more skilled in the bedchamber. "And he's on his way upstairs again, so—"

"It will take more than a moment, Emily. I know things, but I do not carry newspapers and heritage books about in my reticule."

Emily forced a smile. "I know that. When you have a moment, then. You've done me so many favors, Jenny, and I keep asking for more."

"Favors are for strangers. We are family, yes?"

This time Emily's smile was real, and crowded close to rare, genuine tears. "Yes. Thank you."

"Nonsense. Now go find your gentleman before he begins pawing through your private things."

Now that was a thought. As Emily left the common room for her bedchamber, she hoped Westfall *was* going through her drawers and her wardrobe. Because firstly that would tell her for certain he was after her, and secondly there would be nothing for him to find—which might put him off her trail entirely.

Her door stood partly open, and she eased up to it, attempting to ignore her speeding heartbeat as she carefully leaned her head in to peer inside. Westfall was indeed there, sitting in her plain wooden chair by the window and reading *The Scottish Cousin*. Drat. That might have proved him innocent of any spying, she supposed, except that it didn't. She'd found a very long time ago that absence of proof only made one tricky. Not innocent. Unless he *was* innocent.

"There you are," he said, and she jumped.

Westfall adjusted his spectacles, standing rather abruptly and setting the book on the windowsill like a guilty schoolboy. He wore a fine dark gray jacket with black well-fitting trousers and a lighter gray waistcoat, and as she took him in, unexpected arousal trailed down her spine. Whatever else he might be, Nathaniel Stokes was a handsome, well-built man.

"Here I am," she said aloud, walking the rest of the way into the room and shutting the door behind her—after she placed the scarf on the door handle. Thankfully Lily Banks didn't mind being ousted from the room on occasion. "I thought you'd forgotten about me. It's been three days."

"Well, I didn't want to appear overeager. And you did say anytime after noon, did you not?"

Had she? It wasn't like her to be so distracted, especially when he was at least partly the cause of it. "I did," she decided. "You have a good memory, my lord."

He smiled. "Not the best compliment I've ever received, but woefully accurate." Light green eyes lowered, taking in her simple gown and lingering at her bosom. "You aren't working this evening?"

If she had been, she would have dressed in something of a much richer material, with a more revealing neckline. But he'd noticed the difference. Oh, her brain was beginning to hurt with attempting to decipher at least two meanings to every word he spoke. "No. I'm not."

"Ah. Good." He cleared his throat. "I know you said

that you don't leave the club, but I found a very nice inn at the edge of Town. They serve the best roasted pheasant I have ever tasted. Would you care to accompany me there? I promise to behave myself and return you directly to the Tantalus after dinner."

Panic gripped her heart, but she shoved it away. Panic only made things worse and prevented logical thinking. "If you haven't eaten I can have something brought up here. Perhaps an equally fine roast pheasant." It would cost her the price of a regular club dinner, because the common room's fare was never as grand as that. If it could distract him, though, it would be well worth it.

"I accept your challenge," he said. He walked up to her and lifted his arms toward her. Gathering the remains of her resolve, Emily took a step back. "I don't kiss," she announced, far too late to do any good.

He lowered his arms again. "We kissed the other day," he returned, sounding very like a slightly befuddled, bookish fellow.

For the first time it occurred to her that if he was as he appeared, she might well be leading him on. "You surprised me. As a rule, however, I don't kiss."

"Why not?"

"I don't kiss because this"—and she gestured between them—"is only for fun. And temporary. I hate to think I've been leading you on, Westfall. Though it's happened on rare occasion, Tantalus girls as a rule do not marry members of the peerage. Nor am I after a husband, nor do I wish to be kept like some finch in a cage."

Green eyes behind round lenses studied her for a moment. "And kissing is not fun?" he asked, ignoring the rest of her dialogue.

"Kissing is about emotion. Or so it seems to me."

A slight smile curved his mouth. It was a very nice mouth, she had to admit, in a way she couldn't quite describe. *Welcoming,* she supposed. And it made her think of being naked, with him touching her.

"So you have no actual dislike of kissing," he continued. "Merely its timing and application."

"Correct."

He took a half step closer, so that she had to lift her chin to continue to meet his gaze. "Might I beg your indulgence then, for one moment? I have a theory I wish to prove. About kissing and fun."

If this was about him attempting to track her—or someone—down for Ebberling, he had a very odd way of going about it. Of course if he was innocent of subterfuge, this would merely have been a very intriguing way of beginning the evening. And his previous kisses still felt half seared into her. Had that just been surprise, though? She nodded. "Very well."

Westfall moved still closer, so that her breasts brushed against his chest. He slowly moved his left hand up to cup the back of her neck, while the fingers of his right hand brushed her cheek. Then he bent his head, brushing his mouth featherlight against hers. It was so different from the deep, passion-filled kiss of the other day that it surprised her. Before she could classify it at all, he caught her lower lip between his teeth and tugged ever so gently. Releasing her, he brought his mouth down over hers for an openmouthed embrace that found her tangling her tongue with his. Down between her legs she went wet and hot.

"There," he said, straightening, lowering his hands again. "Would you say that was about an emotional connection, or about having fun?"

She just barely resisted the urge to touch her mouth with her fingers. "I would say that that was about sex," she managed, her voice not nearly as steady as she'd intended.

He lifted an eyebrow, the arch rising above the rim of his spectacles. "Is that good or bad?"

Emily grabbed his hair in both hands and yanked him down over her mouth again. "Good," she muttered, the word muffled.

She seemed to have forgotten about her offer of roast pheasant, but as she pulled him down to the bed on top of her, Nathaniel decided that was both understandable and inconsequential. For a chit who avoided kissing she did it well enough, and he stifled a moan as her hands wandered down to cup his crotch.

When she pushed him onto his back and then crawled down the length of him to unfasten his trousers and take his cock in her mouth, the bits of his brain still working wondered how he could even imagine that Emily Portsman was the high-in-the-instep Rachel Newbury. A stiff-backed governess would not be comfortable with doing what she was presently doing between his legs.

She laughed as he pulled pins from her hair, tossing them aside to tangle his fingers through the straight chestnut mass that curtained her face from view. For God's sake, that felt good.

When he felt an inch from bursting he tugged her up his body again. "If you don't stop that at once, Portsman, you'll ruin what I'd intended to be a very lengthy and satisfying performance."

With a chuckle she lifted her skirts and sank down on him. "There's always the encore, Westfall."

As she bounced up and down on him he worked at yanking her arms from her sleeves and then pulling her gown down to her waist. That done, he sat up and kissed her again before he turned his attention and his tongue to her breasts.

"Oh, oh," she panted, then practically leaped from the bed. "Wait!" Fumbling into her bedstand, she removed another of the French condoms she seemed to store in ample supply and fitted it over his engorged member.

His spectacles began to fog, and he pulled them off to stuff the damned things under a pillow where he wouldn't lose track of them. She was absolutely delicious, and he twisted to swiftly undo enough of her buttons and ribbons to pull her gown down her legs. She kicked out of it and straddled his hips again. "Now you may proceed," she murmured breathlessly, closing her eyes and groaning as she lowered herself around him.

At that he left off thinking altogether and surged up into her, matching her pace until she found her release. With a rumble he came, as well, holding her down across his hips until he'd finished. Then he sank back flat on the bed as she folded herself over him.

"That performance definitely calls for an encore," she breathed, kissing him, nipping his lower lip as he'd done to her. *"Meraviglioso."*

He felt her hesitate for an instant, then resume kissing him. She spoke Italian. For a Tantalus girl that might not have been so remarkable, but the fact that she'd evidently regretted saying *marvelous* in perfectly accented Italian spoke volumes. With every passing moment he wanted less and less to discover that she was other than what she claimed, and yet . . .

"Grazie," he returned, keeping his own eyes closed as he felt her lashes flutter against his cheek. It still might not mean anything, but every ounce of his being

thought otherwise. Emily Portsman was hiding something. And now he could only hope that he'd somehow stumbled across a young lady who'd fled from a poor wedding match or an unloving husband. Or that she'd stolen a ring from her former employer. Or anything but a necklace. A necklace and a murder.

In the few minutes he'd had before he'd heard her approaching down the hallway, he had managed to look through her bedstand and flip through the pages of two of the books sitting on the narrow bookshelf across the room. Other than a generous supply of French condoms—evidently Miss Portsman was *very* cautious, indeed, when it came to lovers—he'd found absolutely nothing that pointed to her as a culprit in any crime at all.

So other than her immediate interest in him after Laurie's blunder and that one word of Italian, why did he continue to suspect that she wasn't who or what she claimed? What other than the prickle of something unsettling that touched him whenever he looked at her? Of course that was in addition to the something lustful prickling him at the same time.

Yes, she was intelligent, but so were the majority of The Tantalus Club's employees. Yes, she seemed to have an aversion to leaving the club's grounds—but he had no idea of her background, so her reluctance might have been due to something other than a wish to avoid Lord Ebberling and anyone who might know the marquis.

One thing at a time, then. Eliminate all possible trails, and follow what remained. He'd learned to do that well over the past ten years; anyone who didn't learn that lesson didn't live long enough to regret it.

With her nipping at his ear the blood seemed reluctant to return to his brain, but he could think well enough to remember that she'd been the one to bring up her refusal to leave the Tantalus grounds. He could therefore ask her why.

"I met your cousin, you know," she said before he could decide how to phrase his question. "Gerard, yes?"

"Yes." He sent her a sideways glance. "When you say you 'met,' does—"

"I mean he sat for dinner and faro downstairs on several occasions," she interrupted. "And he seemed a true gentleman."

That was an interesting choice of words. "As opposed to an untrue gentleman?"

"As opposed to someone who is called a gentleman simply because that is the custom. The way a Thoroughbred is a horse and a rag-and-bones man's cart dray is a horse." She flopped down beside him to run the palm of her hand up beneath his shirt. "I don't think anyone would mistake one for the other."

"A very good analogy, Portsman. So why d—"

"Before you became Westfall," she broke in again, her finger idly brushing his nipples, "what did you do? Were you in the army, or a pastor, or an idle gentleman?"

She's interrogating me, he thought, *and attempting to distract me at the same time.* And she was tolerably good at it. Was it casual interest, though, or something more? *Hm.* The fact that he still couldn't decide was in itself telling. Perhaps "tolerably good" was an understatement. "Can you imagine me in the army?" he countered, rather than outright answering. She could draw her own conclusions from that. "And I think being a clergyman would be excessively dull. I did have considerably more time for mathematics and reading previous to my cousin's unfortunate death, though. I miss that."

"You seem in reasonably good physical shape for a dabbler in mathematics and a reader," she insisted, leaning over him to run her lips across his abdomen.

"Well, thank you for saying that. I attempt to go riding daily, and of course walking through London's parks is very invigorating." Good God. He sounded like an old man. Time to counterattack. "But I'm not the only one whose life has been altered over the past few years, surely. What did you do before the Tantalus opened?" It was more direct than he cared to be, but she'd left the door open. If he hadn't stepped through, he wouldn't have been able to call himself a spy any longer.

She sat up. "Me? It's a very dull tale, Westfall. A chit with a yen for a better life who blundered. And I completely forgot that I challenged you not to enjoy Miss Green's roast pheasant." Sliding to the edge of the bed, she donned a dressing gown and stepped for the door. "I'll be back in just a moment. And I think you should remove the remainder of your clothes while I'm gone."

Nate took a breath as she reached the door. "You know, we've all blundered in the past," he said slowly, mentally crossing his fingers. "We're all friends here, aren't we?"

Emily faced him, one hand on the door handle. "Simply because we've been in bed together doesn't mean I trust you, Westfall. In here we're a man and a woman. Out there"—and she indicated the world beyond her window—"you're a lord and I'm a nobody. The balance shifts, loyalties and trust don't signify. If you want a lady with no secrets, Lucille Hampton's bedchamber is two doors down the hallway. She'll blather until your ears bleed."

"Portsman, I—"

"Whatever you think you know, you don't. And I think you should leave."

He sat up, swinging his still-booted feet over the side of the bed. "And what is it you think I know?" he asked, studying her face intently for any sign of ... anything.

For a long moment she met his gaze, her pretty brown eyes serious and searching just as closely. "Don't forget your spectacles," she finally said, and slipped out the door.

Damnation. He'd blundered. And in this instance he didn't feel relieved to have escaped alive, or thankful he would now have a chance to learn from his mistake. No, this time he was angry. He wasn't finished with Emily Portsman. Not finished with his questions, and not finished with sex. Time, then, to step up this game and see if she could still play.

Chapter Seven

Jenny?"

Emily knocked on the door to the small suite of rooms Genevieve Martine had at the back part of Adam House. Jenny had volunteered to room with the rest of the club's employees, Emily knew, but Diane had instead given her the five rooms at the east corner of the main house.

Behind her, even through the thick walls dividing Adam House from the club, she thought she could hear the high-pitched titter of female voices. All the club's employees looked forward to the two Wednesdays every month that had been designated as ladies' days—none of them were allowed to work, and every eligible croupier, footman, and waiter for the rest of London's clubs flocked to the Tantalus to offer their services.

Only women—not members, but those invited by a select group of ladies designated by Diane—were permitted through the doors. They dined and wagered and chatted without having to be exposed to the scandalous flock of Tantalus girls, while those same girls tended to leave en masse for Vauxhall Gardens or wherever chits such as they were could go. Throughout London the aristocrats complained of the poor service they received at their other clubs on those Wednesdays, since all the young lads deserted to serve at the Tantalus.

For tonight all it meant for Emily was that Westfall wouldn't be calling on her. She thought she'd made it clear that he wasn't to do so at any time, but after two days she remained uncertain over whether he would keep away. She knocked at the door again. Mr. Smith of the Helpful Men had said Jenny remained at home this evening, but that had been an hour or more ago.

Finally the door opened, and light blue eyes beneath tightly coiffed blond hair looked out at her. "What's amiss?" Jenny asked.

"Oh. Nothing. I only wanted . . . you're not occupied, are you?" None of the Tantalus girls had ever seen Jenny ask a man upstairs, but that didn't mean she hadn't done so. Jenny very nearly seemed able to disappear at will, after all.

"Only with some reading." Miss Martine backed away from the door. "Come in, my dear."

Emily entered the short hallway and closed the door behind her as Jenny vanished ahead of her into the small sitting room. "I truly didn't mean to disturb you. I only wondered if you'd learned anything about Lord Westfall."

"You don't give a lady much time, do you?" Jenny had seated herself before the hearth, a stack of newspapers three feet high on the floor beside her. As far as anyone knew, she had newspapers dating back ten years or more, all neatly organized in a small storage room together with maps and books and other bits and bobs that no one else could make any sense of.

"I know. It's just that I can't shake the feeling that he's not what he says he is. And that he's after something." He's after *me,* she thought, but she still couldn't be entirely certain that he was anything more than a liar about his poor vision. Feelings might point her in the correct direction, but she needed facts. And the sooner the better.

"And yet you entertained him in your room a second time, did you not?" Jenny queried as she picked up a newspaper, opened it, and handed it up to Emily.

"I did. And then after he began asking about my life and saying I could trust him, I told him to leave."

"That was a mistake, you know. Especially if you had suspicions about him."

Emily sighed. "Yes, I know." It had troubled her from the moment she'd said the words, that in reacting too swiftly to what might—by anyone else—have been construed as harmless questions, from one lover to the other, she'd revealed too much of herself. But she knew—she *knew* that he wasn't what he claimed. Not entirely.

"The column on the left-hand page," Jenny said. "And take a seat, if you please."

She sat, going to the narrow column of print under the headline WELLINGTON'S STRATEGIES ON THE PENINSULA. It had been written three years ago, just after Bonaparte's second capture, and after Wellington had been elevated to duke. In less-than-exciting language considering it talked about war, the article detailed the mission of the foot soldiers, the cavalry, the navy, and Wellington's famed network of spies and turncoats.

"I don't see anything," she said after a moment, looking across the breadth of the fireplace at Genevieve. "Some soldiers being commended for their exceptional service, but nothing about Nathaniel Stokes."

"No? Not the Wellington article. The one at the bottom of the page."

Lowering her gaze to the short article at the bottom, Emily read through it. NOTABLE PERSONAGES ENTERING LONDON SOCIETY, it read, listing several aristocrats who'd recently made the trip back to London after an absence. Most of them were officers who'd been away on duty, along with younger people finally of an age to attend soirees . . . and one Nathaniel Stokes, who had evidently been abroad for the previous four years.

" 'Abroad,' " she said aloud. "That's not very helpful."

"It is if you look at the timing and the lack of information," Jenny returned, in a tone that said she was speaking with an infant. "The others are very specific; Lord Humphries, who gallantly served with the 101st Foot in Spain and Belgium and who has now returned to Grey House on Bond Street to be reunited with Lady Humphries and young Lord Victor. And then Nathaniel Stokes, who has been abroad. For the entire duration of the war and then some."

"Jenny, I—"

"He was a spy," Jenny cut in. "For Wellington."

Emily's blood turned to ice. "You're certain? Just from that?"

"Not just from that, but yes. I . . . have reason to recognize the patterns and the language. Aside from that, the name Nate Stokes is not unknown in certain circles."

"Your circles?" Emily asked, her hands shaking so badly she had to set the paper down.

"If I were ever to admit such a thing I might nod my head. But you will very rarely hear anyone say so directly." She sat forward, pulling the newspaper closer and carefully refolding it. "A spy for Wellington is not an enemy, Emily, but a spy in someone else's employ is a dangerous thing, indeed. Especially a spy named Nate Stokes."

"I—I need to leave," Emily said in a small voice that sounded reluctant even to her own ears. For three years she'd felt safe. Or if not safe, then at least a little protected. And not alone. Now it was over. Her home, her new family—she needed to leave them all behind. Immediately.

"Emily, this thing from which you hide. I think you know you could trust me with it. And Diane. And even Haybury."

Emily shook her head, the ice spreading through her like winter. "No. It's better for all of you if you don't know."

"Perhaps I can judge for myself what is good for me to know or not. And fleeing into the night without a plan is never a wise idea."

Forcing herself to think logically for a moment, Emily had to agree that Jenny had a point. When she'd fled before, she hadn't had a plan, and it had cost her dearly. Finding The Tantalus Club had been an accident, a moment of providence, and she wasn't likely to be so lucky the next time. "I haven't seen him for two days," she said aloud, her voice unsteady. "I asked him to go away, and he has."

"Then I would say that even if he suspects something, he does not yet have proof. A spy is trained to find definitive proof before taking action—because a spy's truths cost men their lives."

"I don't know what to do, then. It's still safer if I go."

"Unless your flight is the proof for which he is waiting."

She hadn't thought of that. The idea that he might be lurking outside the club, waiting for her finally to stick her head out the door . . . She drew a shaking breath. Nothing had happened yet. Nothing other than a few questions she hadn't answered, and a man's visit to her private rooms. Twice. If he was a spy, and he did need definitive proof, he hadn't found it. She'd certainly left nothing for him to discover.

"What do you suggest?" she asked, managing to steady her voice.

"You won't like it."

"I don't like any of this."

Jenny slowly sank back into the plush brown chair again. "A guilty person, a frightened person, acts in a particular way. Acting in this manner might be the last bit of information he needs from you. So do not act in that manner. Do not hide. Do not be cautious. Or do not appear to be. You have fooled most everyone so far, but Nate Stokes is not like everyone else."

And that was what she'd begun to enjoy about him. She clenched her jaw. The tactic would take a great deal of courage. Perhaps more than she had. "When will he stop looking, though?"

"When he's convinced you are not the one he seeks."

"It seems very risky." Especially when she had a very good idea that she was precisely who he was after.

To her surprise, Jenny gave a small smile. "Life is risky, Emily. I don't know what you hide from, but the consequences of it remain hanging over your head, regardless of what you do or where you go. Is taking this risk worth the reward of being able to put those things aside if you can convince Stokes—Westfall—that you are not this other person?"

That was a very good question. Even if she could convince Nathaniel that she had nothing to do with Ebberling, the marquis himself remained in London. Whatever changes she'd made to her appearance, a chance existed that he would recognize her. But once he left, and once Nathaniel turned his attention elsewhere, she might . . . she might be able to walk outside. To go shopping with her friends, or stroll through Hyde Park on a sunny day. Or ride to Dover to see the ocean. Or to Vauxhall to see the Thames.

"Yes," she said slowly, meeting Jenny's gaze. "It is worth the risk."

And it had nothing to do with the fact that she liked him, that she liked sex with him, and that she surprisingly liked kissing him, and that she wanted him to be after someone's lost hound and not Rachel Newbury. Those were just wishes, and wishes were for fools.

"Do you have results for me then, Westfall?" the Marquis of Ebberling demanded, striding into the Velton House morning room where Nathaniel and Laurence had been placed five minutes earlier.

So much for pleasantries. Nate had become accustomed to that greeting, however; in order to indulge his hobby he'd allowed himself to be hired. As far as Ebberling was concerned, they were *not* equals. That would suit, for now. He remained by the window where he'd placed himself. "Not as yet. I wanted a ch—"

"Not yet? I was told you were the man for this task. What am I paying you for, if—"

"You allowed the trail to go three years cold. It will take longer than a fortnight for me to track your lost item," Nathaniel broke in, wondering for a moment why he continued to keep his suspicions about Emily Portsman to himself. It would save him a tongue-lashing from a marquis, certainly. Aside from that, it would be simple enough to learn the truth about her once and for all. He could haul Ebberling into the Tantalus, point at Portsman, and ask if the marquis recognized her.

If he was wrong, though, the true Miss Newbury would know that the hunt for her was on, and she would flee. If he was wrong and Ebberling was hungrier for someone to hang than for the truth, he would be doing Emily a great injustice. And just to himself, at the very back edge of his thoughts, he could admit that he wasn't terribly anxious for this hunt to be over. That he liked having an excuse to make amends with Portsman.

"Yes, my lost item," Ebberling rumbled, seeming to notice Laurie for the first time. "And who are you?"

"His brother," Laurence commented, pointing a finger in Nathaniel's direction.

"Why is your brother here, then? I asked for your assistance. Not for that of your entire bloodline. And I also asked for your discretion."

That he had. They always did. "I wanted to have a chat with your son, if I might," Nate stated, pushing up his spectacles and attempting to look his most harmless. "Young George might have some insights I could use."

"No."

This investigation was becoming more interesting by the moment. "It won't be an interrogation. My brother brought his new mount, and I thought George might enjoy a short ride about the stable yard. Laurence is quite amiable, as is Dandelion."

Ebberling looked from one to the other of them. "George likes horses. Very well. But I expect a full report on whatever information you gain from him."

It might have been that the father didn't want to subject the lad to further trauma, but Ebberling certainly hadn't mentioned anything of the kind. Or it might have been as simple as the marquis not wishing to discuss the marchioness's death. Or it might not. "Of course," he said aloud. "We'll be in the stable yard."

With a curt nod the marquis left the room and called for a Mrs. Peabody—presumably the boy's new governess. Laurence took Nate's shoulder as they left the front entry for the yard. " 'Dandelion'?" he repeated.

Nate shrugged. "It sounds harmless. I'm not going

to say we wish to set his son and heir on Widowmaker while we interrogate him."

"I'm not calling him the Widowmaker. That was only something I was contemplating. I decided on Dragon."

"Ah. Much more acceptable. Today he's Dandelion." Stifling a grin, Nathaniel walked up to the pretty bay gelding and patted him on the withers.

"If a name meant anything, we'd be putting young George up on Blue," Laurie muttered.

"And then we both could join the elusive Miss Newbury in running from a murder," Nathaniel returned in the same tone, putting a smile on his face as young George bounded around the corner, an elderly stick of a woman on his heels. "You must be George," he said in his friendliest voice. "Your father tells me you're an admirer of horseflesh."

"Oh, yes!" the boy shouted, grinning widely.

George Velton couldn't be more than eight or nine, which would have made him five or six at the time of his mother's death and Rachel Newbury's departure. Five-year-olds did not make the most reliable of witnesses. What they were exceptional at, however, was reading a man or a woman's character. And that was what he wanted to know.

Two of Ebberling's grooms were also present, evidently to make certain that the lad didn't break his neck. Considering the care with which he and Laurie had selected the bay, and the reputation of Sullivan Waring's stables for producing reliable mounts, they had nothing to worry about.

What he found more curious was that Ebberling remained indoors. In his experience, fathers, sons, and horses were a nearly inseparable trio in aristocratic circles. But he hadn't been hired to determine his employer's character. Bending, he took George around the waist and lifted him into the saddle. A groomsman and Laurie shortened the stirrups while Nate held the reins and the boy bounced excitedly, all skinny arms and legs and ears. Evidently the boy took after his late mother in looks, because other than the dark hair, he didn't resemble the marquis a whit.

"What's his name?" he asked, patting the gelding's neck. "He's sterling."

"Dandelion," Laurie supplied, even managing to avoid grimacing as he said the name. "From Waring's stables."

"Oh, that's diamond. Waring has the best stables in England! I've been wanting one of his, but Father says I'm not old enough."

"Perhaps this will convince him," Nathaniel put in. "Did your father tell you who we are?"

"He said you were Lord Westfall," the boy returned, then looked at Laurie. "And you were Westfall's brother."

Laurie offered his hand. "Laurence Stokes. You may call me Laurie, if you like."

They shook hands. "I'm Viscount Ryling, but you may call me George."

"George it is, then." Laurie patted the boy's thigh. "Ready to give Dandelion a go?"

"I certainly am," the young viscount replied. "I'm a very good rider."

Nathaniel handed over the reins and shifted his grip to the bridle. Clucking his tongue, he led the gelding into a walk around the perimeter of the yard while his younger brother kept pace beside George, chatting with his usual easy amiability.

As they walked, Nate watched his brother. Seeing

him beside an eight-year-old made one thing clear—
Laurence wasn't a child any longer. And he had a re-
freshing way of being himself that made his older
brother mildly jealous. As did the fact that most people
genuinely liked Laurence Stokes.

"That skinny woman," Laurence said in a confiden-
tial tone. "Is she your governess?"

George scowled. "She is. She's very slow, though. I
can't run anywhere. I can't even walk quickly without
her yelling at me. It's quite disappointing. I'm accustomed to being more active."

"When I was your age, I had a governess named
Mrs. Reed. She knew all the words to 'Drunken
Sailor.' "

"Mrs. Peabody would have an apoplexy if I sang that
song." George giggled. "I think you should teach me."

"No one's taught you any sea chanteys? This is a
travesty," Laurence commented with a grin. "Did you
have a governess before Mrs. Peabody?"

"Yes." George's face fell. "But I'm not supposed to
talk about her."

"Why not?"

"She killed my mother. Father says so. I don't think
she would do that, though, because Miss Newbury and
my mother were good friends. They shared books and
everything."

"Did you like Miss Newbury, then?"

"Oh, very much. She helped me learn about insects
and plants, because when I was little I wanted to be a
botanist. Now I'm going to ride a horse in the Derby."

"Did Miss Newbury know any sea chanteys?"

"Probably, but she would never teach me any. Father
says I'm always to be a gentleman." He bounced in the
saddle. "Did you see Sullivan Waring when you purchased Dandelion?"

Laurence shook his head. "Lord Bram Johns was at Tattersall's with Waring's horses."

"Oh, they're partners. They were in the war together."

Nathaniel stifled another grin. Laurence was finally getting a taste of what it was like to have a conversation with himself. Perhaps his brother would pay more heed to staying on the subject during their own discussions, from now on. "What was your favorite thing to do with Miss Newbury?" he asked, taking pity on his sibling.

"Well, we went for a walk almost every day, and she helped me catch frogs. That was quite fun."

Frog catching didn't quite fit with his vision of a nose-in-the-air governess, but that was why he was there—to gain some insight into her character that the butler and the marquis and the housekeeper had lacked. "What did you do on rainy days?" he pursued, walking backward to keep both eyes on the lad.

He smiled. "Oh, we read. Miss Newbury and I would act all the parts in the stories. My favorite was the one with the hedgehog and the badger." Abruptly his expression collapsed into a frown. "But Father says only silly people read silly stories that can't possibly be true. They're for babies, and I'm almost nine."

Laurie sent a glance over Nathaniel's shoulder. "You're out of time," he murmured.

"Go chat with Ebberling, will you?" Nate whispered back at him. "I need two minutes."

"If I get my head bitten off I'm blaming you." Laurence patted young George on the knee and strode back to the edge of the yard. There he began chatting about . . . something. Whatever it was, Ebberling didn't seem terribly interested. However charming Laurie could be, two minutes might be a bit much to ask.

Nate returned his attention to the young boy sitting on the overlarge saddle. "Was Miss Newbury happy at Ebberling?" he asked quietly. "Did you ever see her cry?"

"I saw her cry two times," the lad returned, ducking his head closer to reply in the conspiratorial tone that Nate had used. "One time Mama was sick, and Miss Newbury took me down to dinner, when usually she ate in her own bedchamber."

"Did she cry before or after dinner?"

"After dinner, when she came back upstairs to tuck me into bed and read to me. I even asked her what was wrong, and she said . . . let me think. She said something about how her own mama had been sickly, too, and she used to bring her flowers to cheer her up. And we picked flowers from the garden in the morning, and Mama liked them very much. Her favorite was the yellow daisies, but Miss Newbury liked white roses."

For a moment Nate ran that convoluted bit of conversation through his mind. Knowing Rachel Newbury liked roses was well and good, but something about the rest of the conversation felt off. "Did she stay downstairs with your father for very long after dinner that night?" he finally asked.

"Not for very long," the boy answered. "I only had time to put on my nightshirt and feed flies to my frogs and review my butterfly collection."

Then she had been alone with the marquis, and for long enough to engage in more than discourse. Had she been his mistress? Had the marchioness died because of some governess's jealousy? Had the tears been because Ebberling had ended the affair? Too many damned questions, and not enough answers. "What was the other time she cried?" he pushed, noting that the marquis's face was growing red. Evidently even Laurie's charms had their limits.

"I remember that very well. It was right when she left. I was playing with my frogs, because I was training them to hop across the keys of the pianoforte, and she ran by the music room and I saw her crying. I went to ask what was amiss, but I couldn't find her, and then Father came into the house and he was very angry and said everyone was to look for Miss Newbury because something terrible had happened and it was her fault."

"He didn't tell you what the terrible thing was?"

"Everyone was shouting it at once. I cried, too, but I was little, then. Only five years old. I'm much older now."

"I can see that." The marquis was approaching now, and Nate stepped up to lift the boy off the horse's back. "Was it a nice day? The day Miss Newbury left?"

"Yes. We would have gone for a walk, but I hadn't finished my sums." He frowned. "I finished them after, but it was too late."

"That's enough questions, Westfall," Ebberling announced, nudging his son in the shoulder to send the boy off toward Mrs. Peabody. "Now do what I'm paying you for, or I'll find someone else."

Laurie opened his mouth, likely to say something about how Nate was an earl and they didn't appreciate being ordered about like servants. But then Laurie likely didn't realize how much more servants heard simply because their masters discounted them. Nathaniel put a hand on his brother's arm. "I *am* doing what you hired me for," he returned mildly, making a show of leaning on his cane. "In fact, I now believe Miss Newbury may well be here in London."

The marquis's eyes narrowed. "What? You've found her?"

Very likely, Nate thought to himself. "The more I

know about her, the more I'm able to narrow down my search. At the moment I believe her to be in London. I'll know more as I continue."

"Then you haven't actually found anything."

It amazed him on occasion, the disdain most self-styled men of action had for those who preferred to use their minds. And yet, Ebberling had come to *him* for aid—not the other way around. "I have found several nothings," he said aloud. "Every one of them tells me where not to search."

"That sounds like ballocks to me. My marriage is a month away. I want her found, Westfall."

With a nod, Nate returned Dandelion's reins to his brother and collected his own Blue from a waiting groom. "I shall do so. Ebberling. Lord Ryling."

The boy waved at the two of them as they trotted down the carriage path for the street, but the marquis only turned his back and stalked toward the house. The moment they turned the corner heading for Teryl House, Laurence grabbed his elbow.

"Why in God's name did you let him speak to you like that? You're as much a lord as he is."

"Not according to him. In his eyes I'm an upjumped nobody whose cousin had the misfortune not to have any more appropriate heirs. And at the moment I find that useful, so leave it be."

" 'Useful,' " Laurence repeated, making the word sound venomous. "Sometimes it's not about your bloody spying games. Sometimes it's about being who you are, and being respected for it. You're an earl, Nate. Nothing's going to change that."

He was quite aware of that, and he'd been discovering that nothing was as uncomfortable as a costume that couldn't be removed. "Don't trouble yourself, Laurie. He wasn't insulting you."

"Yes he was. We're not nobodies. Even if we were, we wouldn't be. No one should speak to anyone like that."

"That's very progressive-minded of you. Don't let any of our new peers hear you say that, or they'll dislike you more than they do me."

"I don't see the bloody reason for encouraging them to discount you," Nate retorted. "Do you mean to spend the remainder of your life taking coins you don't need so you can find baubles they don't need? You're better than most of them. For God's sake, you risked your life for nearly ten years for them."

"Not for them," Nate countered. "For you." He cleared his throat as he caught his brother staring at him. "Now. Would you and Dandelion care to take a turn about Hyde Park? Or would y—"

"Dragon," his brother interrupted. "If we're all assuming the identities we choose, my damned horse wishes to be called Dragon."

Nate chuckled. "Fair enough. Blue and I will race you to the Serpentine."

"You and Blue will lose."

He and Blue didn't lose, but it was a near thing. After an hour of riding about and pretending to be absentminded to half of Society's daughters and sisters who'd decided to drive carriages through the park, however, he'd begun to feel decidedly less victorious. Laurence showed well, though, all charm and warm wits, so he supposed that was worth something. If there had been any justice in the world, Laurie would have been the one to become the Earl of Westfall, and he might have been left to do as he pleased.

As they chatted with all the young ladies he kept a closer eye on their companions, or the governesses of any younger sisters they'd dragged into London for the

Season. None of them came even remotely close to Ebberling's description of Rachel Newbury. And as usual when he contemplated Miss Newbury, the portrait in his mind was that of Emily Portsman.

It didn't seem at all likely that he would have found his quarry on his first attempt, but odder things had happened. And she had found him as much as he'd found her. After all, if she hadn't approached the table again after seating them, he likely wouldn't have looked at her twice. Not to begin with, anyway. But she had, and she'd made a point of seducing him and then asking all sorts of leading questions that only meant something if he happened to be of a suspicious nature, which he was.

Three days ago she'd told him to go away, but that hadn't stopped him from thinking about her, from attempting to puzzle her out. To himself he could admit that it wasn't only Ebberling's task that kept him conjuring her, however. Because even if the sex had been a means to rattle his tongue or his brain loose, the act itself had been exceedingly arousing. He still wished to repeat it.

But he'd looked straight at her, gazed at her sharply, in fact, and she'd noticed that he hadn't been wearing his bloody spectacles. And he'd been so surprised that she'd noticed, that he hadn't said anything artful or amusing or sarcastic. He'd just looked at her stupidly until she walked out her door and closed it. And then one of those large Helpful Men had appeared, waiting until he dressed himself and then following him out to the public area of the club.

He'd felt like—he'd felt embarrassed. Certainly he'd done half-witted things before in his life, but during the past ten years they'd all been intentional. They'd lured someone into trusting him, or believing him capable of being duped—usually to that person's detriment. This time he'd simply stumbled, and in the presence of a chit he liked. Of a lady who'd outsmarted him.

"Laurie, your friend Marty Gayle. Do you know the uncle with the membership to The Tantalus Club?" he asked abruptly.

"Not well. I've said hello to him when he came to visit Marty at Oxford, but nothing more than that. Why?"

"Could you convince him to take you to the Tantalus?"

Laurie drew Dragon to a halt. "Why?"

Nathaniel frowned. The only thing worse than being a fool was having to admit to it. "I may have stumbled somewhat. Miss Portsman—I think she realized that I'm looking for someone."

"*You* stumbled." Laurence stared at him, incredulity warring with amusement on his face. "You."

"Yes. I only want to know what is said when you ask after her. Will you do that for m—"

"Just a moment. I'm savoring." Furrowing his brow, his brother glanced in the direction of Carlton House at the edge of Hyde Park. "Oh, thank God. I thought the monarchy might have fallen because you admitted to making a mistake."

Well, that was enough of that. Nathaniel kicked Blue in the ribs, urging the big gelding out of the park and back toward Teryl House. He still couldn't quite bring himself to think of the large white building as home; he'd grown up outside London in much smaller accommodations, after all. At least he was becoming accustomed to it. Much as Miss Newbury had likely become accustomed to her new surroundings, her new means of employment, her new name, her new hair, and whatever else she'd taken up to protect herself.

A moment later Laurie caught up to him. "I'm not apologizing for gloating," his brother commented, "but I'll cease doing it if you'll agree to stop getting your pantaloons in a twist."

"I'll agree if you'll stop suggesting that I wear pantaloons."

Laurence grinned. "Agreed. You almost sounded human there for a moment. I liked it."

"Surely I'm not that bad."

"Yes you are." His brother rolled his shoulders. "So you think Miss Portsman is this Miss Newbury? That's why you want to know about her?"

"I'm not certain yet."

"But you think she might be. That's cold-blooded, Nate." Laurie's smile faded. "You took her to bed. Did you do it just to get information?"

"Laurie . . ." Nathaniel trailed off. The chasm between imaginings about being a spy and actually being one was very wide and deep and full of sharpened stakes to murder the unwary. If he wanted Laurence well clear of his own path he could merely keep his mouth shut and let his brother draw his own conclusions. But he didn't quite feel up to being painted as more of a monster than he actually was. Not today, anyway. "I allowed her to drag me to her bed because I wanted her," he said quietly. "And I still do, which is troublesome because now I suspect her."

"God's sake, Nate. You *are* human. That's frightening."

"A moment ago you liked it."

"Yes, but now you're admitting truths to me. It's a great deal to adjust to, all at once."

Nathaniel mustered a smile at that. "Oh, shut up."

"That's better."

The moment he stepped into the foyer of Teryl House, the butler held out a silver salver piled high with cards and invitations and notes and letters. "These arrived while you were out, my lord."

"I was only gone for two damned hours, Garvey."

"Yes, my lord. It was quite a busy morning. Several of them are for Master Laurence, however."

"That's something, anyway." Evidently the Season had struck with a vengeance, and he no longer had the excuse of being in mourning for his cousin, or even of being new to the machinations of the London elite.

He took the stack of papers and flipped through it, handing Laurie the missives meant for him. "Your schoolmates, I assume?"

"I asked Rawley to keep me apprised of studies and to copy over his lecture notes for me, so I wouldn't fall behind," his brother returned. "I'll have to charm my way into making up the exams, but at least I won't have missed much before the term's end."

For a moment Nate gazed at his younger brother. He was so accustomed to excluding him from his own life that he'd forgotten that also meant missing out on Laurie's. "You may be less frivolous than I previously believed," he finally said.

"Yes, well, not entirely." His brother had the good grace to blush. "I did have that chit in my room."

This time Nathaniel sighed. "I suppose all I can ask is that you not repeat your mistakes."

"You know, brother, if you surprise me one more time today you may give me an apoplexy. I'm going upstairs to attempt to decipher Rawley's hen scratchings before that happens."

Nate barely heard that last part of his brother's comments. His attention was on the folded note toward the bottom of the stack. The return address at the top read only "The Tantalus Club," while whoever had sent it had written only "Westfall" across the front, in a large, elegant hand.

"Thank you," he said absently, turning his back on the butler and making for his office. He didn't know why he bothered to pretend even for a heartbeat that he didn't know who had sent it; no one else at the Tantalus would refer to him only by his title, without bothering to list the house where he resided or even the street on which it sat.

The question was, did the note state that he'd been banned from the club? Not wearing spectacles seemed a hugely minor infraction. In fact, it would mean that he had indeed found Rachel Newbury. And now he was hesitating to open the missive, damn it all. "Stop it," he said aloud, as he sat behind the large mahogany desk.

What did it matter if he wanted to be wrong? Either he was correct and he'd spooked Portsman into revealing her true identity, or he wasn't and he hadn't. And staring at the bloody note without opening it wasn't doing anything but make his head ache.

Growling, he pulled off his spectacles and set them aside, then broke the plain wax seal and unfolded the note. And blinked as he read the salutation. Perhaps he did need spectacles, after all, because this was not at all what he'd expected. "Dear stupid man," he read to himself again, hearing Emily's voice in his head, "Clearly you have never had a tiff with a lover before. If we are indeed finished, please return this note to me with a large *X* through my text so that you will not have to lower yourself to write any words to a Tantalus girl and I will know what's what. Otherwise, I realized after I stalked off that I would indeed like to go for a drive with you, so you may fetch me at three o'clock this afternoon. Portsman."

After a long moment Nate sat back in his chair. Perhaps he was wrong, after all. If so, in her own right Emily Portsman was a warm, witty, lovely young lady. If he was correct, then Rachel Newbury was absolutely remarkable, and he was in the middle of quite possibly the most interesting hunt of his life. Either way, it seemed he would be going for a drive at three o'clock this afternoon.

"Absolutely bloody remarkable," he muttered. And then he laughed. He *had* discovered one thing about Portsman. If she was truly Rachel Newbury, then she wasn't a murderer. No one short of a monster could be a murderer and play the game as she did—and Emily Portsman was no monster.

So instead of finding answers, he'd found more questions. And because the one thing he'd apparently discovered was that he'd begun to like Portsman a great deal—both in and out of bed—he had an even more pressing need to discover what, precisely, was afoot. The sooner, the better.

Chapter Eight

"Don't hang about me, Grace," Emily said, edging a few inches away from the Tantalus daytime butleress. "You're making me nervous."

"But you're going outside," Miss Davenport whispered, then had to walk forward to open the front door and admit Lord Duncanell and his twin sons. "Good afternoon, my lord," she said with the smile that had garnered her a dozen proposals, three of them for marriage.

Yes, she was going outside, Emily reflected, not that she needed anyone else to remind her of the rarity of that deed. On occasion she'd ventured out to the lovely garden on the club's grounds, but even those high walls had a gate—two gates—and that left her feeling distinctly vulnerable.

Of course today she would be leaving the grounds utterly, and in the care and company of the very man who might well drive her directly to Lord Ebberling. She shivered. Jenny Martine had given her two very vital pieces of advice, and she meant to make use of both of them. She'd said that Westfall would require proof before he acted, and she'd pointed out that only the guilty and the frightened hid behind stone walls.

She shrugged closer into her light blue shawl, then tugged the brim of her blue bonnet forward as far as she could. It wasn't about hiding, she told herself. It was about being protected from the sun. That was to be her lie, after all, that she and the sun did not agree.

Grace returned to her side. "Are you certain you wish to go alone?" the butleress asked in that low, conspiratorial tone she'd been using since Emily had arrived in the foyer. "Lucille isn't working this afternoon."

"No," Emily returned, too quickly. The last thing she needed was for Lucille and her wagging tongue and her jealousy over Westfall to accompany them on their drive. "I'll be perfectly fine, Grace. It's not as if I require a chaperone, for heaven's sake." She forced a smile. "And you have to admit, Lord Westfall is worth the risk of a skin rash."

"He looks well enough," her friend agreed, "but he seems rather dull to me." A smile touched her own mouth. "I suppose the trick is to keep him too occupied for conversation."

That would indeed be the trick, Emily reflected, if she could couple it with keeping him from thinking, as well. "Oh, I excel at that," she said aloud, chuckling.

"You are so naughty," Grace whispered, then moved away again as another shadow showed through the window by the front doors.

This time it was the Earl of Westfall who stepped into the foyer. From the dim corner she watched him for a handful of seconds as he spoke with Grace, all the while fiddling with his cane and his spectacles. Every ounce of him bespoke a mild, learned man—every ounce but his lean, fit body and the eyes behind those spectacles.

Jenny had named him a spy in the employ of the

Duke of Wellington. Most would never know that, or even suspect it, but Genevieve Martine wasn't most people. And neither was she, and neither was Nathaniel Stokes. His gaze found her, and he smiled, the expression rendering him even more sharply handsome.

"You said three o'clock, Portsman," he commented, doffing his hat.

"And here I am. Shall we?"

For a moment he tilted his head, gazing at her. "You're certain you wish to go with me?"

Was he offering her a way out? Or warning her that if she left, she wouldn't be returning to the Tantalus? But only guilty or frightened people hid, and as far as he was concerned, she would be neither of those things. Emily grinned. "It isn't you that troubles me," she returned, straightening her wrap and walking forward. "It's the sun. And it does seem to be rather hidden this afternoon."

She'd pulled on elbow-length white gloves, the better to carry on with the farce of her being sun shy. When he offered his arm she wrapped her gloved fingers around his sleeve. Refusing to hold her breath or hesitate, or to acknowledge that even with her trepidation she liked touching him, she stepped through the front doors of The Tantalus Club and out into the cloudy afternoon.

Though she'd half expected that lightning would strike her or that Lord Ebberling himself would be standing on the front drive waiting for her, instead the usual crush of horses and carriages rolled down the cobblestones, delivering and retrieving lords who'd come to visit the club.

Westfall had arrived in a high-perch phaeton, which she had to consider as a hopeful sign. If he meant to do her harm, he likely would have driven to collect her in a closed coach. On the other hand, everyone would be able to see her seated up on a phaeton. But this was the hand she'd decided to play, and she wasn't about to flinch now.

He handed her up onto the high seat, then moved around the back of the carriage to climb up on her other side. "Do you have a destination in mind?" he asked, nodding at the groom holding the horses and then clucking to the team.

"I thought perhaps we might drive through Covent Garden." There. It wasn't a wilderness like Hampstead Heath, which was where someone who didn't wish to be seen would go, and it wasn't the middle of Mayfair, where someone she didn't wish to see might be riding about.

With a nod he turned the matching gray team east. "I was surprised to receive your note," he said after a moment. "I thought you wouldn't wish to see me again."

She considered her response carefully. She had enough suspicions to confront him directly, but she wasn't certain yet that she was ready for what might come next. Aside from that, this was her first venture away from The Tantalus Club in nearly three years. Turning it into a battle wasn't something she felt quite prepared for.

"You haven't become mute, have you?" he asked, glancing sideways at her as they trotted along. "That would be disappointing."

"I'm not mute. I'm . . . cautious."

"Yes, because the sunlight is such a trickster." His mouth curved in a smile. "I had a wonder."

Emily attempted to keep her shoulders relaxed, even though she felt like hunching them against whatever it was he wondered about. "Yes?"

"All the Tantalus girls dress in rather splendid gowns. Is that a requirement?"

Well, that wasn't at all what she'd expected. "Not strictly speaking, but the club maintains its popularity because of a certain allure. We are part of that." They'd also found that the club's members were more generous with their drinking and wagering and gifts when they were slightly distracted by half-visible bosoms and pretty smiles, but she didn't want to insult him. Not to his face, anyway.

"A very large part, I imagine. I inherited my cousin's membership, but Lord Allen told me there was a three-year waiting list to join."

"Exclusivity makes us more interesting."

He chuckled. "I think the nature of the club itself makes you interesting. If you don't leave the grounds, though, does someone else order your gowns for you, or do you have a seamstress come in?"

"Camille Pryce and I were of a size, so she purchased gowns for me until she married last year. I use the same seamstress, though, and she has my measurements by now."

Westfall nodded. "Camille Pryce. She's the one who married Bloody Blackwood, isn't she?"

"Keating Blackwood," Emily corrected. "Yes."

They turned up Long Acre, and the phaeton slowed in the heavy traffic. "Do you want to walk, or should we just tour?"

The idea of getting out and walking, out where anyone could see her and she couldn't do anything but run away, sent a tremor up her spine. "I'd prefer to stay here, if you don't mind."

"I was hoping you'd say that," Westfall returned. "My foot's aching today."

She almost asked if that had anything to do with the

button he kept in his shoe, but he almost seemed to be baiting her. Was he waiting for a confrontation? If so, he could keep waiting. "Someone said a horse stepped on your foot," she ventured. If he could wheedle information out of her, she could do the same with him.

"Yes. I wasn't paying attention, and the deuced thing spooked."

"That was clumsy, wasn't it?"

His jaw clenched, then relaxed again. "Yes, I suppose it was."

Emily nodded, covering her own smile. He might be a spy, but she'd survived by her wits for as long as she could remember. "Was this while you were in Europe? Lord Haybury said he recollected that you spent at least part of the Peninsular War searching for books."

He freed one hand to push his spectacles up his nose, as if he'd just remembered that he wore them. "Sacking towns means burning things. Some of those tomes were irreplaceable."

"So did you fight any battles?" she asked slowly, a queer combination of dread and excitement touching her. If she wasn't asking questions then he would be, and this felt safer—to a degree. In bed he wasn't at all bumbling, and something in his gaze thrilled her. She had the distinct feeling that the man having sex with her was the closest to the real Nathaniel Stokes she'd yet met, and he was very interesting and arousing. And a sense of danger, for want of a better word, seemed to emanate from him when he relaxed enough to forget that he was a bumbling academic with spectacles and a limp.

He turned them to one side of the street and pulled the matched grays to a halt. Holding the team hard in one hand, he faced her. "What are you doing?" he asked, his voice very level.

Another thrill went down her spine. "What do you mean? I thought we were having a conversation."

"A conversation where you seem to feel the need to continually point out my shortcomings. If you're angry with me for something, simply say so. I do have other things to do if you only mean to insult me with every breath."

Emily studied his gaze. The light green eyes seemed nothing more than annoyed, and if she hadn't had that conversation with Jenny, if she didn't *know* he was a very dangerous man, she would have been utterly fooled. Did she want him to continue to believe that he held the upper hand? Considering their whereabouts, perhaps that was the wisest way to proceed. For the moment.

"I apologize," she said after a moment. "You're an earl, and I'm a Tantalus girl. I feel a bit . . . overwhelmed by all this. I suppose I've been attempting to level the field."

"Mm-hm. You're certain that's all it is? You're intimidated by me?" He lifted an eyebrow, the expression both attractive and amused at the same time.

"Take me driving again tomorrow, and I'll do better," she returned.

An earl would have duties, servants to order about, festivities to attend, Parliament to sit through. But the Earl of Westfall nodded. "I'll bring a picnic luncheon. One o'clock?"

"You're certain you don't mind that people will begin talking? Two of my friends from the club married peers, you know. Your fellows will begin speculating if you're seen driving me about Town again."

He met her gaze, a slight smile touching his mouth. "I'm not afraid if you're not."

Oh, she wasn't afraid. She was worried. And she

was beginning to enjoy this man's company far too much. "One o'clock. I'll dress for the country."

When Nathaniel came downstairs the next morning he had a letter waiting for him from his friend with the government. He showed it to Laurie while they sat down for breakfast together. "No Lady Sebret exists," he said.

"That's what you thought."

"Yes, but I wanted confirmation. I imagine there are quite a few minor titles out there that never make it out of their own little villages."

He blew out his breath. Something had been afoot yesterday with Portsman, but he didn't quite know what. He'd expected her to ask why he seemed to be wearing spectacles he didn't need, but instead she'd drilled into him about his actions during the war. He hated that Rycott had concocted such a stupid reason for his meandering about the Continent, but he had to admit that it had more than sufficed. It had even saved his life once or twice. And he supposed it was the only reason he was able to go about England these days as absentminded Nathaniel Stokes.

"How certain are you that you're on the right track?"

"Fairly."

"Oh."

Nate eyed his brother over the rim of his teacup. "I'll know more today." If she wasn't involved, he wanted to know. Because if she wasn't involved, he would have a different decision to make, since Tantalus girl or not, accused killer or not, he enjoyed being around her. It couldn't mean anything good, but for the moment that sense of—not peace or contentment, but life, liveliness—was something he hadn't felt in years. Whoever she turned out to be, he would miss her when this was over. And if she was who Ebberling accused her of being . . . No. He shook himself. Later was later. And today he was going on a picnic.

She waited inside the club out of sight again, as if she didn't want to be seen by anyone. He didn't believe for a second that it was the sun she feared. Did she know that Ebberling was in London? Because she'd certainly walked among the club's members before now. He couldn't come up with another reason for her caution, try as he might to conjure one.

When she stepped out to meet him, Nate took a moment just to look at her. She'd dressed more conservatively than she did as one of the Tantalus girls, in a pretty yellow and green sprigged muslin that went halfway down her arms and all the way up to her throat. Atop that she'd donned a yellow bonnet that darkened the color of her hair. If he hadn't known any better, he would have thought her some peer's daughter out driving with a beau.

Today he almost felt like that beau. "I tracked down another copy of *The Scottish Cousin,*" he said as he sent them off at a trot. "It still doesn't make sense, but I have to admit that it has a certain amount of whimsy that I appreciate."

"It's not about making sense," she returned. "It's about love and passion. Feelings. Two people who would die for each other."

"And they nearly do, simply because the hero decided not to ask the cousin one vital question." The whole lot of the characters were fools, but they'd been described as pretty, so he supposed that was all that mattered.

"You mean a vital question like why someone would wear spectacles they don't need?" she asked.

He gripped the reins hard, then loosened his hands before she could notice. So today was to be the day. *Damnation.* He'd hoped for a few more drives with her, a few more evenings in her bed. "Beg pardon?"

Emily mentally squared her shoulders, all of her attention on the tall, lean man seated close enough to touch beside her. "I asked a few questions about you. You're a spy."

Even with her watching his lean profile, she couldn't detect a flinch or a blink. "A what?" he asked, chuckling.

"I know someone who knows things that most people don't," she explained, finding that it was much more pleasant to keep her attention on Westfall than to dwell on the fact that she was out in the open once again, after someone might have noted that she'd been seen in Westfall's company yesterday. "You spied for Wellington. Are you still in his service, or do you just enjoy fooling people?"

He glanced sideways at her. "If I was a spy, haven't you just placed yourself in danger by revealing that you know about me?" Westfall edged them around a wagon loaded with hay. "I would imagine that on occasion spies kill to protect their identities, after all."

Had he just threatened her? He said it so mildly that he might have been discussing shaved ices or mules. Considering that she'd expected him to admit to the truth, to be so concerned with securing her cooperation and silence that her own identity would become secondary, she wasn't at all certain what to do. She didn't feel frightened, but she imagined that the best spies wouldn't seem at all threatening before they struck.

"With the number of people who know that we went driving together, that would seem rather foolish," she countered, "especially for a man as skilled as you're rumored to be."

For a moment they continued in silence. Finally he sighed, a grin touching his sensuous mouth. "For a Tantalus girl, Newbury, you are a great deal of trouble. I don't suppose you'll tell me who this source of yours is, will you?"

"No. But I have no intention of telling anyone else about you, if that makes a difference. The—" Abruptly she realized what he'd called her. Ice stabbed down her spine, and she twisted on the high seat, gathering her legs beneath her to jump.

Iron fingers gripped her arm. "Don't," he muttered. "You'll hurt yourself."

"You—"

"I thought it was only fair if you admit to knowing my identity, that I admit to knowing yours." He squeezed her wrist tighter, then released her. "Don't jump. I'll drive us somewhere we can talk."

"Talk?" she repeated, feeling as hysterical as she must sound. "Talk about what? I can't—I need to go. Now."

"Take a moment and think," he shot back, his voice harder. "You have no blunt, no clothes, nothing but what you're wearing. I only wish to talk. Truly."

She didn't seem to have much choice. He was correct, after all; she had a little money with her, in her reticule, but it wasn't sufficient to get her far enough away to be safe. He was supposed to retreat, to deflect, to allow her to gain more insight into what he was about. Three years. She'd felt too safe for too long. And now it was too late.

"Stay where you are," Westfall stated again, his steel tone not at all resembling that of some absentminded scholar.

She never should have approached him. Simply because she was clever and lucky didn't mean she had nothing to worry over. And it certainly didn't mean she could stand toe to toe with one of Wellington's spies. The remains of her breakfast roiled uneasily in her stomach. Perhaps if she cast up her accounts on his fine-fitting gray jacket and waistcoat, it would provide her with a moment or two to escape. Where she would go after that, though, she had no idea. She needed just a few seconds to think.

When the traffic began to clear as the phaeton turned north he urged the team into a trot. Emily supposed she might have jumped to the ground, then, but at that speed it would leave her scraped and bruised—which she wouldn't mind, except for the fact that it would make her easier to recognize if he or any of Ebberling's other dogs should come after her.

He'd clearly made the same determination, because now he didn't even spare her a glance as they left Town for the meadows and scattered woods and farms beyond. Considering that she'd expected to be driven directly to Ebberling, she didn't quite know what to make of this drive to the wilderness—unless the marquis was waiting for them out where there would be no witnesses at all. Another shudder ran through her. The moment they stopped, she would run. Plan or not, she likely wouldn't get a second chance.

Finally they turned off the road along a narrow track that ran alongside a tree-lined stream. Emily kept herself as still as she could, attempting not to tense as the horses slowed once more to a walk. When a heron took flight from the streambed Westfall turned his head to look and she jumped to the ground.

Stumbling to her knees, Emily dug her hands into the dirt, righting herself again, and ran back the way they'd come. She didn't care where she went, but this would slow Westfall down the most as he attempted to turn the phaeton on the narrow path.

Except that he wasn't in the phaeton.

She risked a glance over her shoulder. The earl was on her heels, only a few yards behind her. With a squeak she altered her direction, veering across the stream and up into the woods on the far side. So much for either the button in his shoe or the horse treading on his foot—whichever it had been.

Nathaniel caught up to her amid the tangle of roots and rocks on the stream bank, but held back until Emily—Rachel—reached the meadow beyond. Then he lunged forward, grabbing her about the waist, and twisted so that she fell half on top of him. From the way she jabbed her elbow into his ribs she didn't seem to appreciate his consideration, but that hardly surprised him.

"Stop it," he grumbled, planting her face down amid the grass and flowers with his weight. He grabbed both her wrists and brought them around to the small of her back so he could hold them with one hand. "That was stupid."

"I'm not attempting to impress you," she snapped in between hard draws of breath. She managed a nice kick into his backside with her heels.

He wanted to meet whoever it was who'd identified him as a spy. Not many could, and he or she had not done either him or the woman beneath him a kindness. Subtlety, gaining her trust, or learning more about her before he acted had just been tossed out the window with the morning's piss. And the button in his left boot felt like it had worked its way through half his foot, damn it.

Very well, he had his own suspicions about what had

truly happened at Ebberling Manor. Now he could put
them to the test. With his free hand he drew the knife
from his boot and stabbed it into the earth a foot past
her head, where she could see it. "I'm letting you go,"
he murmured, leaning closer to her. "You can have the
phaeton, if you can get past me."

Before she could conjure whatever reply she thought
might be appropriate to that, he pushed away from her,
rolling to his feet.

Portsman scrambled around to face him, balanced
on her haunches. "Why?" she asked, brushing chestnut
hair from her face with one dirty hand.

"I'm being sporting."

Keeping her sharp brown gaze squarely on him, she
angled her chin toward the knife. "And after I run you
mean to kill me? Fine. Give Ebberling a message for
me, then." Her voice shook, but her gaze never wavered.
"You tell him that I wrote it down somewhere. Someone has it, and sooner or later he'll pay for what he did.
And that he'll never know where or when. Then he'll
have as much peace as I ever did."

"Y—"

She exploded into motion—not past him and not toward the knife, but north and west. Was she making for
Hampstead Heath? It would provide her with a multitude of hiding places, if she could avoid the highway-
men and cutthroats who lurked in the vales and hollows.

Nate gave her a moment's head start while he scooped
up the knife and shoved it back into his boot. She
hadn't seen it as a weapon with which she could defend
herself or remove him from the game. And she'd assumed that once Ebberling found her, he would have
her killed before she could give out information that
she claimed to have passed on in secret.

Just before she reached the edge of the trees he went after her again. If he'd had any doubts about her being a killer, she'd just satisfied them. Emily Portsman, Rachel Newbury—whatever she chose to call herself—hadn't murdered anyone. And she'd also just told him who *had* killed Lady Ebberling.

Portsman, as he'd come to think of her, dodged behind a fallen tree and then down a hill into a brush-filled hollow. Even in a gown she moved fast, and she was thinking about evasion as much as she was about putting distance between them. "Ebberling killed his wife, didn't he?" he asked to the woods in general, sidestepping a tangle of branches and moving to cut her off from the rise beyond. "And you saw it."

Silence answered him. With a curse he realized she'd been waiting for him to make enough noise to drown her out, and then she'd stopped moving. Evidently she'd even stopped breathing and quite possibly she'd become invisible, because he couldn't pick her green and yellow gown out from the green and brown sun-spotted wood.

He knew approximately where she had to be, and he cut back down the hillside toward the thicker growth below. "He did hire me to find you," he continued, keeping himself and his gaze moving, looking for a flinch, an inch of cotton, a lock of chestnut hair. A whisper of sound made him adjust slightly to the east. "He said you stole a necklace and murdered the marchioness over it and then vanished without a trace."

From the corner of his vision a sizable branch rushed at the side of his head. Nate sidestepped and straightened, letting the momentum of the blow carry her into his shoulder. With a twist he pulled the club from Portsman's hands and shoved her into the trunk of a tree.

Still moving, he grabbed her right wrist and swept her arm over her head, using the tree to keep her pinned. She flailed at him with her free hand, and he trapped it, as well. "Stop struggling," he muttered in her ear as he pressed up behind her. "I don't want to hurt you."

"No? You just want to kill me, I suppose?" Her voice broke. "I knew it was stupid to leave the club with you. It went so nicely yesterday, and I thought . . ."

"You thought what?" he prompted, curious.

"I don't know. I'm just tired. Tired of running, tired of hiding, tired of being afraid all the time." A tear ran down one cheek. "Are you supposed to do it, or does he mean to murder me, himself?"

"He's paying me something over ten thousand pounds to bring you to him alive. He implied that you wouldn't be turned over to the authorities."

She shoved backward, trying to set him off balance. But he'd been waiting for the move, and only tightened his grip.

"I'm not going to turn you over to him," he continued, somewhat dismayed to realize that while he'd made that decision when she hadn't tried for the knife, it was still a decision. Was his conscience, his sense of morality, so badly damaged that he'd at one point—at several points—actually been willing to turn this woman over to someone he knew meant to kill her? The amount of money offered had been the first thing to make him suspicious, after all.

It was more money than most people would see in a lifetime, and yet Ebberling hadn't put out a public bounty. Instead the marquis had hired a man he'd known to be a spy, someone who didn't talk about his clients or his work, someone willing to take a great deal of blunt to do a job and not ask too many questions about it. Nate scowled. He'd asked only for clues about where his quarry might be, and had completely ignored the larger question about whether this vanished chit had actually done what she'd been accused of. Worse than that, he hadn't ignored the question as much as he hadn't cared. He'd wanted to hunt, and the whys and wherefores hadn't troubled him a whit.

"You expect me to believe that you hunted me down, took me out here to the middle of nowhere, and chased me through the forest, just to let me go?" she demanded, still wriggling to get free of his grip.

Nate mentally shook himself. "I've been chasing you through the forest because you keep running away," he retorted. "Stop doing that, and we can chat about the rest of it. I have a picnic luncheon packed behind the seat of the phaeton."

For a heartbeat or two she stopped fighting him. "Then you meant to feed me cucumber sandwiches and afterward decide whether to kill me or not? You're an awful, despicable man."

"And what did you intend, my dear? To announce that you know I'm a spy and then have more sex with me while attempting to wheedle out whether I was after you or some other poor chit?"

"You're only annoyed because I thought of that tactic first. And if you did suspect me of killing someone, what the devil were you doing in my bed?"

The question annoyed him. "The first time I only thought you might perhaps know where I could find Rachel Newbury."

"And the second time?"

"Because I enjoyed the first time."

"Well, I only invited you upstairs because I thought you might be working for Ebberling and I wanted to know what you knew. So you're much worse than I am."

That, he was. "I'm letting you loose. Don't run or I'll chase you down again."

He let her hands go and took two long steps backward before she could turn around and kick him in the balls or scratch his eyes out or whatever she might attempt next. The fact that he had no idea what she meant to attempt didn't annoy him. It made him feel the opposite of annoyed. Something he didn't quite have the words to describe, when he generally knew everything. A very precise, very ordered everything.

She turned around, facing him. First she rubbed at her wrists, then she wiped the wet from her cheeks, which had the effect of further dirtying her face. Third she brushed her dirty hands down the front of her dirty green and yellow gown. And the entire time her deep brown gaze held his. Every pretty, disheveled ounce of her radiated suspicion and distrust and fear and anger. He wondered what she saw when she looked back at him. His spectacles were somewhere between here and the phaeton, while his cane had never left the carriage at all. They were only the physical part of the disguise he'd been wearing for the past three years, but at the moment he felt distinctly unlike himself—whoever that was.

Finally she stuck out her right hand. "Rachel Newbury. And you are?"

The damned chit had balls, herself. He shook her hand. "Nate Stokes. But you're still lying."

Chapter Nine

W hen she jerked her hand away, he let her go. For a moment something profoundly sad and lonely crossed her features, but it was gone just as swiftly. "I don't trust you enough or know you well enough to give you the truth," she said aloud, walking past him in the approximate direction of the phaeton. "But for the purposes of this conversation I'm admitting to being Rachel Newbury. That will have to suffice."

It didn't suffice for someone who loved puzzles as much as he did, but for the moment he would accept it. "Very well."

"Do you keep solemn oaths that you swear?" she continued, glancing over her shoulder at him as he fell in behind her. "Or is it merely lip service that enables you to accomplish whatever task you're about?"

"You cut more deeply than a knife, my dear," he said mildly, to cover the fact that what she'd just said had truly hurt. He had sworn oaths in the past, in front of or to people he'd been ordered to stop or to kill, and he hadn't even blinked. "When I was employed by England, I swore an oath to protect her. I never broke that vow. Is that what you mean?"

"I intended to ask you to swear that you would keep

your word when you said you wouldn't hand me over to Ebberling, but I realized I have no idea if your promises mean anything at all."

If she continued to rip away at him like that with mere words, he would be asking her to simply take the knife and finish him off in a matter of minutes. "Look at me," he snapped.

She must have understood the iron beneath his tone, because she stopped walking and turned around to face him. "What?"

"I swear that if you are indeed innocent of killing Lady Ebberling, I will not hand you over to Lord Ebberling. I swear on my life and what remains of my honor."

For a long moment she searched his gaze. Finally she nodded. "I will accept that."

"Then tell me what happened."

"I will tell you over luncheon, Nate Stokes."

They found the phaeton with the left front wheel jammed against a boulder some thirty feet from where he'd jumped off it. The pair of grays looked none too happy to have been left standing there in such an embarassing situation as running off the road, but he'd had little choice and fewer places to aim the team where he could be sure the carriage would be forced to stop.

"My apologies, lads," he said, taking them by their heads to guide them backward until the vehicle was clear of the boulder, and then tying them off to a tree.

"You're not going to blame it on me?" the chit asked, climbing atop the boulder to look down at the proceedings.

He shrugged. "I would have run, too. But I would have grabbed for the knife, so you're a better person than I am." The picnic basket had survived the crash, and he carried it over into the shade beside the stream and set it down.

"Would you have stabbed me to escape?"

No. "I suppose that would depend on whether I'd killed Lady Ebberling or not."

"So that was a test of my innocence? I thought you were threatening me." She hopped down from the boulder and untied the ribbon at the high waist of her gown.

"Also a test of sorts. You didn't take the knife, which meant you weren't a killer."

She pulled the gown over her head and stepped out of her shoes before she walked over naked to dunk the dress in the stream. As she washed it, along with her hands and scraped knees and face, she looked over her shoulder at him. "But you said you would have taken the knife."

"I'm a killer." An aroused one, he thought, laying out the blanket and sitting cross-legged beside the basket to pull off his shoes and shake out the left one. The damned button fell into his hand, and he tossed it over his shoulder.

"And I'm not terribly reassured. And I'm only washing my dress; not seducing you."

"You already seduced me." Nathaniel shrugged out of his jacket and dropped it across from him. "Here."

"No, I'd only planned to befuddle you. But then you kissed me, and . . ." Her cheeks darkened. "You kiss very well."

"Thank you."

Once she'd laid her dress across the boulder to dry she took a seat on the blanket and pulled his jacket on over her naked form. It was too big for her and did a splendid job of covering her from the hips up, but her long legs folded to one side, drawing his gaze and his attention. "And thank you," she said, and reached for the glass of Madeira he poured her. "You say you're a killer the way some people would say they had some tea."

"I've had time to reconcile myself to the truth." He pulled a plate free from the basket and lifted off the cloth wrapped around it. She'd been correct about the meal; a dozen triangular cucumber sandwiches were artfully arranged across the porcelain. Taking one, he handed them over and watched as she daintily consumed one of the delicate little morsels. "Tell me what happened with Lady Ebberling."

"You know it'll be my word against his," she returned, sipping at her Madeira. "It doesn't mean anything. Except that you'll be even deeper in this mess than you are at this moment."

That seemed to be secondary to learning what had transpired and whether he could help her. "Just tell me. And what should I call you?"

"Portsman works as well as anything else. I'm accustomed to the name. And I don't want you or me mistakenly calling me something else."

"Then tell me, Portsman. Don't leave anything out."

Her shoulders rose and fell, the movement opening his jacket and revealing a tantalizing partial view of her round, soft breasts. "Very well. I applied for the governess position at Ebberling, and Katherine—Lady Ebberling—hired me on the spot. She said she took an immediate liking to me, but I think the marquis had been . . . driving governesses away. He was very demanding and particular about who was looking after his son."

"It wasn't about sexual advances?" he asked, well past the point of cynicism.

"No. Not with me, anyway. I don't know about the previous ones. He told me I was pretty several times, but he never attempted to visit my room."

"Hm. I'm surprised."

"So was I, actually. He did have a very bad temper, and there were a few occasions when he was cruel simply because he could be, but mostly he was fairly easy to avoid, and I was happy to be employed."

Abruptly he remembered his conversation with young George, about the first time he'd seen Rachel Newbury cry. She must have been *very* happy to be employed, if someone with her spirit could be brought to tears and not either leave her employer's service or level him. "Was he affectionate toward his wife and son?"

" 'Affectionate'?" she repeated, lifting an eyebrow. "He killed his wife."

"I mean, was it a moment of rage, or . . ."

"Ah. Before that day, then, I would have said that he seemed as devoted to Katherine as any man might be to his wife."

"Devoted as any man? That's a rather large canopy," he interrupted.

"I wasn't that interested in discovering the whispers and cracks of the household," she returned, glancing down at the half-empty glass of Madeira. "I was happy to be employed, and Katherine and her son were both very pleasant to me. We went along well for nearly three years."

He wondered again what had made her so content simply to have employment, and whether it had anything to do with the Lady Sebret reference on her resume. That could wait for another time, however. She didn't trust him, and she didn't have much reason to do so. Hell, sometimes he didn't trust himself.

"Until . . ." he prompted.

"Until one morning George decided he would rather stay inside and play with his toy soldiers and frogs than go for our daily walk. It was a bit brisk, so I agreed and set Mrs. Hanworth the housekeeper to keep an eye on him while I went out." She sighed. "I used to love to go walking."

Walking. She hadn't done much of that for three years, Nathaniel knew, hidden inside the walls of The Tantalus Club. The run for her life today hardly counted against that. "What did you see?"

She blew out her breath. "You're assuming that I trust you, or that I think you can do something to assist me."

"I could remind you that we're here, alone, chatting over luncheon rather than on our way to Velton House and Lord Ebberling."

"Simply because I'm free at the moment doesn't mean I will remain that way. You're a spy. How do I know you're not simply attempting to ferret out how much I saw and precisely what I know before you drag me off to him? After all, it would still come down to my word against Ebberling's, with us each accusing the other. In that battle, he wins." She selected a peach and bit into it. "I'm safer keeping my own confidences."

Nate reflected that he'd had easier chats with men who hated him. Whatever had happened to her at Ebberling Manor, he didn't think it had been the first time she'd paid a price for something not of her own doing. Everything about her said she trusted no one but herself, and that she had learned that lesson through experience.

"I *used* to be a spy," he said slowly. Perhaps a secret for a secret would convince her to confide in him. And for the moment he refused to ruminate over why he'd decided he could trust her when he didn't trust anyone. "A little over two years ago my cousin drowned, and as his heir I abruptly became too valuable to risk in the field. Or so Wellington informed me, on the day he handed me my papers and told me to go be an earl." He frowned at his ridiculously small sandwich. "I don't like being an earl. I know too many things about these hypocrites and fools to be comfortable with smiling at them and dancing with their daughters."

"And your brother? Why not give him the title?"

"Because he was sixteen when I inherited, and the last thing my mother said before she died was that I was to look after him better than I'd been seeing to myself." He hadn't actually had that conversation with his mother; he'd been in Belgium when she'd become sick. A solicitor and Laurie had been the witnesses, and it had been the solicitor who'd sent him the letter with her last words. He'd ignored them for nearly a year, until Gerard went and drowned himself.

"If you're no longer a spy, why are you taking money from Ebberling to find me?"

"Because being a spy is all I know, and I can't abide sitting about smoking cigars and chatting about who might win the Derby. I overheard Lady Trumble say she'd misplaced one of her uncle's paintings, and that she needed to find it before his visit. It was a Gainsborough, easily identified, and on a whim I tracked it down and retrieved it for her. She didn't trust the kindness of my heart, however, and insisted on paying me a hundred pounds for doing the favor. They all insist on paying me. To buy my silence and my discretion, I suppose."

"Then you went to Ebberling and told him you would find Rachel Newbury because you're bored with being an earl," she commented, lifting her gaze to meet his before she looked away again.

"He came to me. And he hadn't seen or heard a trace of you for three years. It seemed like a challenge, so I accepted."

"And what is your intention now? To tell him that you couldn't find me, after all? To say you had me and then lost me again? You don't seem the sort to enjoy admitting to failure, Westfall."

She was correct about that. He detested failure, and even more, having to admit to it. But this was different. She wasn't a painting or a necklace or even a long-lost heiress with a large supply of wealth waiting for her. She was Portsman, and he liked her. *Him*. The fellow who could generally assess any companion's lies and shortcomings and failures within two minutes of beginning a conversation with him or her.

"No answer?" she prompted. "Then I think this conversation is over."

If he allowed that, he would never learn precisely what had happened. And he would never know what came next in this odd, adversarial . . . friendship, he supposed it was. "I'll make you an agreement," he said aloud.

Her brow furrowed. "What sort of agreement?"

"A truth for a truth, a secret for a secret, until you feel that you hold enough of my life in your hands to trust me with yours." Laurie would be howling with laughter—or annoyance—to hear such a thing, since he'd told his brother almost nothing of his life in Europe. But he wanted to preserve that sense of innocence Laurence still managed to keep about himself, and Portsman had lost hers long ago. And it would be nice to have someone in whom to confide—if he could trust her.

It would be a dance, certainly. They both knew the steps, but not where it would end. And apprehensive as it left him, he also found it exciting, and interesting. And arousing. If she agreed to it.

"Well?" he prompted after a moment.

Emily cleared her throat. "I'd like a bit of time to consider."

Damnation. "Very well. I can't fault you for that."

"Yes, well, that said, I don't mind spending a bit more time in your company. But if you lie to me from this moment on about anything—your spectacles, your limp, anything—any agreement between us is over."

He stuck out his hand just as she had earlier. "Agreed."

She gripped his fingers and shook. "Agreed."

Emily knew she'd been lucky. If Westfall had been determined to turn her over to Ebberling, she wasn't certain she could have gotten away from him. Not without killing him, anyway—and she was beginning to realize that the Earl of Westfall was quite a bit more formidable than she'd first thought.

By agreeing to his little exercise in secret-sharing she'd earned herself a little more time, but for what? Once he returned her to the Tantalus she could gather up her things, ask Lord Haybury for the money he'd invested on her behalf, and go. If she could make it to Brighton and purchase passage on a ship, Ebberling would never find her in America. She glanced again at Nathaniel as he sat cross-legged opposite her. Ebberling might not have any idea how to hunt her down, but she couldn't say the same thing about this man eating luncheon with her.

And then there was that odd thought she'd had when she shook his hand, that it would be pleasant to be able to trust someone. That in a perfect world Nate Stokes would heroically work to defend her, to protect her from Ebberling, that he would prove to be as gifted in gentlemanliness as he was in looks. But experience told her that was just foolishness.

"Has Ebberling sent anyone else after you?" he asked, momentarily interrupting the birdsongs and frog chirps coming from the stream and the woods beyond.

"I don't know. I thought he would, but everything's been so peaceful until now that I'd begun to think he'd convinced himself I was already dead or some such thing." She tilted her head. "Did he give you a reason for hiring you now?"

"He's remarrying."

Dismay ran through her. "The poor girl." Somehow, she'd never considered that, never thought that once a man murdered his own wife he would go seeking another one. It made sense that he would begin his search for her anew now, though. His marriage would be in the newspapers, in the Society pages, on the tongues of every wag in England. If she ever meant to emerge from the shadows, it would be now.

Did she mean to emerge, though? It could cost her her own life, or her freedom. After all, she still wasn't entirely certain she could trust the man currently studying her face. And Ebberling might have hired more than simply one man. If she stayed hidden, though, and if something happened to Ebberling's new wife, it would be her fault.

"You feel guilty," he stated. "For the first wife, or the possible fate of the second one?"

"I liked it better when I thought you needed spectacles," she returned, shifting. "You didn't seem as keen-eyed then."

"That was the idea." Light green eyes lowered to take in his oversized jacket pulled over her breasts. "Did he threaten to kill you?"

"I didn't give him the chance. Why?"

"Because you don't strike me as a chit who turns tail, is all. Of course his butler and half the staff said you were a pointy-nosed, high-in-the-instep snob, and I don't see that, either."

He'd spoken to Ebberling's staff. A shiver ran down her spine despite the warm jacket that smelled of him and leather and the warm, sunny day about them. "I was . . . overly proud back then, I suppose."

He sighed, handsome as sin in his shirtsleeves and waistcoat, and more dangerous than the devil. "I thought we were being honest, Portsman."

Emily scowled at him. "I find you annoying. I told you that I'm not discussing anything before my employment with Ebberling, so leave be."

"I find you to be a conundrum," he responded, emptying his glass and setting it aside. "I can't seem to stop attempting to decipher you."

"Well, stop it anyway. And you haven't told me anything about yourself, Westfall. Tell me about the people you betrayed in the name of duty, why don't you? That should help me decide whether I can trust you or not."

Nathaniel rose up on his hands and knees, then reached out to grab one of her legs and pull her toward him. She flailed backward, but before she even realized it she was flat on her back, looking up at him looming over her. "I betrayed nearly everyone I ever met, all in the name of duty," he said in a low, rumbling voice, reaching down to lay open the loose jacket covering her. "Since I left the service, it seems I've only betrayed one man's trust."

"Ebberling," she whispered.

He lowered his head, taking a breast in his mouth, teasing at her nipple with lips and tongue and teeth. Emily gasped, tangling her hands into his disheveled brown hair and arching into him. Was this why she was still a free woman? Because he desired her? That seemed only fair, since she'd already half decided to tell him everything, and she couldn't come up with a reason for wanting to do so other than the fact that she couldn't push the feeling of his hands, his body, the weight of him, the color of his eyes or the sound of his voice from her thoughts. It was ridiculous and heady all at the same time.

She'd never trusted any other man she'd been with; she'd only decided she could fool them. Nate Stokes, as he called himself, knew when she was lying just by looking at her face. He was dangerous, and he already knew more about her than even Jenny did. What she needed to do was run and find another place to hide. Immediately.

Instead she reached between them to unbutton his waistcoat, shoving it down his arms until he lifted away from her a little to shrug out of it. He pulled his shirt off over his head, flinging it somewhere behind them, then took her mouth in a hot, openmouthed kiss. And to think she'd avoided kissing because it seemed too intimate, because she didn't like the idea of kissing men to whom she was lying. But she wasn't lying to Westfall.

Lowering her hands still further, she opened his trousers and pushed them down past his hips. He'd already removed his boots, so kicking out of the buckskins only took a moment. His cock pressed against her inner thighs, hard and full. Emily arched her hips, opening to him, and without lifting away from her he slid inside.

She closed her eyes at the heated, filling sensation. Good God, what was she doing, trusting a man who lied for a career? But she did trust him. Or at least she trusted that today she would be returning safely to the Tantalus. Tomorrow . . . was tomorrow.

He entered her again and again, both of them breathless and so aroused it almost hurt. She came hard, stifling her ecstatic moan against his shoulder before she remembered that they weren't in her small room with its thin walls and close neighbors and that only frogs and birds and rabbits could overhear them. Harder and faster he thrust inside her, and Emily dug her fingers into his shoulders, their gazes locked. How could she have ever thought him dull and absentminded? People saw what they wanted—what they expected—to see, she supposed. And now she saw him as strong and hard and sharp, and perhaps her best, last, and only hope.

"Westfall, wait," she panted, feeling him tense against her.

"I know." At the last moment he pulled away, spilling himself across her stomach, burying his face against her neck.

For a long moment they lay there, arms and legs entangled so that she couldn't tell where one of them ended and the other began. For the first time in a very long time she felt safe. And content. And . . . No, not happy, but hopeful. Or something more, that she couldn't quite name. It wouldn't last, but for the span of a few heartbeats it was oh, so very welcome. She kissed his ear, drawing her fingers slowly through his thick hair.

Slowly he pushed up on his arms to gaze down at her. "Well, it likely won't matter," he murmured, a wicked grin touching his mouth, "but I apologize."

Suspicion darted through her again. "For what?"

"This."

He straightened, slid his arms beneath her thighs and her shoulders, and lifted her up. Standing, Nathaniel walked them over to where the stream widened and deepened, and—

"Don't you dare!" she shrieked, grabbing his shoulders.

Instead of dropping her, he simply fell forward, submerging both of them in the cold, clear water. A surprised fish darted by her face, its tail whipping her lightly on the nose. With a gasp she surfaced again, wiping water and sagging brown hair from her face.

"Good God, that's cold," he rasped from directly in front of her, laughing.

"A fish slapped me," she exclaimed, splashing at him when she could see again. Emily opened her mouth to curse at him, but the sight of him waist deep in water, rivulets running from his hair and down his face and chest, was simply too magnificent for her to complain about. She grinned back at him.

"Shall I attempt to capture him? We could fry him up for dinner as punishment."

"Nonsense. I can hardly blame him for it, with what his poor fish eyes must have beheld falling from the sky."

"True enough." Still chuckling, goose bumps appearing on his arms, he reached over and pulled pins and leaves from her hair. "What do you dye it with, to turn it this color?" he asked, brushing the disheveled mess it must be out of her eyes again.

"Henna and very strong tea," she returned. "I began with just the henna, but it turned a terrible shade of orange. The tea darkens it to a more believable color."

"It's a lovely color. Chestnut, or teak."

"At least those are pretty colors of wood," she returned, splashing him again. "A lady prefers that her hair be compared to a degree of sunlight, or autumn leaves."

"Autumn leaves, then," he said, sweeping both thumbs slowly across her budded nipples. "Cold, sweetling?"

"Aren't you?" She reached beneath the water for his cock. "Ah, yes, you are. Poor thing."

A rueful grin softened his abrupt grimace. "You're an evil woman, Portsman."

"Ha! I'm not the one who threw us into the water."

Before she could begin shivering, she stepped onto a water-smoothed rock and climbed back up to the bank. Nathaniel followed her, stepping naked and barefoot and utterly breathtaking over to the picnic blanket. He dumped the remains of their luncheon into the basket and pulled up the blanket, wrapping it around her shoulders.

It was quite chivalrous of him, but she had a better idea. Holding the light covering open again, she stepped forward to envelop him, as well. His skin against hers was cool, but the goose bumps the sensation caused weren't entirely from the cold. However much he'd deciphered about her, whatever insights he seemed to gain into her character and her thoughts and her past at every instant, he was an enticing, arousing man, and she enjoyed his company. More than was likely wise, or safe.

Nate left Emily off at the front door of The Tantalus Club. He would have preferred to see her safely through the door, back into the employees' area, and to her own private room, but then he wouldn't be able to resist removing her clothes and having at her again. Which wouldn't be so terrible except that he'd already had her twice today, it was growing dark, and he had several rather thorny details to think through.

And if he'd discovered one thing, it was that thinking clearly and Emily Portsman did not go well together.

When she'd agreed to a second outing he'd reckoned either that she meant to confess her identity, or that he could use the opportunity to wheedle the truth from her.

Instead she'd announced that she knew him to be a spy, and he'd stupidly counterattacked with her name. Or rather, the name she'd gone by while in Lord Ebberling's employ. He didn't think Rachel Newbury was her true name any more than Emily Portsman was. So who the devil was she? And what did he mean to do with her?

He hadn't found the answer to either question by the time he reached Teryl House and handed the phaeton and team of grays over to Clark, the head groom. As much as he loved a good puzzle, this felt like three or four of them. And he didn't think he had all the pieces to any single one.

"You have a leaf on your arse," Laurence announced as he strolled into Nate's bedchamber.

"When the lord and master of the household is changing clothes in his private rooms you are supposed to knock and announce yourself before you come barging in," Nathaniel countered, brushing off his backside before he stepped into a clean, dry pair of trousers.

"I tried that same faddle on the headmaster when he came storming into my room at Oxford," his brother said mildly, taking a seat by the window. "Except I said 'brother to an earl' and not 'lord and master.'"

"I imagine it didn't suffice any better for you than it did just now for me," Nate returned, pulling on a shirt but leaving it untucked. He had no plans to go anywhere else this evening, and he might as well be comfortable for once. "Have you eaten?"

"I was waiting for you."

"Have Garvey bring dinner up to the billiards room then, will you?"

"Certainly." Laurence cracked open the door and

called down to the butler, then resumed his seat while Nate padded over barefoot to run a comb through his damp, disheveled hair. "You have scratches on your back."

"Yes, I know."

"You had sex."

"I did."

"With a woman."

Nate glanced at his brother's reflection in the dressing mirror. "And did you do anything useful today?" he asked, to change the subject.

"I took young George out riding, if you must know."

That surprised him. "You did? Just you and the little viscount?"

"And one of Ebberling's grooms, but yes. I'm half convinced to change Dragon's name to Dandelion, after all. That's what the poor fellow thinks it is by now, anyway. George must have said it a hundred times."

Nate knew how the horse felt. There were some days he hadn't remembered his own name, he'd gone by so many. "Did you and the lad discuss anything interesting?"

His brother led the way down the hall toward the billiards room at the back of the house. "Interesting to an eight-year-old boy, yes. The Derby, fox hunting, the mummies at the museum, the war, and especially anything to do with insects."

A few months ago Nathaniel would have made some comment about the boy and his brother having much in common. Lately, though, he and Laurie had been dealing surprisingly well together. He'd excluded his family from his life for their own safety, and when the time had come to return, he'd had no idea how to manage a sixteen-year-old boy. It couldn't all just be about logic and facts, but he hadn't realized that three years ago.

Now things had changed—or they'd begun to, and in part because of a very bright chit running for her life.

"Did our young lord divulge anything more about his governess?" he asked aloud, pulling a billiards cue from the rack on the wall and tossing it to his brother.

"More of the same, mostly. He hates her because his father said she killed his mother. That bit's always in there—'his father said.' And otherwise everything he says about her tells me that he adored Miss Newbury."

With a slow nod, Nate racked the billiards balls. Although Portsman had told him nothing specific about the murder, he knew she'd either seen or overheard Ebberling kill his own wife. Young George's comments only supported that; the lad only knew what his father had told him, and it had been drummed into his head so many times that it was spoken by rote rather than with any feeling.

"Did you discover anything more?" Laurie pursued. "Or were you otherwise occupied?"

He wasn't certain that he wanted to admit to finding Rachel Newbury. For one thing, it wouldn't give him the excuse of going to see her again on the pretext of hunting her down. For another, it meant that he would have to decide what he intended to do next.

What he wanted to do was arrange for another picnic or two or three with Portsman, take her about London where she'd been too fearful to venture for the past three years, because he could ensure that she would remain safe. He wanted to chat with her, learn not just what she knew about the murder, but also simply about . . . her. It wasn't merely her secrets that intrigued him, he was beginning to realize, but the woman herself.

In the past that would have been dangerous. Hell, it would have meant his own death, more than likely. A spy learned what was needed to perform the assigned task, then went on to the next task. And frequently that meant killing the very person who'd just confided in him. Becoming acquainted with that person, coming to appreciate their wit and their company, only made the task more difficult. It made him hesitate, and that was death.

"Nate, your hair's on fire."

He blinked, looking across the table to see Laurence eyeing him. "My apologies. I was thinking."

"You looked sad."

"I'm never sad. Sad isn't logical," he said absently, and bent over the table to line up his shot. The balls cracked against each other, rolling smoothly across the green velvet covering of the table. He wasn't sad; sad meant that he regretted what he'd made of his life. And he'd done well, not just for himself, but for England. Wellington had told him so, invited him to dinner at Welsley House and thanked him personally for his services. He would never have a medal or a shiny button on a uniform, but he'd done his duty. And he'd done it well.

"So which chit were you visiting?" his brother pursued, taking his own shot and then cursing. "The pretty, brown-eyed one from the Tantalus? Emily Portsman?"

Nate straightened. "Don't talk about her."

Laurence's expression hardened, the old familiar scowl furrowing his brow. "That's where we are again, then?" he snapped. "I do you a favor or two and then I'm useless again?"

For a long moment Nathaniel looked at his brother. Ten years separated them, too much for them to have been friends as children. And if he didn't take care, he would lose that chance now that they were both grown. He took a breath. "If there is one man in this entire world that I trust, Laurie, it's you," he said quietly, then had to stop when Garvey knocked at the door to bring in their dinner.

Once they were alone again he gestured for his brother to sit at the small writing table, and took the seat opposite him. Two plates of roast duck in orange sauce, a pile of onions and carrots and leeks surrounding them, covered the entire surface. Trust. Trust was the most difficult thing in the world, because it meant making a decision.

"I found Rachel Newbury," he continued, nodding when Laurie lifted a bottle.

"You did? Where is she? Have you turned her over to Ebberling? George never said anything, but—"

"I don't think she killed Lady Ebberling," he interrupted, taking a swallow of the deep red wine.

Laurie was nodding. "I'm not convinced of that, either. It's odd, but from what I read of your notes, everyone seems to tell the exact same story. Even George. It's too perfect."

"Good for you," Nate said, covering his own uneasiness at the thought that his younger brother had the instincts of a good spy. *Never.* That could never be allowed to happen. "I had the same thought. The problem is, I agreed to do a job."

"Return the blunt. It's not as if you need it."

"And what would Lord Ebberling think if I did that? It's a bit too early to admit defeat, and even if he did accept that I failed, he might well just turn around and hire someone else." Someone who wouldn't care if Portsman had done what she'd been accused of. Someone who would drag her away from the small, safe life she'd made for herself and turn her over to a likely murderer.

"Then we turn Ebberling in. Give him to the Old

Bailey or Bow Street or whoever takes care of men who murder their own wives."

"And for proof we give them . . . what?"

"Rachel Newbury's word."

"All we know for certain is that she's an accused murderess. Is she Ebberling's scapegoat, or did she see something? And why would anyone take her word over that of a marquis? She's been in hiding for three years, while he's been peacefully raising his son and planning another marriage."

Laurence frowned as he devoured his duck. The conundrum hadn't stolen his appetite, anyway—but then he was nineteen. Nothing stole his appetite. "Then what are you going to do?"

"I don't know."

That made his brother choke, though Nate was fairly certain it was only for show. "You don't know? I've never heard you say that before."

"I don't make a habit of it. I need some time to figure things out."

"And you can do that in bed with Emily Ports . . ." Laurie's eyes widened. "It's her, isn't it? She's Miss Newbury! But how did you—when did—"

"Keep your damned voice down," Nathaniel hissed. "I trust you, but that's where it ends."

"But—"

"I suspected when she invited me upstairs after you blurted out that bit about me looking for someone. That didn't make her Rachel Newbury, but it did make me think she knew someone or was someone in hiding. From there it wasn't that difficult to figure out." That wasn't strictly true, but the hows and wherefores didn't signify. "She admitted it to me today."

"Did she say that Ebberling killed his own wife?"

"Not directly. She doesn't trust me."

That made his brother snort. "Can't imagine why. You being so warm and romantic and gallant."

That made Nate pause. He wasn't any of those things. They'd been leached out of him years ago. But when he was in Portsman's company he remembered them. At times he could almost taste them again. Perhaps that was why he wanted to do nothing so much as throw Ebberling's blunt back in his smug face. It seemed a very poor reason, but he couldn't quite let go of it. Or of her. Not yet.

"Regardless, I need more information before I can act, in whichever direction I decide to go. And you need to never mention Emily Portsman's name in the hearing of either young George or his father. I don't want Ebberling's gaze turning in her direction."

"Easy enough. George hasn't asked me about The Tantalus Club. I don't think boys of eight are overly concerned with Tantalus girls."

At that Nate cracked a smile. "You would have been, if there'd been such a thing when you were that age."

"I was always wise beyond my years." Laurie ducked his head. "And I wanted to be you."

It was said almost shyly, and indeed Laurence blushed as though he regretted speaking the words the moment he'd said them. Considering the number of times Nate had verbally slapped him down for saying such a thing, it made sense. "The me back when you were eight was very stupid and foolish. You are neither of those things. And I intend to see that you have better choices and opportunities than I did."

"And I thank you for that, Nate. Truly." Laurie stirred at his vegetables. "I'll go back to Oxford when I'm permitted, and I'll make up my exams and whichever papers I've missed. But let me help you with this, first. Please."

"One way or another, a woman was murdered, and someone did it. This will be dangerous." Their mother would be whirling in her grave to hear him even considering putting her baby in harm's way, but as Nate had been realizing over the past fortnight or so, Laurence Michael Stokes wasn't a baby any longer. He was a young man, with the makings of a better gentleman than his older brother. "You realize that, yes?"

"Yes, I do. I still want to help you. You're my brother."

Nathaniel sighed. "And I apologize for that. Very well. I have a few tasks in mind for you. And you should meet Emily Portsman again. Perhaps she'll trust you more than she trusts me."

And for the moment he attempted to ignore the way that merely speaking those words, meant half in jest or not, made him jealous. What he couldn't ignore was the fact that he meant to help her, meant to save her, meant to enable her to live a life she seemed to long for—and *had* longed for, years before she ever took employment with Lord and Lady Ebberling.

Chapter Ten

E mily hadn't slept for a moment last night. Instead she'd sat looking out her small window while Lily snored delicately in the second bed behind her, and she'd considered her very limited options.

Westfall—Nate, because that fit him better in her thoughts, whatever she'd told him that she meant to call him—had asked her not to flee. That wasn't the reason that when dawn came she still sat in her chair within the walls of The Tantalus Club, of course. She remained because she still felt safe there, and because a flight without a plan had never served her well.

At the least she meant to ask Lord Haybury to assist her in withdrawing a large sum from her account at the Bank of England, and to have his man write up a paper enabling her to do so on her own from elsewhere in the country. The marquis had seemed to understand her reluctance to leave the grounds even to open an account and so he'd done it for her, but he wouldn't be fleeing with her. If she left.

The only thing she'd decided, actually, was that she needed to speak to Diane and Jenny. She'd made them a promise, and it was past time she kept it.

"Have you been sitting there all night?" Lily asked

sleepily, when Jenny knocked at their door to announce time for the morning shift to rise.

"No," Emily lied. "I only woke a short while ago."

The pretty daughter of a high-ranking member of the Church and a baron's daughter, Lily Banks had come to the club only a few months ago. With her quiet smiles and warm wit Emily had liked her immediately, and had decided that sharing a room with the petite, black-haired girl would be much preferable to taking on Lucille Hampton and her ceaseless prattling.

When Sophia White, the unacknowledged daughter of the Duke of Hennessy and his wife's maid, had come to the Tantalus even before it had opened its doors, London had been scandalized. Now that sweet Sophia had married the Duke of Greaves, though, every young lady born on the wrong side of the blanket to a lord or a diplomat or a member of the clergy or a high-ranking officer had been appearing at the back door of the club.

Not all of them were allowed entry, either. As sympathetic as Diane was to their varying plights, the Tantalus came first. If they weren't able to read and write, if they didn't have pleasant conversation or a brain between their ears, if they weren't young and pretty, if they couldn't at least cook or mend clothes, they couldn't become Tantalus girls.

She herself had been at least as fortunate as Lily, because she'd come to the Tantalus when it had still been an idea. Diane, Lady Cameron, had been hiring desperate young women, and had asked the scandalous and devilishly handsome Lord Haybury to teach them what he knew of wagering. Adam House had been full of men doing construction, tearing down the entire interior at the front of the huge old mansion to turn the morning room into a gaming room, to make the dining room into a dining hall fit for half a hundred lords.

It had been chaos, and when Emily had refused to supply the name of her previous employer she'd been certain that Diane would turn her away. Instead Diane had only asked her to make one promise, and she'd done so. And now it was time to keep her word.

She left Lily dressing for her morning shift in the main gaming room, and went to find Jenny. Genevieve Martine had returned from the Continent with Diane, and the two ladies had been friends since childhood. Whatever one of them knew, the other soon learned, though she suspected that Jenny hadn't been telling Diane everything where Emily was concerned.

Luckily or not, she found both women together with Diane's husband Lord Haybury in the private hallway opening out into all the club's rooms on the east side of the building. They were speaking in low voices to each other, and none of them looked pleased. Even the characteristic cynical glint in Haybury's eyes was missing.

When Diane caught sight of her approaching, the marchioness broke away from the other two. "Emily," she said in an even quieter voice than they normally used in the private hallway. "I was just about to send for you."

"What's happened?" Her first thought, as always when something upended the club, was that Lord Ebberling had arrived at the front door to have her arrested or dragged away somewhere. Her second thought was that something ill had happened to Westfall, and that thought bothered her far more than it should have. After all, he knew. And that made him trouble.

"Lord Hemfell brought a guest with him to breakfast this morning," Diane returned, as Jenny and Haybury joined them. "It's—"

"It's Ebberling," Emily finished for her. Ice slammed down her spine, but she kept her feet. Only a thin, unlocked door separated her from Peter Velton, the Marquis of Ebberling. But if he was having breakfast, he didn't know she was there. She repeated that to herself with every heartbeat, making it a kind of prayer. He didn't know she was there. *Did he?*

What if she'd been wrong about Nate? What if he'd told her not to flee only so he could ride off and inform Ebberling where to find her? No, he wouldn't do such a thing. She'd looked into his eyes, and even if he were the world's best liar, a professional spy of great skill, she would have seen something if he meant to betray her. All she could see when she imagined his face and his voice, though, was that slight, sensuous smile and the feeling of hope when he'd told her to stay at the club. No. Ebberling didn't know she was there. *He didn't.*

"We seem to be the only ones who know we should be wary," Haybury put in, "and you haven't fainted, which is good."

"Not yet, anyway," she said, managing a brief smile. "I need to speak to the three of you, though. Now, more than ever."

With a nod, Diane gestured her toward the far doorway that led back to the employees' area of the club and the private Adam House beyond. "We were about to sit down for breakfast when Grace sent word that Ebberling had come by. Join us."

Emily didn't know how much of an appetite she could muster, but she appreciated the invitation. Once they knew how much trouble she might be bringing to their doorstep, it could be the last meal she ever ate under the roof of The Tantalus Club. "Thank you."

It had always amazed her that as busy as the front of Adam House was, with its gaming and dining rooms, the rear part of the house could remain so calm and peaceful. Lord and Lady Haybury resided there almost year round, though she knew that Haybury Park in Devon was said to be one of the most splendid country homes in England. Jenny Martine also had her own private rooms there on the uppermost floor. All the rest of The Tantalus Club staff, with the exception of the grooms who lived above the stables, resided on the third floor above the club.

Today Adam House seemed almost too quiet, as if the house was holding its breath and waiting for her to begin burning down the curtains. That was nonsense, though; she would leave before she brought harm to this house and anyone who lived within it. If nothing else, she owed them peace.

"What did you want to tell us?" Diane asked as they selected breakfast from a sideboard and sat around the small breakfast table.

Emily took a slow breath that shook at the edges. "I promised you that if my past troubles became my present troubles, I would tell you."

The marchioness nodded. "You told us you wished to avoid Ebberling."

"I used to be employed in his household, as a governess to his son, George." Emily kept her gaze on the uneaten ham slices decorating her plate. "As Rachel Newbury. The . . . I . . . He's been looking for me for the past three years. He accuses me of murdering Lady Ebberling. I did no such thing, but that won't matter if he learns I'm here. The authorities will come, there will be arrests, and you could be accused of harboring me here."

"Then he'd best not find out you're here," Diane said after a moment, taking a sip of her tea.

They knew, Emily realized, her heart stammering.

They already knew who she was. She sent a glance at Jenny, to find Miss Martine salting her boiled eggs. "But I never told you who I was, or where I came from," she blurted.

"You said you'd served as a governess," her employer returned in her mild voice. "Once you gave us Ebberling's name and we realized how determined you were to evade him, it wasn't difficult to piece the rest together, my dear."

"But what if I'd done it? What he says I did?"

"You just said you didn't." This time it was Haybury answering her. "And not to offend, but you didn't react like a murderer when you heard the news that Ebberling was in London."

She nearly asked him how a murderer would have reacted to the news, but then decided she didn't want them to examine the facts that closely. If they changed their minds about her innocence, she likely wouldn't have a chance to flee. Instead she took a sip of squeezed orange juice, wishing it was whisky. "Lord Westfall knows who I am, too. Ebberling hired him to find me."

That made Haybury frown. "Westfall? I'm surprised he remembers to tie his cravat."

"Don't be fooled by Westfall," Jenny put in, speaking for the first time. "He is not what he seems. Or rather, he is more than he seems."

And even more than that, Emily added silently. How much more, and what it meant, she had no idea. She both anticipated and dreaded learning the answer to those questions.

"More, how?" the marquis demanded, no humor at all in his light gray eyes.

"We all have our secrets, Haybury," Jenny said in her faint French accent. "His is . . . similar to mine."

"Sim—" Haybury cursed. "I'm supposed to be the

biggest scoundrel under this roof," he stated, scowling. "You people need to stop sneaking out from the wood-work."

"You can fight over who is the naughtiest later," Diane broke in, reaching across the table to squeeze Emily's fingers. "But I would win. What I want to know is when you learned about Westfall's dealings with Ebberling, and what we need to do about him."

"I suspected Nathaniel shortly after I met him." Emily met Diane's green-eyed gaze, waiting to see the censure and disapproval there that she felt, herself. She'd been so stupid, tempting fate by insisting on knowing Westfall's business. If she'd kept her distance, he might never have known who she was. He'd as much as said so, himself. But he was like a flame, and she a very light-starved moth. "But yesterday he told me."

"Is that why Ebberling's here?" Haybury rose. "If Bow Street is on its way, you need to go, and I need to throw some guests out on their arses."

That made tears well up in Emily's eyes. These people had known nothing about her three years ago, and even now when she hadn't told them much of anything, they still stood up for her. The family she'd found after what felt like a lifetime of looking. And now she risked losing them. "Lord Westfall said that he wouldn't turn me over to Ebberling. He said I could trust him. I would like to, but that would mean all of you trusting him, as well. I didn't think that was right. That's why I wanted to talk to you this morning."

"I don't trust anyone," Haybury rumbled, pacing to the garden window and back again. "Least of all men who call themselves trustworthy."

"Well, short of going about bashing people for no good reason, I believe we must wait and see," Diane put in, her gaze following her husband's pacing. "Won't we, Oliver?"

"It isn't up to us, now is it, Diane?" he countered, stopping in front of Emily.

"Do you wish me to go? It would certainly make things easier for you." She refused to cry. In the end, everyone would look out for his or her own best interest. That was simply the way of things, and she couldn't blame them for it.

"The heart of my life has decided that as much as she adores The Tantalus Club," Lord Haybury said, before either Diane or Jenny could answer, "she has an even greater interest in protecting her employees."

"I stand by those who stand by me," Diane amended. "I cannot tell you to stay or leave, Emily, because that's your decision. All I can say is that you are welcome to stay."

She was welcome to stay. That was perhaps the nicest thing anyone had ever said to her. Swallowing, she nodded. "I would like to stay. At least until I have a better idea what Westfall is up to, and what Ebberling knows." She glanced over at Jenny and back to her untouched plate of breakfast. "As long as I may continue to earn my keep. I won't sit about doing nothing and expect to be provided for."

"A great many titled men strive for that very thing," the marquis put in, his half grin returning now that the denouement was finished with. "And women, for that matter."

"That is fairly close to the opposite of our policy here." With a smile of her own, Diane nudged the edge of Emily's plate. "Eat something. I think I shall go and greet our guests this morning. And you have more than earned your keep, Emily. I have no fear that you'll continue to do so."

Lord and Lady Haybury left the breakfast room, but Jenny remained behind, seated at the table beside her. Emily wasn't surprised that she now required supervision; if she was discovered now, she would be accused of murder. Whether she'd done it or not, the reputation of the club would be badly damaged, if not ruined. There were people who saw the Tantalus as a blight on Mayfair's landscape, a scandalous den of iniquity in the middle of the blue bloods' haven. Those people would welcome the excuse to see the club closed. She would not allow that to happen. She wasn't the only desperate soul who'd found refuge here, after all.

"Out of the blue Westfall admitted that he was hunting after you?" Jenny asked after a moment.

Emily chewed and swallowed a slice of ham. "I tried to set him off balance by announcing that I knew he was a spy," she admitted, feeling her cheeks heat as she spoke. It had definitely not been one of her brighter ideas, considering the consequences. But at least she knew for certain now that Ebberling was still looking for her.

"How did he react to that, I wonder?"

"He denied it at first, and then he wanted to know how I knew. Don't worry, I only said that a friend of mine knows about such things."

Jenny nodded. "Whether you decide you trust him or not, I expect I'll be keeping an eye on him, then."

That didn't sound terribly friendly. "He's suspected who I am for days," she returned. "And he might easily have told Ebberling where to find me, or even have brought me to see him yesterday." At that thought, a shiver ran through her again. However mad things had become, she only needed to think of that to know they could have been so much worse. "He didn't. I have to give him credit for that."

"Perhaps so, but I have never been fond of giving someone my secrets," Miss Martine commented. "It gives them far too much power over me."

"I'm not precisely worth blackmailing, Jenny."

"Ebberling is," her friend returned flatly. "Which would make you the prize, or the pawn, depending on what you know or what Stokes—Westfall—tells the marquis you know."

Emily frowned. "He wouldn't do that."

"My dear, a spy will do anything to accomplish his mission. And Wellington prized no spy higher than Nate Stokes."

The niggling uneasiness Jenny's previous words had brought to life deepened. Emily knew what it meant; she would be wise to leave the Tantalus. To leave London, and even to flee England. She'd nearly done so three years ago. On the day she'd meant to book passage for the Americas, however, she'd seen that advertisement for young, educated women willing to work at a gentlemen's wagering club. It had seemed a godsend, and it had been one. Until now, apparently.

"I want to talk to Nathaniel before I decide," she heard herself saying.

"You will hear what he wants you to hear, Emily." Jenny pushed away from the table and stood. "What reason in the world would he have to keep your secret? The man who hired him is a fellow lord, one with wealth and influence. You leave him the choice of either announcing his failure to find you, or to confront one of his peers with only a Tantalus girl to support his accusations. Be logical."

"I . . ." She trailed off. For the past ten years she'd let logic rule her life. It had seen her to a good education, a good position, and then to what she'd thought was safety. It made no sense to abandon it now. Jenny was absolutely correct. She had nothing to offer Nate Stokes, and even less to offer the Earl of Westfall. She was a Tantalus girl, an accused thief and murderer.

And she still wanted to talk to Nathaniel before she fled.

"I will consider what you've said," she stated aloud.

"Good. Come along. I'll see you to your room."

Even though no one had ever come out and directly said that Genevieve Martine had also been a spy, Emily knew it with as much certainty as she knew anything. So whether Jenny's company was meant to protect her or to protect the Tantalus, she welcomed it.

In her room she closed and latched the door, then knelt to reach under her bed for the nondescript portmanteau she kept there. Inside was a small amount of money, some clean clothes, and several faux reference papers. She pulled them out, looking through them. In America she could be Jane Halifax or Mary Nexton; both girls had good references from very upright, prominent families of her creation. Isobel McQueen wouldn't do; that was her favorite invented name, but Isobel sounded too Scottish. Prominent families in America wouldn't hire someone who sounded like she'd come directly from the Highlands.

With a sigh she returned the papers to their place and added another twenty pounds to her funds. Then she pushed the bag back under the bed. Not yet. Not until she spoke to Nate one more time. Because whatever logic told her, she did trust Nathaniel Stokes. And deeper than that, she wanted to see him again. Not at his convenience, however. It was past time she took the reins to her own destiny.

*   *   *

Indoor plants were one of the most clever inventions in the world, Nate decided as he carefully tipped most of the contents of his glass into the potted palm behind him.

They were lovely things, giving a bit of greenery to a world of iron and fabrics and dead wood, and they had all that lovely dirt that could absorb dozens of glasses of liquor without giving away a single secret. As his tablemate looked at him again, Nate lowered the nearly empty glass from his mouth and grinned.

"You are bamming me, Henning," he drawled, sloshing a bit more liquid from the glass as he set it down a bit too emphatically. "No one is that lucky."

Francis Henning refilled both their glasses with the fine vodka Nate had requested from the helpful footman at White's. Even the vapors were intoxicating, but on top of the fine lamb and kidney pie he'd dined on earlier, he was more sober than a judge. Not so Mr. Henning, but that was the idea, after all.

"No, I swear it," Henning returned with a chuckle. "Four matches in a row, and Ebberling had the winner in every one of them. At damned astronomical odds, too. The man walked away with two thousand quid, and the rest of us bloody paupers. My grandmama nearly peeled my ears from my head, she shouted so loud when I had to tell her I'd lost my rent money for the month."

"Did anyone think Ebberling had . . . influenced the direction of the breeze, so to speak?" Nate pursued, spinning a penny with his fingers and then dumping half his glass again when the coin distracted his exceedingly drunken companion.

"I thought he might have, but it would have cost him more to bribe the boxers to lose than he won in wagering on them who did win." Henning scowled. "Or the other way around."

"I know what you meant." And he also knew what it signified. Ebberling would have lost money overall, but the boost to his pride seemed to have been worth it. Everything he'd noticed about the Marquis of Ebberling bespoke his need to be admired, even if he had to make bribes to arrange it.

For another hour he listened to tales of every nonesuch and rakehell and blackguard admired by Francis Henning, until he'd heard every rumor and supposed fact known about Peter Velton before and during his tenure as the Marquis of Ebberling. And Henning was only his latest source—in the past day he'd purchased more drinks and meals for his peers than he had in the previous two years.

Whether it had been worth it or not, he wasn't certain. But he did have confirmation that his instincts concerning Ebberling were precisely plumb. The man would go to any expense for the sake of his pride, and he detested losing. Embarrassing the marquis was a mortal sin, and was paid for in kind tenfold. Nathaniel wondered if the late Lady Ebberling had cuckolded him or had merely defeated her husband in a horse race or a wager over which of two birds would perch higher up in a tree. Any of those might have caused her death.

When he'd finished with the genuinely amusing Henning he made his way back to Teryl House to change for the evening. "Welcome home, my lord," Garvey intoned, taking his hat and gloves. "Master Laurence requested me to inform you that he—"

"Nate, where the devil have you been?" his brother broke in, practically vaulting down the last twenty feet of staircase.

"—wished to speak to you," the butler finished.

"Thank you, Garvey."

"Never mind that." Laurence grabbed Nate by the arm and practically dragged him toward the stairs. "Where were you?" he repeated in a loud hiss.

"Working." He shook Laurie off his arm. "Did someone expire naked and bloody in the drawing room?"

"What? No."

"Then simply say 'Nate, I'd like to speak to you upstairs, if you don't mind,' and I swear that I'm very likely to follow you there on my own two feet."

Laurence stopped his scrambling ascent of the stairs and faced him. Taking a breath that visibly lifted and lowered his shoulders, he straightened. "Nate, I'd like to speak to you upstairs, if you don't mind," he enunciated

"Oh, certainly. Lead the way." Stifling a grin, Nathaniel gestured for Laurence to precede him.

On the landing they turned not for the drawing room, but Nate's private study. "You have a very odd sense of what a household emergency might be," Laurie said over his shoulder. "A nude, murdered corpse? Christ, Nate, you'll frighten the servants."

"I didn't actually think that," Nathaniel retorted, ignoring the fact that for a brief half a heartbeat, he had thought exactly that. "I was trying to keep you from fainting in excitement over whatever it is you're up to."

"I'm not up to anything. And this is important." He knocked at the study door, then shoved it open without waiting for a response.

Ignoring for a moment that no one, including Laurie, was permitted inside his private study without his permission, Nathaniel followed his brother through the door. Then he stopped in his tracks.

Emily Portsman sat behind his writing desk, her hands neatly folded on the smooth red mahogany surface.

"See? Important." Laurie folded his arms across his chest.

Nathaniel barely noted him. All his attention was on the slender young lady with the rich chestnut hair currently gazing at him with eyes the color of purest chocolate. The knot of something hard and cold and unsettled that had been roosting in his chest all day broke loose and vanished. "Laurie, go away," he said, not shifting his gaze from her face.

"What? I—"

"Out."

"Well, that's a fine thank-you."

"Thank you. Out. Bring tea."

His brother seemed to deflate. "Fine. Two cups only, though, because no one else knows she's here," he said, whispering the last bit. "And you're welcome."

Once the door closed behind him, Nathaniel reached back and locked it. "Hello," he said.

"Your brother knows about me." Her voice was oddly flat. She was angry, he realized.

"He's my brother. I trust him." Grabbing one of the reading chairs from beneath the window, he twisted it around to face her and sat down in it.

"He's not *my* brother, and I don't trust him. He's just a child, for heaven's sake."

"He's only five years younger than you are. And he's known what I am since the beginning, and has never breathed a word about it to anyone. Your secret is safe with him." He leaned forward, setting both hands flat on the writing table between them. "Now what's amiss?"

"Ebberling had breakfast at the Tantalus this morning."

Damnation. Something heated and dark wrenched to life in his gut. He reached out to grip her folded hands. "Did he see you?"

Portsman shook her head. "No. Lord and Lady Haybury saw him first and warned me away. They thought you might have sent him there. Haybury wanted to shoot you."

Nathaniel narrowed his eyes. "So they know about me. It seems both of us are spilling secrets every which way."

"I trust them."

Her expression was defiant, daring him to question her despite the fact that she'd just done the same thing to him. Rather than turn this meeting into a wrestling match over whose friends and family were more trustworthy, he inclined his head. There were other questions he had for her. "Very well. Is it Haybury who knew I was a spy, then?"

"No. And I'm not telling you who it was."

"Ah. Because you trust this person, too?"

"Yes. Now, th—"

"With my life?" he interrupted. "And my brother's life?"

"You were Nate Stokes, spy. Is there any other spy who doesn't know who you are?"

"I was not Nate Stokes, spy," he grated, tightening his grip on her hands. "For God's sake, Portsman. Wellington knew that, and my direct superiors. And me, of course. There were times I had to remind myself that that was my name. To the world at large I was Nate Stokes, wastrel and gaddabout with the lack of common sense and patriotism to go abroad during a war and look for nice, fat old books to purchase and study. To sundry and various people of interest to England I was John Cobbins, Adam Genning, Heathrow Parks, Mohammed Ziffari, and so many damned others I just wanted to forget after I shed their skin.

"I had scars and beards and accents and languages and gray hair or black hair or blond hair and names and stinks and fat and gristle that I put on and took off every other week, every other hour, sometimes," he went on in a torrent of words that he wanted to stop but couldn't, "and I still wake up every morning and have to lie there and try to remember who I am today. That is who I was. Am."

So bloody much for keeping his own secrets from her. He'd blurted them out like a schoolboy with his first whore. Glaring at her, breathing hard, he shoved her hands away and slammed to his feet. He needed some damned air.

As he stalked to the window and pushed it open he flung his spectacles onto the floor behind him. He hated the damned things, sometimes, as much as he felt like he needed them. Nate Stokes. They told him he was Nate Stokes, and he needed to remember that, now. Whoever he truly was, the world had come to know him as absentminded, bumbling Nate Stokes, accidental Earl of Westfall. And so he was.

Supposedly confession was good for the soul. It left one feeling lighter and freer or some such nonsense. Mostly what he felt as he breathed in the air of his garden, spiced roses mixed with the smell of horsehit from the stables and the city beyond, was fear. He'd told her everything. And now his life was literally in her hands. Why? Why would he do that?

Part of him wanted to answer that it was because he was tired of living twenty different lives and of never knowing which one was actually him. The other part was shouting that he'd spoken because he trusted her— which was idiotic because he didn't even know who she was. She'd said she hadn't killed anyone, but Rachel Newbury was as much her real name as Emily Portsman was.

He heard her stand up, but he stayed where he was. The next sound would be her opening the study door, and then he would have to decide—not whether to turn her over to Ebberling, but whether he could let her leave at all, knowing what she did. It wasn't just about his life, but Laurie's, as well. There were men who wanted Nate dead. Or rather, there were men who wanted Heathrow Parks and the others dead, and now she knew that all of them were him.

A hand touched his back. A second hand joined it, and both together moved around to circle his chest. Her cheek pressed lightly against his shoulder.

"Eloise Smorkley," she whispered. "My mother was a washerwoman, and my father was a poacher. I ran away when I was twelve because I knew I would end up as some gentleman's fancy girl at best, and an alleyway whore at worst. I lied and stole my way into finishing school, and because I was pretty and witty I got away with it. The governess position at Ebberling Manor was my first. And then I saw him kill her, and it was my last."

He stood unmoving, listening, his hands braced against the windowsill and her arms quietly around him. All the power he'd given her, and she was giving it back to him. Not because she was angry and couldn't stop her tongue from wagging, but because she chose to do so.

"I was going to say that we're alike, you and I," she continued, "but that isn't so. You've lived your lies for the sake of king and country. My lies were because I didn't want the life I'd been handed and I decided to make another. I don't have any right to drag you into my troubles, and I'm sorry I ever tried to. You're a good man, Nate Stokes. That's the part you should be remembering."

Her touch left his back, and he heard her walking for the door. And then it struck him. "Eloise Smorkley?" he said, facing her. He laughed. He couldn't help it, any more than he could help the torrent of words a few minutes earlier. "Smorkley? Really?"

Emily lifted her hand off the door's handle and turned around. *For heaven's sake.* She'd just bared her soul to the man, just as he had for her, and now he wanted to laugh at her very unfortunate name? The sound of his laugh, though, deep and rolling and genuine, stopped the retort she'd been about to make. She found herself grinning back at him.

"It's awful, isn't it? And I had the poor fortune to be tall as a child. Smorkley the Storkley, the other children called me. Oh, I hated that name." Emily chuckled.

Nathaniel's shoulders lowered, and he crossed the room to stop in front of her. "I swear I will never call you that, Portsman," he returned, still laughing. "If you'll let me help you, that is."

She studied his gaze for a moment. Humor touched his light eyes, but there was determination there, as well. Flight still seemed the wisest choice, but at the moment she didn't feel in the mood to discount the brave, devious, troubled man currently gripping her shoulders. "I will take a chance," she said, sobering. "Because I don't want to have to begin all over again."

Nate leaned down and touched his mouth to hers. "I'll hold you to that, Portsman."

Chapter Eleven

Nathaniel swung down from Blue and retrieved his cane, then limped up the drive of Velton House. The last time he'd been here, he'd wondered if Lord Ebberling had told him the entire truth about Miss Rachel Newbury and the events that had befallen his wife, Katherine. This time, he knew he was about to speak with a murderer.

He'd done so before, of course, back when the information he was after outweighed the crime of the moment. Today he needed to tread even more carefully.

The butler pulled open the door as he topped the shallow marble steps. "Good morning, Lord Westfall," he said politely.

"Good morning. Is Lord Ebberling in?"

"If you would care to wait in the foyer, I shall inquire, my lord."

Once the butler had closed the front door he vanished up the stairs and into the bowels of the large house. Nate stayed where he was, his back to the wall, and listened. Every household had its own peculiarities and quirks, and they all meant something.

What he noticed first about Velton House was that it was silent. No servants chatted about the weather or about his lordship's request for fresh flowers. Young George, wherever he was, seemed to be going about his morning in silence. An odd thing for an eight-year-old boy.

Mentally Nate shrugged. It was entirely possible, he supposed, that the lad was out of doors, the servants were finished with their morning duties and were in the kitchen having breakfast, and he was reading sentences onto blank pages.

The butler reappeared at the top of the landing. "This way, my lord, if you please. Lord Ebberling is in his library and will see you now."

Ebberling sat before the fireplace, a thick book resting in one hand while he flipped pages with the other. Curious, Nate dipped his head as he adjusted his spectacles. *Grain Supplies in Europe during Bonaparte's Conquest.* Ah. The book was only meant to look impressive, then—a serious-sized tome for a serious man.

"Good morning, my lord," he said, inclining his head again.

The marquis lifted a finger, evidently intent on finishing a paragraph before he could tear himself away from the book. "Westfall. Have a seat."

Taking the chair on the opposite side of the fire, Nate leaned his cane against the arm and sank back into the soft cushions. Emily was afraid of this man. She hadn't said so directly, but her expression and her tone of voice had spoken volumes to anyone who knew how to listen. The heavy jaw, the straight line of his back even while seated, the immaculate, expensive clothes, all bespoke a man of wealth and power. There was more, though—the lack of laugh lines, the clenched jaw, the slightly narrowed eyes, things he'd noted before but put to the man's anger at a thief and murderer escaping—that he now saw as marks of a foul temper, or even possibly of cruelty.

If he was now seeing things from Portsman's point of view he needed to stop, however; whatever and who-ever Ebberling was, Nate wanted to see him clearly. Facts only, body language only. Anything else was dangerous and counterproductive.

"Do you have news for me, then?" the marquis finally asked, closing the book and setting it aside.

"I have news that I have no news, I'm afraid," Nate returned in his most harmless tone.

"Rycott said you were competent."

"Yes, well, I've never attempted to find someone who's been missing for three years, and could well be anywhere in the entire world. For a moment I thought I'd tracked her to London, but that young lady had green eyes and a shortened left leg. In fact, I have found no trace of her at all. No one of her description that anyone recalls has boarded a ship, or taken work, or turned up dead, or married, or . . . anything." He pulled the uncashed banknote from his pocket. "And so I cannot, in good conscience, take your money."

"You've only been looking for four weeks. Are you so certain she's completely vanished?"

"If I thought there was a reasonable chance of locating Miss Newbury, I would continue looking."

Ebberling gazed at him levelly. "What is your fee, then, for looking and finding nothing?"

Nate smiled, pushing at his spectacles again. "This is my hobby, Ebberling. It was entertaining, attempting to find a ghost. But I won't take your money when I have no results."

"Not even a penny?"

"I haven't earned it."

"But you know that she hasn't boarded a ship or married or died, do you not?"

The low arrogance permeating the room chilled into a tense hostility. Nate shifted his elbow, checking that his cane and the rapier inside it remained within reach. "No, I don't know that. I could not find anyone who recalled seeing someone of her description. In three years people leave positions or die or simply forget."

"You offered bribes?"

"Where they seemed appropriate."

The marquis sat back again. "Then I do owe you some money. Tell me how much you spent, at least, and I will recompense you."

Nathaniel didn't want his money. Not a shilling, not a penny. But Ebberling was after something, and he didn't quite know what it was, yet. "The amount came to twenty-one pounds, if you insist, but it isn't necessary. I was looking for the woman you believed may have killed your wife. With no results, I won't—"

Pulling money from his pocket, Ebberling counted out exactly twenty-one pounds and set the blunt on the table beside him. "Then we are finished here. I will hire someone who can produce results and find me Rachel Newbury. Good day, Westfall."

Rising, Nate set the banknote on the table next to the cash, which he scooped into a pocket. "Good luck to you, Ebberling," he returned, the words tasting like ash in his mouth.

If the marquis found Portsman, he would kill her. Of that, Nathaniel was certain. Which left her with two choices—running again, or striking first. Legally, or physically. That was a question he would leave up to her, though he had his own preferences. He'd killed for his country, and while he hadn't enjoyed it, he hadn't hesitated, either. This was the first time that the idea of removing someone from the equation, as Wellington tended to put it, was something he could look forward to.

He found a groom holding Blue, and climbed back into the saddle with his practiced lack of grace. His first thought was that he wanted to go see Portsman, or Smorkley, or Newbury, or whatever name she chose to go by. *Smorkley.* He couldn't conjure a less likely name for a more interesting, elegant, clever woman. No wonder she'd left it behind.

Instead, though, he turned for Teryl House. He'd promised to let Laurie know how the meeting had gone, and he needed to find some perspective where Portsman was concerned. He liked her. He wanted her. But were those things worth further tangling himself into her life? She'd confessed to being a poacher's daughter, after all. And while that might have done for bumbling Nate Stokes, bookish cousin to an earl, he wasn't that man any longer. He'd never regretted his cousin's death more than he did at that moment, either.

This past winter the Duke of Greaves had raised eyebrows all over England by marrying a Tantalus girl, and she'd been a duke's daughter. An illegitimate one, but even so, half aristocrat. Because he was now an earl, he'd be expected to marry and father little heirs himself, though he'd already half decided to pass the title on to Laurence and let him have the worry of procreation and parenthood.

Nate shook himself. He'd bedded Emily Portsman on several occasions, and had enjoyed each and every one of them. She wasn't his first lover, however. So why the devil had the word *marriage* popped into his head? Because she knew who he was? That only made her dangerous. Except that he didn't think of her that way, however much logic urged him to do so. In his mind

she was simply Portsman, of the deep brown eyes and
witty, sinful mouth. Someone with whom he no longer
had to pretend to be anyone but who he was—whoever
that might be.

A horse reined in beside him. "What did you say to
Ebberling?"

He looked over at the black Thoroughbred. "Isn't
that the Duke of Greaves's horse? Zeus or some such?"
he asked, leaning sideways to scratch his calf—and
loosen the knife in his boot.

The Marquis of Haybury nodded. "It was. Now he's
mine. What did you say to Ebberling?"

This was Portsman's employer. Or rather, the husband of her employer, since if the rumors were to be
believed Oliver Warren had signed a paper upon his
marriage to Diane Warren promising never to take
ownership of The Tantalus Club. The marquis was rich
as Croesus in his own right, so he certainly had no need
of the income from a gentlemen's club, anyway. The
more pressing question where Nate was concerned,
however, was how much Haybury knew, and how much
he cared to share. "Ebberling and I had a business ar-
rangement, which we have mutually terminated. I don't
believe that to be any of your concern, however."

"Terminated in that you let him know where to find
Emily, or in that you told him to go stuff himself?"

Haybury kept his voice low, but Nate flinched anyway. "I beg your pardon, Haybury, but I was tasked
with finding someone named Rachel Newbury. My
friendship with Emily Portsman, if that is the Emily to
whom you are referring, has nothing to do with that."

"Hm. You're more slippery than the French twist,
aren't you? Spies. Bugger 'em all."

He and Portsman were going to have to have a chat
about her confidence-sharing, if she meant to continue

exposing him every time he turned around. Haybury had given him a bit of information, anyway. This French twist had to be the one Emily had spoken to, the one who'd identified him as a spy. And *French twist* sounded like a female. Someone else at the Tantalus? Bloody hell, that place was turning out to be quite the interesting hive of buzzing bees.

"I suppose you're completely straightforward and aboveboard in everything you do?" he shot back.

"I do what's necessary to protect myself and mine," the marquis retorted.

"As do I. The *mine* you speak of merely means all of England, in my case. And I'm retired. So keep your damned mouth shut about it."

To his surprise, Haybury grinned at that. "That's better. You're flesh and blood, anyway. So you told Ebberling you couldn't find our girl?"

"I did." Denying it to this man seemed utterly pointless.

He knew Haybury's reputation as a gambler and a rake with a penchant for causing trouble when it amused him. Everything he saw riding beside him, from the steady gray gaze to the easy hold on a formidable-looking mount, spoke of confidence and charm and happiness. The marquis was deeply in love with his wife. And Nate liked him for it. And for his direct, straightforward manner. There was a world of difference between this marquis and the one he'd just left.

"Did he believe you?"

"He thought I was an incompetent ninny, and he said he would hire someone better at the job than I was. There is no one better at the job, but I did find her, so another man might, as well. And a new fellow might be less inclined to question his employer's motives than I was."

"She's still in danger, then."

"Yes." And that was what troubled him more than anything. He might have turned Ebberling's offer down, but he hadn't saved her from the man. Far from it. In fact, he might have made things worse.

"What do you mean to do about it?" Haybury asked on the tail of his own thought. "Assuming you mean to do something and not simply walk away."

Nate eyed him. "And what do you know of Portsman's background and parentage?" he asked crisply.

"Nothing."

"Then consider why she trusts me more than she trusts you. I'm not walking away."

He kept his expression cool and blank, but Haybury nodded anyway. "Good. If you need assistance with not walking away, come see me. I've a certain lack of affection for any man who would harm his own wife." With that he kicked his heels into the black's ribs and turned toward Hyde Park.

Well, that had been interesting. Nate wondered if Portsman had any idea that she had allies. Powerful ones. More than likely, she didn't. As a spy he generally trusted to no one's counsel but his own. However, this wasn't about him. And if it meant keeping one Eloise Smorkley safe, he was somewhat troubled to realize that he was willing to do anything. Even trust. Even be himself.

"Haybury," he called, wheeling Blue after the marquis. "There is something you can do for me, actually."

"Are you too good now to work in the dining room?"

Emily looked up as Lucille Hampton plunked herself down at the communal dinner table opposite her. "I haven't been feeling well," she returned, thankful she'd taken time to consider that one of her fellow Tantalus girls might not look too kindly on her altered duties. "Diane and Jenny thought it best if I remain out of the club for the time being."

"Are you pregnant, then?"

"What? Good heavens, no." Her cheeks heated. All she needed was for that rumor to get about. None of her friends would talk about anything else, and all her plans to remain quietly in the background would explode in her face.

Lucille stood up again. Rather than flounce away as Emily had expected, though, Miss Hampton walked around to her side of the long table and slid onto the bench directly beside her. "Then what's truly going on?" she whispered in a much quieter voice. "With you and Lord Westfall spending so much time together I thought perhaps you were after a wedding. If you're not carrying his babe, though, and you're still seeing him, and you're claiming to be too ill to work out with the gentlemen, then something is afoot."

Evidently Lucille did have a mind; she just used it only rarely. Even so, Emily had no intention of telling her what was truly going on. "Oh, very well," she whispered back. "You know that I came here to avoid my previous employer, yes?"

"Yes, we all know that story. You worked for some old couple and the lord of the house made advances."

Telling herself that not all lies could be sins, when they saved people's lives, Emily nodded. "Exactly. Someone saw my former employer in London, and I've been worried that he might make an appearance here. There would be a terrible scene, and . . . well, I just don't want to set eyes on him again. He smelled like mold, and oh, it was just awful." There. It was partly the truth, at least, and if Ebberling ever did discover

that she was at the Tantalus, it would be worse than awful. At least for her.

Lucille patted her on the shoulder. "You know, I was
mad that you stole Westfall from me, and I still am, but
we're all sisters here. I won't mention your name to
anyone. And if some moldy old lord comes here asking
after you, I'll say that I've never heard of you."

"Thank you." And even if Lucille was sincere, Emily was still thankful that no one would come here
looking for Emily Portsman. Just in case.

"Since today is ladies' day, I'll even invite you to
come have dinner with my cousin and me," Miss Hampton continued.

"Thank you again," Emily returned, "but I'm accustomed to spending ladies' day upstairs here. And Jenny's given me more accounts to do, since I'm not out on
the floor working shifts."

Wrinkling her nose, Lucille stood again. "I'd rather
kiss a moldy old lord than do accounts."

By mid-afternoon most of the Tantalus girls had left
the premises or were making plans to do so. And the
replacement staff—footmen and croupiers and waiters
Diane hired for two days each month from Pall Mall's
most auspicious clubs—was beginning to arrive. At first
the owners of White's and Boodle's and the Society,
among others, had refused to allow a portion of their
own employees the evening off to go serve the ladies
who flocked to the Tantalus to dine and wager together
twice a month. Once they'd realized that all the ladies'
husbands would be the ones flocking to *their* clubs in
the absence of the Tantalus, however, their tunes had
changed.

As the common room began to fill with young, attractive men, Emily gathered up her things and retreated

to her own room. As accustomed as she'd become to the upheaval that occurred every other Wednesday, this time it unsettled her. None of the men would be Lord Ebberling, of course, and it was likely that none of them even knew the marquis, but they were strangers. And she disliked strangers.

Two hours later one of the cook's helpers came knocking, and Emily went to unlock the door. "You're early, aren't you, Betty?"

"I've not got your dinner, Em," the girl replied with her usual easy smile. "You've a caller. Miss Charity says she don't want no men in the kitchens, ever, but he couldn't come in the front way tonight."

Her heart started pounding. "Did he give his name?"

"Oh, yes. Forgot. It's Westfall."

Thank goodness. Her heart sped even further, but with anticipation now rather than dread. It felt like far longer than three days since she'd last seen him, and he'd said that he meant to leave Ebberling's employ. A chill swirled down her spine. Whether Nathaniel would be able to convince Ebberling that she was far, far out of his reach she had no idea, but that was what she wanted him to tell her. Even if it was a lie.

"I'll be right down," she said, when she realized that Betty was eyeing her curiously.

"Don't hurry. We don't get men in the kitchen much, and he's pretty."

Emily choked back a laugh. "I shall take my time, then."

She wouldn't have described Nate as pretty, herself. Even with his long eyelashes and light green eyes he was every inch a man. Handsome, devilishly so, but not pretty.

Betty gave her another grin. "Thank you."

Closing her door again, Emily dug through her wardrobe for something less demure than she'd worn to the picnic. She had daring gowns aplenty, since that was unofficially the uniform of the club, but it still took her several minutes to find just the one she wanted. Finally she settled on a low-cut gown of sky blue with silver bands at the arms and waist and the squared neckline. That should do, she decided as she took a last look at herself in the dressing mirror. And it only belatedly occurred to her that she wanted to see Nate more than she wanted to know what he'd learned from Ebberling.

It was foolish, but to herself, at least, she could admit that she was quite smitten with the former spy. Of course nothing would come of it, because nothing could come of an earl and a poacher's daughter, but she could at least have him in her bed. And that was very nice, indeed.

As she walked down the attic hallway one of the temporary men nearly fell over himself he was so busy gaping at her, but she only nodded and continued on her way. In the past she might have stopped to flirt, or even asked him to stay after he was finished with working, but not tonight. Tonight all her dances were taken, so to speak.

When she reached the kitchen she stopped to one side of the doorway while the male staff hurried back and forth with plates and baskets and pots of hot water. Nate stood beside the largest stove, chatting with Charity Green as the head cook spooned what looked like the remains of one of her famous peach tarts into his mouth.

He looked up and met her eyes, then said something to the cook and walked up to her. "There you are, Miss Portsman."

"Here I am, Lord Westfall," she returned, gazing at

his face as he stopped only a foot in front of her. "Did we have an engagement?"

"Oh, did I forget to tell you?" He pushed at his spectacles, his eyes dancing behind the glass lenses. "How dull of me. Are you free this evening?"

"Not any longer." She tossed her head and sent a wink at Betty. "Don't wait up for me, dear."

Nathaniel led the way outside. Once she'd closed the kitchen door he turned around and backed her into the wall, lowering his mouth over hers in a kiss that left her breathless, and damp between the legs. "There," he murmured, lifting his head a little, "that's better."

"For you. I feel thoroughly ruined," she managed, chuckling.

"Not thoroughly enough. Not yet."

And to think, a few weeks ago she'd disliked kissing.

In a sense, though, she'd been correct; almost from the moment they'd met, Nate Stokes had not been just any man, someone with whom to dispel her boredom and loneliness. She'd worried that kissing would mean she'd forged a connection, and as she looked at the man currently leading her toward his big, black closed coach, she'd been correct. Of course he was likely the worst man she could ever hope to like, not foolish, not dimwitted, and not self-concerned, but there he was.

"Where are we going?" she asked belatedly, balking at the coach's open door. "I'm not dressed for Vauxhall, or a picnic."

His light green gaze roved across her from head to toe and back again. "You're dressed perfectly, as it so happens. In fact, I may change my plans and simply drive you back to my home."

"I'd prefer that, actually," she returned, "and I'm not going anywhere until you tell me our destination."

Nathaniel nodded, reaching out to tuck a straying strand of her hair behind one ear. "Promise you'll listen to the entire presentation before you flee into the night."

That sounded dismaying. Cautiously taking a step back from the vehicle, she inclined her head. "Very well."

"We're going to the theater."

Her heart stopped. "We are not going to the th—"

"Ah, ah, Portsman. The entire presentation," he broke in. "*A Comedy of Errors* premieres tonight, and a group of my friends are all joining me in a box. You're one of my friends, so you're coming, as well."

She backed away another step. For heaven's sake, she'd never been to a proper London play. It was unfair, to tempt her with such things when he knew she couldn't go. "I don't know your friends, and I barely trust you, Westfall. No."

"But you do know my friends. Better than I do, actually." He began ticking them off on his fingers. "Lord and Lady Haybury, His Grace the Duke of Greaves and his duchess, K—"

"Sophia?" she interrupted, her heart beginning to beat again. "I didn't even think they were back in London."

"They arrived three days ago, along with a pair of their friends. I believe you're also acquainted with Mr. and Mrs. Blackwood."

Keating and Camille. Oh, goodness. They didn't know all her secrets—only the man currently gazing at her with a half smile on his handsome face did—but they knew some things. They were her sisters, who'd begun at the Tantalus when she had. "You swear— *swear*—that you're not bamming me," she demanded.

"I swear it. I asked Haybury for assistance, and he

arranged it. I'll be the outsider, not you. Well, Laurie and I will be. If I wouldn't agree to take him, he threatened to cry."

That made her pause again. "If you don't know any of them, why are you doing this?"

He sighed, leaning against the side of the coach. "Because I wish to spend time with you, and because I've returned Ebberling's blunt and he might be eyeing me at the moment. If I went somewhere alone with you, he might notice. A group of old friends, though, is safer. And he has no idea that I'm not already aquainted with everyone in your circle."

A few weeks ago the idea of going out anywhere when she knew that Ebberling was in Town, and possibly even looking in her general direction, would have sent her straight back into hiding. It nearly did, even tonight. But what Nathaniel had said, that he wanted to spend time with her, that lure was strong enough to overcome even her well-honed sense of caution. "Very well," she breathed, and leaned up to kiss him on his smiling mouth. "You are very persuasive."

He handed her up into the coach. "At times my skills become useful for things other than subterfuge," he returned, sitting on the well-padded leather seat beside her.

Once he leaned over to pull the door closed, they rumbled down the drive. "Are we going to Drury Lane?" she asked, attempting not to sound like an excited schoolgirl.

"We are. It's a good twenty-minute drive, especially if Sams goes the route I instructed him to." Nathaniel cupped the nape of her neck and pulled her closer for another plundering kiss. "And whatever shall we do in the meantime?"

With a chuckle, Emily ran her hand up his thigh. "It seems you already have something in mind, sir," she said, brushing across the bulge in his trousers.

"That I do."

She unbuttoned his waistcoat and then continued down to his trousers, reaching in with delicate fingers to pull him free. With a groan he lifted her over him to straddle his thighs. For a moment she hesitated; she certainly hadn't thought to bring any French condoms with her, and there wasn't a stream or a cloth anywhere in sight.

Then he dipped into his pocket and produced one of the little confections. Emily smiled at him. "What if I'd refused to go with you?" she asked, slipping it over his member and tying the red ribbon.

"Then we would have been in your room doing this very thing," he returned, pulling down on one of her sleeves to bare a breast, which he promptly took into his mouth.

Breathing unsteadily, she gathered her gown up around her waist and settled down over him, sighing as he slid deep inside. Emily flung her arms around his shoulders, bouncing enthusiastically as he held on to her hips, pulling her down on him again. Sex had always been about chasing away the dark, for her, at least. Over the past days, the past fortnight or so, however, it had become about . . . him. About Nathaniel Stokes, Earl of Westfall. About the way he looked at her, listened to her, parried and danced about their conversation like a master swordsman, the way he'd told her things about himself that no one else knew, and the way she'd been able to tell him things about herself that she'd never meant to speak.

She came around him, whimpering into his neck as

he thrust hard up into her again and again. Finally he shuddered, pulling her down over him and kissing her openmouthed, tongues tangling. This could not end well—not for her heart or her happiness or her future—but she'd never been so tempted by the present. Or by any other man, ever.

For a man who kept himself out of gossip, under the notice of Mayfair's wags, and away from politics, Nate reflected that he'd certainly chosen an odd set of box mates. He kept himself between Portsman and the rest of the crowd filing into the theater, not that anyone was likely to make note of either one of them on the way up the long, curved staircase. The return trip back to the coach was likely to be much more difficult, and all because of the seven people currently greeting her with great enthusiasm. Well, six of them, anyway. Laurie hadn't become notorious yet, though given a few years he just might.

However much time Nate had spent away from London, away from England, over the previous few years, he'd made a point of learning everything possible about his peers upon his return. Once he'd inherited the earldom, it had become even more important to know the minds and characters of the aristocrats around him.

"Westfall," Haybury greeted him, offering a hand. "Have you met Keating Blackwood and his wife, Camille?"

Nate inclined his head. "I have not. Thank you for joining us tonight."

Sharp blue eyes gazed back at him. "Didn't do it for you," Blackwood commented, but shook the hand Nate proffered him.

I know all about you, Blackwood, Nathaniel might have said, but he needed the man's assistance tonight. And Keating Blackwood wasn't the only killer in the box. At least the dark-haired gentleman farmer had been tried and found guilty only of self-defense. Nate couldn't make the same boast, himself.

"Don't mind him," the lovely sprite with the buttermilk-blond hair broke in, stepping in front of her husband. "I'm Camille," she said, smiling. "And if you truly mean to assist Em, then thank you, my lord."

Emily stepped up beside him again, another young female in tow. "Westfall, this is my good friend Sophia White. I mean Baswich. The Duchess of Greaves. And her husband, the Duke of Greaves."

This was the pair that had scandalized England over the winter. The young lady with the easy smile and the deep red hair was the illegitimate daughter of the Duke of Hennessy, and the tall, lean-faced Greaves had thrown over several far more eligible women and stolen her from a parson in order to marry her. Inwardly he sighed. Evidently a Tantalus girl, even one who wished to remain hidden away, could not have subtle friends. "Your Graces," he said, bowing.

The duchess laughed. "Oh, don't bow to me," she whispered. "You'll make Lady Velling in the box across from us faint, and she'll fall on the orchestra."

"She'd kill the lot of them, with her girth," Greaves seconded, kissing his wife on the temple. He eyed Nate much as Blackwood had. "But I thank you for the courtesy, all the same," he said, and offered his hand, as well. "Evidently Haybury judged you rightly."

Nate glanced at the marquis, already seated with Lady Haybury at the back of the box. He'd asked for a group that would take attention from the pairing of himself and Portsman as anything more than a pair of lovers, and Haybury had certainly provided it. How much assistance being grouped with this notorious crowd would be for Laurence, he had no idea, but his brother looked happy enough to weep as he chatted animatedly with Blackwood and Haybury about horses and wagering. *Bloody hell.*

Then Portsman took his arm and pulled him toward the back of the box. "It's about to begin," she murmured.

"We could sit in the front, with your friends," he said, holding the back of her chair for her.

"No." She spoke a bit too sharply, but he understood her reluctance. In the dark he couldn't tell if Ebberling was here or not, and he couldn't look about without drawing attention to the fact that he was searching for the marquis.

He sat beside her. "You have very interesting companions."

That made her smile. "Yes, I do." Emily slipped her hand around his arm. "You, included."

"I'm the opposite of interesting," he murmured back, for the first time wishing he could stand up and toss his spectacles and cane aside and shout that he was a damned hero, for the devil's sake.

"Yes, because only a dull, sensible man would arrange for a night like this, with people like this around us." She leaned a breath closer. "I very much want to kiss you right now, Westfall. Thank you for dragging me out of my hermit's cave."

"You are welcome."

The curtain opened to tumultuous applause, and Portsman sat forward. What would her fellows think, if they knew she was the daughter of a poacher and a washerwoman? After all, everyone else in the box bled blue. Even the illegitimate chit had a duke for a sire, and the other one, Camille, was an earl's daughter, and

Blackwood a marquis's cousin. Lady Haybury was a viscount's daughter and an earl's widow and now a marquis's wife, thrice blue-blooded.

And even with all that, he still found Emily, or whatever she chose to call herself, the most fascinating female—the most fascinating human, in fact—he'd ever encountered. She'd said they were different because his lies were for the benefit of England, while hers were only to save herself from a life of poverty. However far she'd managed to raise herself up from the mud, though, and considering their company tonight that was very far indeed, she'd earned it. She'd fought for every inch of ground, and she'd earned it. She belonged here, as much as anyone else in this box.

And no one, least of all the Marquis of Ebberling, was going to be allowed to take it away from her. No matter what he had to do to see that she had a happy life.

The Marquis of Ebberling set down his glass of wine as the play began.

Around him his fiancée and her family kept chittering about this lady's necklace and that duke's rumored wealth, but he wasn't in the mood to enjoy either the gossip or the play. He sent another glance at the box three closer to the stage than his own. Damned clod. He should have known better than to hire a crippled slug to do his spying for him.

For a short time he'd thought Westfall might have found Rachel Newbury's scent. After all, he'd gone to Shropshire, questioned ship's captains and reviewed their records in Brighton and Dover, and then he and his dolt of a brother had come by twice, at least, to chat with the boy. Once he'd learned that the earl had begun to frequent The Tantalus Club he'd even taken himself there on the chance that his quarry might have found a refuge among those scandalous chits. Westfall had said he was on a trail, after all.

In all that, nothing. Nearly a month of nothing, and he had a wedding now only four weeks away. That damned sharp-nosed chit had enjoyed nothing so much as pointing out his supposed shortcomings to the boy and Katherine. Now that he meant to marry again, she would know. Now that he meant to marry the daughter of the wealthiest banker in England, she would know. And she would find a way to ruin things, again. Blackmail would be the best he could hope for, but he didn't intend to wait for her to find him. No, he would find her first, and then it would finally be over with.

What he should have realized was that he'd been foolish to go to a broken-down, retired cripple when the man who'd recommended him was still in the game. Well, he learned from his mistakes. And he would see that Rachel Newbury learned from hers. Except for her, it would be too late.

Beside him his betrothed laughed at someone on the stage, and he joined in. By this time tomorrow Jack Rycott would be on the chit's trail. And then he would see who won out in the end.

Chapter Twelve

Emily took Sophia's arm as they waited for their various coaches to thread their way through the crowd. "You look so happy," she whispered, kissing her friend on one rosy cheek.

"I am happy," the new Duchess of Greaves returned, grinning. "In another few weeks I'll begin waddling and complaining, but I'm still happy. Ecstatically so."

Putting a hand on Sophia's belly, Emily shook her head. "I can't believe I warned you not to go to Greaves's house party over Christmas. If you'd listened to me, you would be Mrs. Reverend Loines by now."

With a shudder, Sophia shook her head. "Don't remind me. Spending three days in the company of that hideous man and his mother was enough to last me a lifetime."

Camille joined them after she nudged Blackwood toward the other men. "The lesson I choose to take away from all this is that Sophia and I both made narrow escapes and found a great deal more happiness than we thought we deserved." She glanced in Westfall's direction and back again. "And so will you, Em."

Oh, she would give a great deal for that to happen. Just thinking about him started delicious shivers running through her. But she'd ruined her own chances of an auspicious marriage when she'd told Nate about her true parentage. Lying to him, though, after what he'd told her about his work during the war—she wouldn't have been able to look him in the eye ever again if she hadn't spoken. "I will be happy simply to come and visit you two from time to time," she said aloud.

"Yes, why have you suddenly decided to venture out of doors?" Sophia asked. "Haybury's note to Adam only said to come here tonight and be pleasant. Adam said he only complied because he wants a chance to win his horse back, but I think he was touched that Haybury thought of him when he wanted friends about."

Camille nodded. "Keating says the two of them have nearly patched things up between them, though he refuses to tell me what the difficulty was in the first place."

"Men and their stupid secrets." The duchess sighed loudly, then grinned again. "Speaking of secrets, Em, you never said you had a penchant for bookish earls."

"Westfall and I are friends, is all," Emily returned, wishing for once that she hadn't been speaking the truth. "I'm perfectly happy at the Tantalus. And as for me finally walking outside, I thought it was time."

As she glanced back toward the well-lit theater entrance, however, her words died in her throat. He stood there. *Him.* Golden-haired and handsome as ever, with a woman on his arm. She was likely his new wife-to-be, but Emily couldn't tear her gaze from him for long enough to get a look at the unfortunate lady. He was talking with another man, but at any moment he would look in her direction. He would see her looking back at him, and he would recognize her. How could he not? She'd only changed her hair and the way she dressed, but otherwise she was the same. It would happen, and she needed to run, but—

"Steady, Portsman," Nathaniel's low drawl came, and he stepped between her and her living, breathing nightmare. "He didn't see you," he murmured. "He isn't looking for you here. You were a governess to him, not a lady in the company of a duchess."

"Em?" Camille whispered, squeezing her arm. "What's amiss?"

"Nothing," she blurted. "Nothing. I just . . . I need to go."

Before she could move away, though, Sophia took her other arm. "If Lord Westfall troubles you," her friend breathed, "only nod your head and we will see to it that he never does so again."

"What? Oh, no. It's not Nathaniel. It's . . . someone else. The reason I . . ." *The reason I'm always afraid,* she almost said, and only stopped when she felt Nate's hand brush the small of her back. "I saw someone from my past," she amended. "We did not part well."

"You're certain?" Camille pressed.

"I promise. Nathaniel is my friend. I trust him. Truly."

"Tantalus girl's word?" Sophia prompted.

"Yes. Tantalus girl's word."

Her friends released her, and Nathaniel took her arm in turn. "The coach is here. And I promised to have you back by midnight, didn't I? Or was that Laurie?"

"I'm going to the Society with Blackwood and Greaves," his brother put in, with such perfect timing that Emily wondered if Westfall had rehearsed the conversation with him.

"Very well," Nate said slowly. "But you're to be home by two o'clock, as you're still being punished for your ill deeds at Oxford."

"Nate."

Keating Blackwood laughed. "Got sent down, did you? You're not the only one here who's managed that."

They all might have continued chatting together, but Emily could practically feel Ebberling somewhere out of sight behind her, and she quickly said her good-nights and tugged Nathaniel over to his coach. Only when the carriage had begun rolling back down the street did she let out the breath she'd been holding. "I think I'm going to be ill," she managed, shuddering.

Nathaniel removed his coat and put it around her shoulders, topped by his warm, strong arm. "Nonsense. He glowered at me, but didn't even give you a first look. Much less a second."

"You're certain?"

"Absolutely certain."

Emily looked up at him, at his light green eyes behind his useless spectacles and at his serious, kissable mouth. "Why are you taking these risks for me?" she finally asked, even as she reflected that it would likely be wiser to accept the help he offered without causing either one of them to question it.

"I do have a sense of right and wrong, you know, dim though it may be." He smiled, but the expression didn't touch his eyes. "Ebberling killed his wife. You've lied about your past. Weighed one against the other, I choose to side with you."

"And it has nothing to do with . . . us?" She gestured between them.

"It has a great deal to do with us. I said I knew right from wrong. I never claimed to be a saint." This time he looked genuinely amused. "Even we sinners can see justice done, though, don't you think?"

That one word, even in the middle of all the very nice ones, alarmed her. " 'Justice'?" she repeated. "What do you mean?"

"I mean that if you ever want to be able to walk out of doors without having to look over your shoulder,

Ebberling needs to be dealt with. At this moment I don't favor murdering him. Do you?"

"I've thought about it," she admitted, leaning her head against his shoulder. How was it that he made her feel so safe? No one else had ever managed to do that. Not until this remarkable man beside her. "But that would make me no better than him. Even so, saying he's guilty and proving it are two very different things." She took an unsteady breath. "And either would involve me talking to people. Officially. I can't do that."

"I think it's time we did some strategizing, don't you?" He rapped his cane against the roof of the coach. "Take us to Teryl House, Sams."

"Yes, my lord," the driver's voice returned dimly.

"I thought I needed to be home by midnight," Emily commented, smiling.

"Did we say which home? I don't recall." He lifted her chin in his fingers, then leaned in to kiss her. "Tonight you're mine, Portsman," he muttered roughly, cupping her face in his hands and kissing her again.

Tonight, she wanted to be. And tomorrow, too, but one impossible miracle at a time.

It was odd to sit up in bed and see a glorious spill of red-brown hair on the pillow beside him. Even odder was the way he, always bored with the present, always looking for the next thing to occupy his mind, wanted to do nothing more than lie there and watch the unusual woman curled up next to him sleep.

Nate turned on his side to face her, folding one arm beneath his head. This morning he didn't need to squint and fumble for his spectacles the moment his companion's eyes opened. He didn't need to reach for his cane the moment he sat up. He didn't need to search the events of the previous day or evening to remember which name he happened to be going by. He could simply be . . . himself.

Portsman stirred, sliding a hand along his chest, and he frowned. He couldn't keep referring to her as Portsman any longer. It wasn't her true name, and it didn't feel personal enough. What to call her, though? Even if it hadn't been dangerous to call her Rachel Newbury, that wasn't her name, either, and he'd promised not to let Eloise or Smorkley pass his lips. Truthfully, that wasn't who she was any longer, either. She'd made herself into someone all her own, through her own sweat and blood.

Deepest brown eyes opened, blinked sleepily, then focused on him. And she smiled. "Good morning."

He could drown in that smile, he thought. "Good morning. I've been thinking."

She sat up, running her fingers through the dishevelment of her hair and stretching deliciously enough to make his cock twitch. "You're always thinking. What about?"

"Your name. Who are you, truly? What do you wish me to call you?"

Her brow furrowed. "That's a complicated question for so early in the morning, isn't it?"

"Not really."

For a long moment she sat, looking down at her hands. Long, elegant fingers that if not for her strength of character might have been crooked and callused from washing other people's clothes, or if not for an accident of birth might have been floating lightly across the ivory keys of the finest-made pianoforte. "Of all the people I've been," she finally said, in a quiet, thoughtful tone, "I like Emily the best. So Emily."

Nathaniel smiled. "Emily it is, then." He sat up beside her and kissed her, tangling his fingers through her lemon- and tea-scented hair.

His bedchamber door slammed open. Emily yelped, diving beneath the rumpled covers, while Nate reached for the knife he kept beneath his pillow. Before he could pull it free, though, he opened his fingers again. "Laurie, what the devil do you think you're doing?"

His brother sagged against the door frame, his gaze on the wriggling mound of sheets. "Have you ever been to a club called Jezebel's?" he drawled with a loose grin.

Eyeing his brother more closely, Nathaniel frowned. His cravat was a ruin, his boots scuffed, and his eyes rimmed with red. "You're drunk."

"What I am, Nate, is three—no, five, at least—sheets to the wind. Greaves and Keating know all the worst places in London. It was . . . stupendous. Do you have any idea how spectacular it is to go about with men that everyone else practically shits at the sight of?"

Beneath the covers, Emily chuckled. Nate was fairly certain he didn't feel that amused, himself. "Did you happen to inform these shit-inducing gentlemen that you were nineteen?"

"I may have added a year or so," Laurie admitted with another lopsided smile. "But I was being helpful, too. Greaves doesn't like Ebberling, at all. Says he's so swellheaded they have to open both doors to let him into a room."

All the rapidly fading humor in Nate vanished. "You told them about Ebberling?" he demanded, sliding to the edge of the bed and standing.

"I say, you're naked."

Nathaniel grabbed his brother by the shoulder. "You. Go take a cold bath, drink some damned coffee, and meet me in the breakfast room in thirty minutes. If you aren't sober enough to tell me what the devil you talked

about with your new friends, I will send you to Westfall Manor, and you can spend the rest of the Season
there doing my accounts. Is that clear?"

Laurence swallowed, brushing light brown hair from
his eyes. "Yes. Damnation. Yes."

"Good." Nate shoved him back out the door and
slammed it shut. Then he cursed, in several languages.

When he turned back around, Emily was sitting up
in bed, sheets gathered around her, and her expression
dismayed. "How much trouble am I in?"

Still swearing, Nate grabbed for a pair of trousers
and yanked them on. "I'm not certain, but more than
enough if Greaves or Blackwood talk to the wrong person. Get dressed. I need to get them over here. Now."

She didn't like it; he could see that quite clearly. He
should have known better. In the beginning this had
only been a puzzle for him to solve, and perhaps a way
for his brother and him to heal the chasm that had
formed between them. Now the puzzle had a face—
a face that had become absurdly dear to him over the
past weeks, and everything had changed.

"Nate, send for their wives and for Haybury, as well,
if you would. And Jenny Martine, with a change of
clothes for me."

"You're certain you trust all of them?"

Emily cleared her throat. "I trust myself, and I trust
you. But I have friends, now, and I'm . . . I'm so tired of
lying. Sophia and Camille are my sisters, and so even is
Diane. So I suppose their husbands must be worthy of
my trust, as well."

He nodded, slipping back out the door and down the
stairs for paper and ink and Garvey the butler. He could
claim that it was his old caution as a spy that so disliked anyone else knowing what he was about, but it
wasn't that. Not entirely. The fact was, he liked the idea

that this had been between him and Emily. That she trusted him, and that he would somehow ride to her rescue and save her from the evil marquis who wanted her silenced, everyone else be damned.

Whether that was the wisest way to approach this conundrum, he didn't know. Not yet. But that path had been tromped all over by Laurie last night, anyway, and so he would make do with what he'd been given. All that mattered was that Emily be protected. His own heroic role was mere stupidity. He'd given up on the idea of ever being a hero when he'd agreed to work as a spy.

Once the messages were sent out he returned upstairs to finish dressing. Emily had moved over to the chair beside the window to gaze out over his garden, and he took a deep breath and walked over to sit on the sill beside her. "I'm sorry," he murmured. "I should never have told Laurie. In my own defense, when I first did so, I didn't know anything more than what Ebberling had told me. I didn't know you were the one he was after."

She met his gaze. "Oddly enough," she returned in the same, soft tone, "when you went scrambling out of the door, I sat there in your bed for a moment because I realized that something was missing."

" 'Missing'?" he repeated.

"Yes. And it took me a good minute to realize what it was. I wasn't afraid, Nate." She reached out and gripped his hand. "A few weeks ago if I'd learned that someone else might know of a connection between Ebberling and myself, I would have been packing my things and booking passage on the next ship out of England. I probably should be now, even so."

He turned his hand up, twining his fingers with hers. "No, you shouldn't be." The idea of letting her slip away from him because of his own stupidity . . . It was utterly unacceptable.

"The thing is, I suddenly realized that I'm not alone in the world. Not any longer. I do have friends. I have people who . . . care what happens to me. If I disappeared, someone would notice." A tear ran down her cheek, and he brushed it away with his free thumb. "Don't you think someone would notice?"

"I would notice." He leaned forward and kissed her.

The way she'd said it . . . He couldn't count how many times he'd had that same thought over the years, that if he failed at whatever his current task happened to be, if he died at it because he'd misjudged someone, would anyone notice his absence? And for a time he hadn't been able to answer that question.

"I would notice," he repeated fiercely, kissing her again and again, sliding to the floor with her slender, sheet-wrapped form in his arms. "I would notice."

She began sobbing, and for a long time he simply sat on the floor beneath the window, holding her. And she'd said they weren't alike. Christ. One day, he would tell her. Not now, because they had other things to worry about. But one day, he would tell her that this was the moment he'd realized that he loved her.

Nate told them everything. Well, not everything, because he left out the fact that she was a washerwoman's daughter from Derbyshire, but he told them all the bits about her being Rachel Newbury and witnessing Ebberling kill his wife, Katherine.

Camille had been out having breakfast with her sisters, but Sophia came with her husband, and Jenny was there, as well. If Nathaniel was surprised that she'd asked the club's manager to join them, he didn't show it, but then he wouldn't. Or perhaps by now he'd figured out that Genevieve was her source for information about him—she certainly wouldn't have put it past him.

When he finished, Sophia was staring at her, and Emily scooted her chair closer to her friend. "I'm so sorry," she whispered. "I should have told you ages ago, but I didn't know how."

The pretty redhead kissed her on the cheek. "I always thought you'd changed your name and run away because some old, wrinkly lord at your previous employment had been after you. I had no idea." She squared her shoulders. "For heaven's sake, how would you have told me? I'm not angry. Well, not at you. Ebberling is another matter, entirely. He's a monster."

"He may be a monster," the Duke of Greaves took up with a fond glance at his wife, "but he's a cunning one. And a wealthy one, which is nearly as dangerous. People overlook the sins of rich men much more easily than they do the sins of poor ones." Steel-gray eyes glanced at Nate's brother. "You need to learn to watch your tongue, whelp."

Young Laurence looked as though he couldn't decide whether to vomit or weep. "You tricked me into chatting with you," he said accusingly.

Greaves nodded. "Of course I did. Haybury wouldn't tell me what last night was about, and there you were."

"That isn't very nice."

"No one has ever accused me of being nice."

"Adam, he feels bad enough," Sophia put in. "And no harm has come of it, thankfully."

The duke sighed. "My wife, however," he amended, "has on occasion told me to be nicer. And luckily for you, lad, I listen to her. So I will admit to you that you never actually gave us Miss Portsman's name. Keating and I figured it out, but only because we'd all spent the evening at the theater together."

"That's bad enough," Nate commented, not looking mollified. "If someone had overheard—"

"No one overheard." Keating finished off a slice of chicken breast. "He might be a pup, but Greaves and I aren't. If you want to be angry at someone, we're more to blame than he is."

Emily reflected that somehow, somewhere in her life of lies, she must have done something good. She had no other explanation for why four very formidable men would take her side when for a very long time she'd thought she'd had no allies at all. She forced a smile. "I'm not angry at any of you."

"I may be mistaken, of course," Jenny said into the silence, her French accent thicker than Emily had ever heard it, "but my thought is that you gentlemen could be using your time more wisely than accepting everyone else's shortcomings onto your own shoulders, yes?"

Finally Haybury stirred. "Much as I hate to agree with the French twist, she has the right of it. Blame whomever you please, but I'd prefer to hear how we mean to deal with Ebberling."

We. That might possibly have been the best word that Emily had ever heard, and the least expected one. Still, she hadn't managed the life she'd chosen for herself by allowing other people to make decisions on her behalf. Slowly she climbed to her feet. "I thank each and every one of you for coming this morning and listening to my sad story, but I don't expect you to shoulder my troubles."

"Emily, d—"

"I saw him pull Katherine off her horse and strangle her, and I just . . . stood there. Then when he looked up and saw me, I ran. Not to the authorities, and not for a weapon. I simply ran." She paused, gazing at Nathaniel and daring him to interrupt her again. When he only glared at her, she continued. "I knew what it would be; my word against his. And for many reasons no judge, no jury of his peers, would ever listen to me. That hasn't changed."

"We would seem to be his peers," Greaves commented dryly.

"You are married to my dearest friends, Your Grace. You don't count." Emily very much wanted to stop there, but because whatever they claimed, they were true gentlemen and would likely attempt to help her regardless, she made herself continue. "I'm not of aristocratic lineage. In fact, I'm the very opposite of anything aristocratic. And I'm asking you to stay out of this. No one will thank you for it."

"That's not the best way to ask for help, Em," Sophia commented, her green eyes serious despite her light tone.

"I'm not asking you for your help, Sophia. Truly, I'm not. Ebberling is a marquis with money and power, and he's planning on marrying yet more money. Your Adam and Keating married ladies they likely shouldn't have, and as much as they love you and Cammy, it's hurt their reputations. I'm a common girl who works at a gentlemen's club." She glanced at Haybury. "I'm an employee. Would you risk the Tantalus for one of the kitchen girls? Would you let Diane do that?"

"If you don't want our help, why are we here?" Blackwood snapped, standing. He strode to the nearest window and turned his back on them.

"Lord Westfall asked you to come here to make certain you wouldn't mention who I am or my whereabouts to anyone. That's all. And that's all I ask. Your silence."

Silence was what she got. For a long moment no one said anything, or moved, or looked at anyone else. It was the worst sound in the world, but they had been the truest words she'd ever spoken, and she refused to feel sorry for herself for saying them. If anything, she felt proud. Desperate and back to being alone again, but proud.

The one person she couldn't make herself look at was Nathaniel. She didn't want to see if he was angry with her, or disappointed that she might have pulled the carpet out from under his feet. Worse than that, she didn't want to look into his light green eyes and see that underneath it all, he might be relieved. Relieved that she'd given him an excuse to walk away from this mess, and from her.

Finally Oliver Warren, the Marquis of Haybury, pushed back slowly in his chair and stood. Then he walked over to the breakfast sideboard, selected a nice plump cinnamon-sprinkled muffin, and sat down again to slice it in half and spread butter over it. "Seven, nearly eight years ago," he said calmly, "I had a chance to do something right by a young lady who was destitute and alone, and trapped in a foreign country. Instead, the moment she turned her back I literally leaped from her bedroom window and fled. I'm married to her now, but that doesn't signify. Because what I most think about now when I recall that day, is how . . . disgusted I feel with myself. Back then I thought I'd narrowly escaped a lifetime of misery and obligation. Now I look back and am certain I did the absolute wrong thing. Because someone, a person, a woman, needed my help, and I walked away. I won't do that again."

"What are you?" Greaves put in abruptly, looking at Emily. "You said you were common. A common what?"

"That's enough, Greaves," Nathaniel growled, clenching his fist.

"My father was a poacher, Your Grace," she answered. "My mother washed clothes at the Blue Dove Inn for all the travelers who came by."

"Hm. And you said you're what, now? A Tantalus girl? You can read and write, can't you? Learned how to dance, I'll wager, and play the pianoforte?"

She felt as if she was being ripped to shreds, and she nearly decided to argue that his own wife was a former Tantalus girl, but that would only counter her own statement of earlier, so she only nodded. "Yes."

"You worked as a governess for Ebberling, Westfall said. For nearly three years."

"Yes."

"I beg your pardon then, Emily, but that doesn't sound common at all."

Over by the window, Blackwood turned back around and raised one hand. "Killed my lover's husband. Self-defense or not, they've hanged men for less. Then I stole my cousin's betrothed from her own wedding. Not throwing any stones from inside any glass houses. I'm in."

Sophia took Emily's hand and pulled her back down into her chair. "Em is Cammy's sister, and she's my sister, and she's Jenny's and Diane's sister. We're in."

Laurence sat forward in his chair. "I'm an idiot, and I want to do something right. I'm helping."

That left only Nate, and to her, his silence spoke volumes. No, he hadn't liked it when Greaves seemed to be insulting her, but that only meant he was kind. Which he was, whatever he might say about that. Without him, the effort the others now said they were willing to go through, while miraculous, wouldn't be worth it. Why would she wish to stay and fight, when victory would mean . . . nothing? She still couldn't even force herself to look at him. Oh, she was pathetic. If they knew how broken her heart felt, none of them would still even be in the room.

Nathaniel stood. "Emily."

She closed her eyes.

"Emily."

No. She wouldn't look, and she wouldn't listen. If he would just leave the room, she would know, and she could slink out the back way, return to the Tantalus, pack her things, and leave.

Her chair tilted backward. Hard. Flailing for balance, she opened her eyes and looked up, to see Nate looking down over the back of the chair at her. "Don't worry," he said, his voice not quite steady. "I won't let you fall."

Chapter Thirteen

The unusual meeting adjourned with everyone's promises of discretion, but little else actually helpful. Nathaniel had a few ideas, himself, but he couldn't claim to be comfortable with the notion of saying things aloud. Not without anything tangible, and not to anyone he'd met less than twenty-four hours earlier.

Assistance was a very nice notion, but he meant to reserve judgment until he saw results that demonstrated that these additional people were more of a help than a hindrance. Emily lingered, which he found much more interesting, anyway.

The French woman remained, as well, and he spent a moment studying her as she tied a bonnet over light blond hair pulled into the tightest bun he'd ever seen. When Laurence touched his shoulder, he actually jumped.

"Nate, I—"

"No," he interrupted. "You go upstairs, and go to bed. I'm not speaking to you until you're sober."

"I'm sorry," his brother said again, his shoulders lowered and his entire demeanor one of utter misery. "I thought . . . Greaves and Blackwood, for Lucifer's sake. They asked me to go with them. *Me*. I . . ."

"Later," Nathaniel repeated, though most of his anger had fled. It wasn't Laurie's fault that he had no clue how to be suspicious of everyone, that he didn't expect a dagger in his back every time he turned around. "Be glad you have a chance to learn from a mistake. You're more fortunate than most."

Once his brother disappeared upstairs, he turned back around to the foyer. Emily had dressed in a rather plain green walking dress and a pretty matching bonnet. If he didn't already know who she was, if he'd simply seen her walking down the street, he would have thought her a fetching young lady, some lordling's daughter taking the air. And without knowing what secrets lay beneath her smooth, fair skin, behind her dark brown eyes, he likely wouldn't have looked at her twice.

"What is it?" she asked, tilting her head at him.

"Considering the twists and quirks of fate," he returned with a brief smile. "You could stay here, if you wish. I'd see to it that Ebberling never came near you."

"I know you would." She put a hand over his heart, and he wondered if she could feel it speed. "I, however, would simply be a prisoner in a prettier cage. At the Tantalus I'm earning my way, and you are free to leave your own house, as well."

It made sense, damn it all. He'd found the key to some vital piece of information before and been forced to walk away from it until a more opportune time presented itself, but he couldn't remember it ever bothering him as much as this did. "I've a few things to look into," he said, covering her hand with his, "and I will keep you apprised."

"You'd better." With a nod she turned for the door, and Garvey pulled it open. Then she abruptly stopped.

"I left my reticule upstairs," she said, her cheeks darkening. "I'll be back in a moment."

The butler wordlessly shut the door again, and Nate angled his chin at the man. "That'll be all, Garvey."

"Very good, my lord."

Then it was only him and the French woman in the foyer. She stood gazing up the staircase and completely ignoring him. Or so she would have it appear. "Haybury called you the French twist," he said after a moment.

She glanced at him. "I believe it is because of the way I wear my hair, monsieur," she said in her soft, heavily accented voice.

"That's interesting, because previously he referred to a French twist who had her fingers in a great many different pies."

With a smile, she nodded. "I do like pies, yes."

Nathaniel narrowed his eyes. "Emily doesn't have stupid friends, Miss Martine. And we're both her friends. So shall we continue to waltz, or would you prefer to see what the two of us together might accomplish?"

Miss Martine faced him. "I saw you once, at one of Bonaparte's assemblies," she said, her accent mostly vanished. "You had a terrible scar down one side of your face, and one of your eyes was milky. I only learned who you were later, but I have to say, Nate Stokes, you were impressive."

That answered the nagging question of why she seemed familiar. "You were the black-haired Spanish chit who had that note relaying the location of two of Bonie's advisors."

She sketched a shallow curtsy. "I apologize for telling Em that you were a spy, but the war is over, and she is my friend. My sister, as Sophia said."

"I can understand that," he said, meaning it. "It

seems to be easier to find enemies than friends, even now. Friends are to be treasured, and enemies, destroyed."

Genevieve Martine offered her hand. "For as long as you are Emily's friend, I shall be yours. Not a moment longer. Does that suffice?"

He gripped her fingers. "It does. And likewise."

Emily leaned over the balcony. "Oh, dear. I should never have left you two alone."

"All is well," the French twist said, smiling. "We have reached an understanding."

"That sounds somewhat frightening," she continued, descending to the main floor. "Jenny, would you wait for me outside?"

"Certainly. Don't be long, though. I am to be on duty for luncheon."

Once Miss Martine was outside and the door closed again, Nate reached out to straighten Emily's sleeve. "Not very subtle of you, Emily."

"That shows what you know. I never forgot my reticule. I thought with the way you've been studying Jenny all morning, you'd want a private word with her."

He laughed. "Well done, then. One spy chatting with another?"

"Exactly. I'm glad you know who she is, now. I'm becoming rather tired of lies." Placing her hands on his chest, she leaned up and kissed him. "You were very gallant this morning. There's still nothing that can be done, but it was . . . very nice to hear that there are people in the world who care about my fate, even given who I am and who they are."

She would have moved away, but Nate gripped her by both shoulders. "If there's one thing the past ten years have taught me, my dear, it's that there is always something that can be done."

Emily touched him on the cheek. "Not about everything," she murmured, kissing him again. Then, before he was ready, she slipped out his front door and was gone.

He knew what she meant; if by some miracle they could stop Ebberling from pursuing her, she would still be a washerwoman's daughter, and he would still be an earl. An accidental one who would have preferred something entirely different, but an earl nonetheless. "Damnation," he muttered, and went to have his horse saddled.

Where previously his task had been tracking down the elusive—and nonexistent—Rachel Newbury, his new assignment looked to be both easier and more difficult. Locating the Marquis of Ebberling would, at the most, take him an hour or two, and that was if the man wasn't at home this morning. Much more complicated would be finding a chink in the man's armor.

It needed to be done, however. Because the arithmetic was simple; in order for Emily to be free, Ebberling needed to be removed. Killing him would be the easiest method, but murdering a marquis in the middle of Mayfair would only have everyone digging deeper. In that case, someone else might find Emily, and she would be by far the most likely culprit. Aside from that, Nathaniel had had his fill of killing, even for king and country. With no alternative he wouldn't hesitate, but he kept it as a last resort only.

No, for all the pain and fear the Marquis of Ebberling had caused over the past three years, to his wife, his son, and to Emily, he deserved something less . . . clean. Something he could consider for a good long while—and something that rendered him harmless.

That would take some consideration, and a detailed survey of his quarry. As Nate swung up on Blue and headed off to White's Club, he realized that he'd never been as thankful as he was now to be a spy. Because someone else might have found Emily, someone else might have handed her over to Ebberling, and the man might well have gotten away with ending two lives for his own satisfaction. Nate gave a grim smile. He'd always relished the chase, but he'd never cared about the prize, until now. My, how things had changed.

So. First he would find the man's friends, then he would get them talking, and then he would find that one misstep the marquis had made in all this. Because if he'd learned one thing, it was that everyone made a mistake. He'd thought that he'd made one in taking on this little puzzle, but as he glanced down the way in the direction of the unseen Tantalus, he couldn't think that any longer. This had happened for a reason, because otherwise he couldn't name the point of putting himself and his family through the past ten years.

And still he continued doing equations and calculating the logical odds of success. Nathaniel snorted, making Blue flick his ears back. When he'd become the crusading knight he had no idea, but it was pleasant, for once, to feel like a hero. For Emily's sake he hoped he would still prove to be one at the end of this venture.

As Emily had expected, once the coach reached The Tantalus Club, Jenny vanished in the direction of Adam House. Emily'd decided that Lord Haybury was more likely to keep the tale of her low birth from his wife than his wife's closest friend was. At the thought of that conversation, a sliver of uneasiness ran down her spine.

Diane preferred to have highborn ladies employed at the club, because wrapped in scandal or not, well-bred women attracted well-bred men. And in that case, any scandal the ladies brought with them actually helped the popularity of the club. Emily was certainly well educated, because she'd seen to it that she was. Before this point, though, she'd made certain that she had nothing scandalous attached to the name Emily Portsman, and she'd minimized her contact with the club's member. That had all been by design, to make her useful with the least number of questions asked about her past.

Now, however, the potential for an interest-raising scandal was rather outweighed by actual legal difficulties if Ebberling discovered her and decided he preferred to accuse her of murder rather than simply kill her out of hand. And that had become a possibility now that she'd made the acquaintance of people who claimed that they wouldn't let her vanish without comment.

She sighed as she went to collect the ledger for the produce purchases. They had all sounded sincere, and at the least she finally knew why Diane and Oliver's relationship had been so volatile when she'd first met them. And if she was arrested, she didn't doubt that they would all express their dismay with the proceedings. As for whether they would do more than that, she had her doubts.

With one exception.

The way Nathaniel had looked at her this morning had stopped her heart. All sorts of silly, girlish notions had flitted lightning-fast through her mind—marriage and children and peace and safety, and Nate waking up beside her every morning, holding her in his arms and telling her that he would never let her fall. That silly dream could never be, but she believed that he would aid her with Ebberling, if only for his own pride.

As for the rest of it . . . It might be easier to flee, after all, so she wouldn't be present to hear him tell her they were finished with, and she could go back to finding

random, dim-witted men to share her bed when the
loneliness started roaring in her ears. Because without
him, none of the rest of it was likely to matter. She'd
spent most of her life alone, relying on her own wits to
survive, and she could do it again. Knowing what she'd
almost had, what she might have made of her life if either of her parents had been even distantly related to a
baron or a knight, had to be far worse than never knowing about it at all.

The common room was fairly empty at this time of
morning, with the day staff all on duty and the evening
staff not yet ready to gather for luncheon, and she spread
the books out on one of the long tables to work. Juliet
Langtree, the evening butler, had delivered a note to
her room last night, and she opened it first. Lord Gil-
bert Parglen missed her and wished to call on her this
evening.

She tucked the note into her pelisse pocket to answer later, actually somewhat surprised that Lord Gil-
bert knew how to write. He certainly must have missed
her, if he'd gone to the trouble of thinking of words and
putting them to paper. But she would be declining his
request, regardless. The occasional evening's entertain-
ment had lost most—all—of its allure now that she'd
found someone whom she could imagine as more than
a midnight friend.

"Emily."

Starting, she looked up as Diane, Lady Haybury,
strolled into the room. The marchioness was dressed in
black as always. Even her hair was black, which made
her deep green eyes all the more luminous. "Diane. Jenny
spoke to you, I imagine?"

"She did." Emily's employer seated herself on the
bench opposite. "In your opinion," she continued in a
low voice, though the only other people in the room

were Mr. Jacobs, the largest of the Helpful Men, and his evening coworker Bartholomew, playing a game of whist by the fire, "is Ebberling more likely to attempt to murder you, or to have you arrested?"

She said it in such a matter-of-fact tone that for a moment Emily thought she'd misheard. "I'm . . . I'm not certain," she answered. "If he could do as he wished, I think he would prefer me silenced. The arrest would make it a longer, more messy process, and there's always the chance that he couldn't bribe everyone involved to make certain it went his way."

Diane nodded. "That was Jenny's opinion, as well." She reached over, taking the pen from Emily's fingers, and set it aside. "Haybury Park will be fairly empty this time of year, but it has the benefit of being better than two days out of London, and Oliver will hire a few additional footmen to make certain you don't have any unwelcome visitors."

"I—thank you so much for offering me your home to stay in, but I'm not leaving London, Diane." Her first instinct had been to flee not only the city, but the entire country. Things had changed, however. She'd met Nathaniel Stokes, and even if their relationship were to end, she had him now. She was loath to give him up. "I've done some things of which I'm not proud, but I never did anything to Lady Ebberling but flee from the man who killed her."

"This is not about being ruined, Em. This is your life."

"I know. And I'm not going to do anything foolish, but neither will I run again. Not yet, anyway."

The marchioness sighed, though she didn't look terribly surprised. "Then you are not to leave the Tantalus again without telling either myself or Jenny precisely where you're going and when you expect to return. You

will not set one foot into the club itself until this is resolved, and you will pack a portmanteau in the event
that we need to smuggle you away quickly. Is that clear?"

"You realize that if he does find me and decides to
have me arrested, I will be found guilty. The club will
not fare well if that happens."

"The Tantalus is my concern. Do you agree to abide
by those rules, Em?"

"Yes." Tears welled in her eyes, and she looked down,
willing them away. "You know the rest, do you not?
Jenny told you about my parentage, I assume."

Diane stood. "She did. If I haven't made it clear before now, you're here because of who you are, not who
you were. We are not a charitable organization."

Her employer had said that before—many times, in
fact, and in the past Emily had always considered it a
good thing that the marchioness didn't know the truth
about her. Now, however, she'd abruptly begun to look
at it differently. None of the Tantalus girls was here out
of the kindness of Lady Haybury's heart. They were
here because they were strong, competent women.

With a slight smile she lifted her head to return to
her work, then paused, setting the pen aside once more.
She'd spent her entire life running from her past, and
the previous three years actively hiding from it. So what
did she mean to do now, continue peering out from
behind the curtains while she waited either for Nate to
solve her problems or for Ebberling to return to Shropshire? And then what? Did she continue as before until
Ebberling returned to London with his new bride—or
worse, as a second-time widower? Would she send for
Nathaniel again and hope that he still liked her enough
to ride to her rescue once more?

"Piffle," she muttered, and gathered the ledgers up

in her arms. Simply because she'd found herself with friends, and one dear, dear man that she'd already begun to dread losing, didn't mean that she could no longer look out for her own well-being.

Once she'd returned the books to their place, she retreated to the room she shared with the very tolerant Lily, where she closed and latched the door. Then she walked over to look at herself in the dressing mirror. Over the past three years her face had thinned a little, and to her own eyes she looked . . . wiser, she supposed it was, but what would Ebberling see?

Her, if he looked beyond the darker color of her hair and the much less governess-appropriate clothing. Rachel Newbury, governess and witness to a murder. That would never do. In fact, the only two things in her favor were her red-brown hair and the fact that he would never expect to see her walk directly up to him. "Heavens," she muttered, putting a hand over her pounding heart. She sat down at her dressing table. Could she do such a thing? Even to save herself?

A knock sounded at her door, and she jumped. "Who is it?"

"Betty," came the answer. "Lady H said I was to bring up luncheon for you, but you weren't in the common room."

Emily rose again and went to open the door. She'd always had a special place in her heart for the cook's assistant. Not only was the girl far too young to have to be fending for herself in the world, but she'd found a place where she could improve upon the life she'd been given. In some ways, they were very similar.

"Why are you looking at me like that?" Betty asked, setting the luncheon tray on Lily's bed. "Do I have something on my nose?" She rubbed at the offending member, which did serve to smear a dot of soot, but didn't matter a bit to the smattering of freckles across her nose.

"Do you think we're of a size?" Emily asked, taking the girl's hands and spinning her in a slow circle.

"I think you're a tad taller than me, and I'm not near as skinny. And your bosom's grander than mine. Why?" The cook's assistant eyed her suspiciously.

"Because I thought I might loan you one of my gowns, if you would lend me one of yours."

"Mine? I don't have any gowns. Just this work dress, one other like it, and a blue one for church."

Emily went to her wardrobe and lifted first a pretty yellow gown from a drawer, then a slightly more practical green one. "I think this one would fit you," she said, holding it up to the younger girl's shoulders. "Would you care to try it on?"

Betty fingered the soft silk. "I'd love it, but where would I wear it? Not into the kitchen. Miss Charity would have my head, for putting on airs."

"There's to be a troop of Russian acrobats at Vauxhall tomorrow night. A group of the day girls are going. I'm not, so you could take my place. I know April would be happy to sit with you. And so would Sophie, or Lily."

"Acrobats?" Betty breathed. "Yes, please!"

With a chuckle, Emily set the dress on the bed. "Then let's go find your other work dress and a sewing kit. We'll let this gown out a bit, and lengthen your dress hem out. It'll be fun!"

"For me, yes. I still don't know what you're about, wanting one of my dingy dresses."

"I've a mind to visit someone," she said slowly. "And I want to surprise him."

She wanted to do more than that, but if she could fool Nate, then Ebberling would be simple. If she could make herself walk close enough for him to see, that was.

Once she had Betty's dress let out at the hem enough to reach her ankles, she went to find Jenny. However much courage she might have found to attempt this, she wasn't quite ready to face the world without the assistance of someone as skilled in subterfuge as she knew Genevieve Martine to be.

"What are you doing?" Jenny asked, when she opened the door of her own private sitting room. "This is not what Diane asked of you."

"No, it isn't. But I am not a damsel in distress. I want to be free of this, Jenny, and I'm the only one who can do it."

"I could do it."

Emily frowned. "Very well, I concede that you would likely be better at this than I would. But I *should* be the one to do it, nevertheless." She forced a smile as she pushed past her friend into the room. "I do imagine I have the makings of a better servant than you do."

Jenny put her hands on her hips. "And what do you mean to do, then? Find employment in Lord Ebberling's house and trick him into confessing that he murdered his wife? He will never do that, not to a servant. And even if he did, you already have that information. He needs to confess in front of witnesses that a court would listen to." Her eyes narrowed. "Unless you mean to murder him. I will not assist you with this."

"Jenny, pl—"

"No. You know another spy. Go convince him."

This, she hadn't expected. "Jenny, I may not have everything planned completely yet, but I do not mean to murder anyone."

"You do not understand at all what you may be facing, my dear," Miss Martine said in an easier tone after a moment spent glaring at Emily. "What you mean or do not mean to do is not necessarily what you could be required to do."

Blowing out her breath, Emily inclined her head. "Very well. I'll ask Nate for his assistance. But do you at least have a portmanteau with wigs and face paint or something? I thought all spies carried such a thing about with them."

"I'm not a spy any longer, Emily." Grimacing, Jenny turned her back and walked toward her bedchamber. "Wait here. I may have a thing or two that would suffice."

She returned to the sitting room a few minutes later with a leather-bound case that looked more like a well-used physician's satchel than a portmanteau. Emily would never have given it a second look, which she supposed was the point of it. "Thank you, Jenny. Truly."

"My thanks would be you forgetting about this and simply waiting here in safety until Lord Ebberling leaves London."

"But he'll return, won't he? Sometime when I'm less ready for him to appear."

Jenny gazed at her for a long moment. "You may have the right of it. Only promise that you'll be careful, whatever you decide to do. Running is always preferable to dying, Emily, Rachel, and whoever else you have become. And whatever heroic men may say, dying is preferable to nothing."

"I'll be careful. And if Nate doesn't think my plan, whatever it is, will work, I won't do it." Well, probably not, anyway. Emily pulled open her friend's door to leave, until Jenny pushed it closed again.

"Oh, bother. I can at least help you learn to look like

someone else. Come along. But if your gentleman asks, you forced me to assist you."

Her gentleman. Nate. He wasn't hers, though. Not the way she wished for. Not forever. "I agree," she said aloud. He was hers for today, at least. And she would take all of those todays she could.

Chapter Fourteen

"S hooting him would be easier," Nate snapped, flinging a stack of his notes across his office.

"It would solve Emily's troubles," Laurence agreed,
squatting down to pick up the pieces of paper, "but it
would begin several new ones for you."

"Not if no one knew who'd done it."

That made his brother straighten again. He could
read Laurie's face like a book—was he serious, had he
done such a thing before, what was it like to kill a man?
"But you wouldn't, would you?"

"No. I make a point of not killing anyone who isn't a
direct threat to the safety of the nation." Though at this
moment he'd met someone whose safety he prized more
highly than that of England's. That was likely the reason Rycott had made a point of recruiting only single,
unattached men and women; evidently a man in love
was prone to taking insane risks to protect the woman
he loved.

"That's . . . good. You only need to continue what
you've been doing, then. You'll find something you can
use. You said that you always do."

So he had, back when he'd been stupidly naïve and

hopeful. "The man's remarrying in just over three weeks."

"Once he marries, then, won't he think that Emily's not going to make an appearance after all? Won't he let everything go back to the way it's been for the past two years or so, when he wasn't trying so hard to find her?"

"He might," Nathaniel conceded. "Of course he might just as easily decide that he's become even more vulnerable to blackmail. Or that he now has a taste for killing his wives. We have that chit to think of, too, now that we know what he's about."

"Can't we warn her, then? What's her name, Harriet?"

"Harriet Danders. Yes, we could. If she believed us, then Ebberling would wonder how we discovered that little bit of information, and he'd figure we'd found Rachel Newbury, which would put Emily in even more danger. If she didn't believe us, she would definitely tell Ebberling, with the same results."

Laurie planted his face into his hands. "This is very complicated."

"I don't believe I've ever mentioned that it would be simple." Moving away from his office window, he clapped his brother on the shoulder. "Straightforward is for soldiers, Laurie. Straightforward is often also bloodier."

His brother twisted around to face him. "What would the ideal solution be?"

He considered that for a moment. "Ideally, he would still trust me, and I could buy him a great deal of liquor and convince him to chat all about it while a half-dozen uninvolved lords, ministers, judges overheard him."

"Then you likely shouldn't have told him you wouldn't help him any longer."

"I know."

That small misstep had kept him awake for the past few nights. If he'd still been thinking as a spy he would never have burned the best bridge to a suspect like that. But he'd been thinking as a man with a conscience, and worse, one who was more than halfway to being in love with his target. It had been foolish and stupid, and the idea that it might cost him Emily terrified him.

"Evidently, Nate, you're human. I'm rather glad to see it."

Nate glared at his younger brother. "I'd be gladder not to have erred."

"Yes, but that's you. I was talking about me."

"Mm-hm. Thank you for your—"

The butler knocked at the closed door. "My lord?"

"Come in, Garvey."

The servant opened the door partway and leaned in. "My lord, you have a message."

Hopefully it was from one of his new friends, who'd learned something that he hadn't. "Let's see it."

"The message is still in the hands of the . . . person who delivered it. She will only give it to you directly, she says."

Well, that was curious. "Send her in, then."

The butler hesitated again. "I . . . do not think it wise to give her access to the house, my lord."

Nate straightened, walking to the doorway. "And why is that?" he asked, moving past the butler and into the hallway.

"She has a certain . . . odor, Lord Westfall. An unpleasant one. I had her wait on the front steps."

Who would send him a smelly messenger? The Duke of Greaves, perhaps, but it was more likely that she'd come from one of his less highborn sources. And that meant the information was more likely to be useful to someone of his background. Hurrying his steps, he descended the stairs and strode into the foyer, pulling open the door before Garvey could reach it again.

The odor that hit him as the door swung back was indeed unpleasant. Sour milk and rotted eggs, he decided, as the female bearing the scent faced him. "You Westfall?" she asked.

He eyed her. Plump, with an ill-fitting gown of uncertain color under a dirty silk shawl and matted black hair that likely housed a colony of lice. There was also the beginnings of a moustache, bad skin, and what looked like a syphillis sore on one cheek. Nate made her for some very poor quality inn's resident whore. "I am," he said. "What do you have for me?"

"I don't think ye'd want yer highborn neighbors t'see," she drawled.

Hm. Charing Cross, or Whitechapel, from her accent. That could be Abel Dooling, then, though he doubted that Ebberling was even acquainted with anyone from the area. "Come in, then," he said, opening the door wider and stepping back both to allow her room and to keep upwind of her. "Into the morning room, if you please."

"My lord," Garvey squeaked in protest.

He leaned toward the butler. "We'll open the windows and air it out after she leaves."

"Or burn it down," the man grumbled under his breath.

Nate followed the woman into the morning room, watched as she took in the furnishings and decorations. When she turned around he noticed the heel of one shoe, which made him narrow his eyes. They weren't anything special, but they were of better quality than the rest of—

"Here ye are," she said, producing a slip of paper from somewhere he didn't care to question too closely.

He stepped forward, and the female grabbed his wrist, lifted up on her toes, and kissed him full on the mouth. Her tongue raked across his lips, and Nate recoiled. "What the devil are you—"

She started laughing. And then he realized what the devil she was about.

"Emily?"

Dancing a swift circle, she curtsied. "I fooled you," she chortled, in her own cultured, careful accent. "I told Jenny it would work. She reckoned you'd see through it, but when I found that rotten egg in the alley on the way here, I knew you'd never get close enough to me to even guess."

Torn between genuine, surprised delight and horror, he held out one hand. "The egg, if you please."

She pulled it from her reticule, and the stench intensified. At least she'd wrapped it in a handkerchief, but she'd be lucky if she didn't have to burn her entire wardrobe and cut her hair off to be rid of the smell. Arm outstretched, he carried the bundle to the open morning room doorway. "Garvey, bury this or something," he ordered.

The butler took it and practically ran out the front door, no easy task for a man of Garvey's age. Nate shut the door, then strode past his visitor to open the two windows on the garden side of the room.

"Did I overdo it?" Emily asked, still chuckling.

"The smell was a bit much," he returned, facing her again and looking at her more closely, "but otherwise you're nearly perfect. Except for the shoes."

"I couldn't find any wretched ones that fit." She lifted her hem a little and stuck out the toe of one black walking shoe. "I didn't think you'd see them."

"I noticed them at the last moment," he conceded, "just before you assaulted me."

Abruptly she stopped laughing. "I might have stabbed you instead of just kissing you, Nate. What were you thinking?"

"I was thinking first that I could see both your hands and that you weren't carrying a knife, and second that one of my men might finally have found something useful for me." And that he would have risked an armed assault in order to find the information that would save Emily Portsman from having to leave London and find yet another life for herself—one that didn't include him.

"Oh."

He closed the distance between them. "Assault me again, why don't you?" Taking her chin in his fingers, he lifted her face to his and kissed her softly.

"Better?" she asked breathlessly, once he'd released her.

"You still stink, but yes. Much better."

Now that he looked, she was quite impressive. Most people wearing a disguise overdid it, adding warts and moles and becoming far too hideous to pass as someone unmemorable and unremarkable. He could see that she'd had some practiced help, though, nothing to make her too ugly, but merely too dirty to warrant a second look. And in her favor, the smell had worked, too, if only to keep anyone from getting too close to detect her true identity.

"Why are you wearing a disguise?" he asked finally, though he could guess the answer. And he didn't like it at all.

"Because I refuse to hide while you and Haybury and Jenny and everyone else are trying to help me."

"What if we're all just waiting for Ebberling to leave London?" he shot back. "Did you consider that?"

"Yes, and they might be doing just that. You wouldn't be."

"And how do you know that?"

She touched his cheek, and he just kept himself from leaning into her palm. "Because you're Nate Stokes."

The morning room door opened again. "What the devil is that smell?" Laurie asked, walking into the room with his hand over his nose. His eyes widened. "And why is that . . . woman touching you?"

Lowering her hand, she gathered her skirt and waddled over to his brother. "So this is the boy ye want me to break in? Seems a bit skinny."

His brother's face went white, and he backed toward the door. "I don't need to be broken in! What—"

"It's Emily, Laurie. Calm down and shut the door."

"Em . . . What? Why the bloody hell are you dressed like that?"

Once Laurence had shut the door, Nate faced his stubborn, exasperating, impossible love again. "Yes, why are you dressed like that?"

"I wanted to see if I could change my appearance enough to fool you. Which I did. Which means I can fool him, even more easily."

Nate shook his head. "No. Absolutely not."

Laurie circled them, then reached out to poke one finger into Emily's plump side. "What are you wearing under there?"

"Several pouches of beans and rice," Emily returned. "Jenny said they hang more like real fat than cloth or feathers would."

"Yes, they do," Laurence agreed, poking at her again. "But I don't think you'll be able to seduce Lord Ebberling looking like that. Or stinking like that."

"She's not seducing anyone," Nate snapped, too vehemently. She was his, damn it all. For as long as he could hold on to her. "And stop jabbing at her."

Laurence lifted both hands in surrender. "I think I'll

leave you two to figure this out," he said, backing away and slipping out of the room.

Nate strode over and locked the damned thing before someone else could barge in. "You want to go work in his household. No."

"Then you have a better idea?" she retorted. "I am not going to sit by waiting for him to find me any longer! So I can either leave London, or help you stop him before he can murder anyone else, including me!"

He looked at her for a long moment, then frowned. "Take that off, will you? I can't think with you looking like a Gorgon."

Emily blew out her breath, then reached up to pull off her black wig. "Very well. But I'm not going away until you have a better plan than mine, or you agree that this is the best way to proceed."

If he'd ever needed something to prove that Emily was unlike anyone he'd ever met, she'd just provided it. He knew that Ebberling frightened her, yet there she was, prepared to beard the lion in his very den. "And what is your plan, then?" he asked, just barely resisting the urge to pull the pins from her hair and set it loose down her shoulders.

"I . . ." She frowned. "I'm not certain yet. I wouldn't dress like this, of course; that was only to see if I could fool you. But I do know how to be a servant. I watched my mother for twelve years, after all. Once I was in his household, I could watch him."

"You're the only witness, my dear. If you caught him at doing something else wrong, or admitting to killing his wife, you'd still be the only witness."

She plunked her plump, smelly form down on his couch. "I know that. But I can't simply sit in the Tantalus and hide. I've hidden enough. I have . . ." She trailed off. "Good things are happening to me now. Finally. I don't want to give them up."

By "them," did she mean him? He'd never been anyone's "good thing" before. And as desperate as he was to keep her in his life, a small part of him hoped that she wanted him in her life just as badly. A friend, a confidante, a lover—while previously and occasionally he'd been able to find, separately, two of the three, he'd never encountered them all in one person. Nate wanted to tell her just that, tell her that he'd fallen in love with her. But to do so now, when she might need to make a quick decision that could cost her or ensure her freedom, if not her life—he didn't want his own sentiments to muddy the equation. He could wait until she was safe, though that would only mean an entire new set of obstacles.

Nate sat down beside her, running his thumb across her cheek and then examining it. "What is that she's put on you, talc?"

"Yes, mixed with charcoal, to make me look unwashed."

"It makes me want to give you a bath, so call it successful." He took her hand, pulling off the worn black gloves she'd donned. "I want to help you, Em. You're not forcing me to act."

Abruptly she stood again, pulling her fingers free of his grip. "But I'm—I'm not—You're a hero, Nate. More than most people will ever know. This is . . . it's beneath you."

He tilted his head at her. "Have you looked at my life, love? I became a spy because it paid enough for me to support my mother and my brother. I became an earl because my cousin, who was a nice enough fellow, but not so nice that he ever offered to provide for a widowed in-law and her two sons, fell into a lake while fishing and drowned." Nate gestured at the well-appointed morning room around them. "I don't belong here, any more than you think you do."

"Yes, but you're still an earl, and a cousin to a former earl, the son of an earl's younger brother. I'm a Tantalus girl at best, and a common thing who's put on airs above her station at worst."

Standing, Nathaniel slid his arms around her enlarged waist and tugged her up against him. "Wouldn't they all wag their tongues at us, if they only knew?" he murmured, and leaned down to kiss her.

"Nate," she breathed, wrapping her own arms around his shoulders. "You're going to break my heart."

"Never. There's always a way, and I don't mean to let you go." As he spoke, he realized that he meant every word of it. She was not getting away, even if it meant giving up what he'd received by accident. Even if it meant killing one very powerful marquis.

"Don't make promises you can't keep," Emily whispered, almost hoping she'd spoken too quietly for him to hear. His words sounded so very lovely, and it would be so pleasant to be able to sink into that dream, if only for a moment.

"I never do," he whispered back, which was even nicer.

It would all cut even more deeply when this was finished with, but she'd made something of an art at pretending. For now, she could imagine that Nate Stokes, Earl of Westfall, could be hers, could marry her, could be the one thing in her life that was permanent. She certainly wanted him to be.

He reached up under her frumpy, ill-fitting gown and found the tie that held most of the pouches of rice and beans in place. When he untied it, ten pounds of weight fell about her feet. Ten more followed a moment later, and then he tugged her oversized dress down her shoulders. It puddled to the floor, the shift she'd donned to keep the pouches from itching at her skin joining it a second later.

"You still smell," he muttered, lifting her up and dumping her onto his couch.

Emily chuckled. "My perfume doesn't seem to have dampened your enthusiasm." She reached up to brush her fingers across the front of his trousers, and he jumped. "Not a bit."

"Your face paint doesn't seem to matter, either," he returned, shrugging out of his coat, then swiftly unbuttoning his tan waistcoat and dropping it somewhere behind him. "It's you I want. The you behind all that nonsense."

Heat deepened between her legs. "That is a very nice thing to say."

Nate shook his head as he opened his trousers and shoved them down past his thighs. "If I was nice I would be conjuring a way to get you out of this mess instead of doing . . . this." He lowered himself onto the couch over her, kissing her openmouthed while his hands roved over her breasts, pinching and nipping until she couldn't breathe.

Then he shifted, sliding down the length of her, his mouth and lips and teeth following his hands until she moaned, bucking beneath him "Nate, stop teasing me," she managed, gasping when he slid two fingers inside her.

"You want me," he rumbled. "You're wet for me."

"I want you," she agreed. "Now."

Rising up over her again, he slid deeply inside her. "You're mine," he groaned as he pumped his hips forward. "No one else's. You're mine."

Emily dug her fingers into his shoulders, panting in time with his thrusts. At this moment, she believed him. And he belonged to her, as much as she to him. "Yes," she agreed. "Yes."

He gazed into her eyes, his light green with the black rim around them. "I'm not leaving," he went on, deepening his thrusts.

She'd already thought of that, and while a few weeks ago she would have argued, today she only nodded. Everything was about to change, whatever became of her and Nate and Ebberling. For the first time, she thought she was ready for it.

Then she drew tight and shattered, clutching at Nate as he continued his rhythmic assault. Groaning, he held himself hard against her as he spent his release deep inside her. "You're mine," he repeated, lowering his head to her shoulder.

"And you're mine," she agreed, tangling her fingers through his hair and wishing with all her heart that it could just this once be true.

The Marquis of Ebberling looked up from his morning newspaper as his butler showed the caller into the breakfast room. "Colonel Rycott. How pleasant to see you."

Jack Rycott looked nothing like a spy, which was likely why he was so good at his profession. In fact, in his dark green, well-tailored jacket, gray waistcoat, and brown buckskins tucked into his polished black Hessian boots, he looked like any well-heeled aristocrat come to Mayfair to enjoy the Season.

Even his dark blue eyes and raven-black hair a bit disheveled from horseback riding, the lean jaw and straight nose, all made him look a landed gentleman.

Much better than the moth-eaten, spectacle-wearing professor.

"You paid a great deal to convince me to come down here, my lord," Rycott drawled in his cultured tones. "So I'm listening. Let's get to it, shall we?"

"I sent for you nearly a week ago."

"I'm not your dog. I serve a very different master, in fact."

The marquis attempted to ignore the insult. "Would you care for some tea? And you'll find Velton House always puts out a splendid breakfast. Help yourself."

Instead the colonel pulled out the chair at the foot of the table and sat, one leg out to the side. "If you want me to be your friend, it'll cost you another thousand quid. Otherwise, get to the point."

Ebberling clenched his jaw, then forced himself to relax again. The idea that he would have to pay someone to befriend him was beyond insulting, but he let it pass. After all, he did have another duty in mind for his guest. "You recommended Westfall to me."

"I did."

"The man's a fool."

Rycott cocked his head to one side. "How so?"

For a moment Ebberling had the distinct sensation that he was being eyed by a leopard, sizing him up for a meal. He picked up his cup of tea and drank to cover his discomfiture. He made men nervous; not the other way around. "He bumbled about for a several weeks, spending more time asking my son questions about Rachel Newbury than going about looking for her, and then he returned my money and said she couldn't be found."

"Interesting." The colonel sat back an inch or so. "If you wanted to complain about Stokes, you might have written me a letter and saved us both some time."

"I didn't ask you here to complain; I'm telling you what happened." Ebberling put both hands on the tabletop and leaned forward; Rycott wasn't the only one who could cut an imposing figure. "And now I'll tell you what I want. I want *you* to find Rachel Newbury, and I want you to bring her to me. No authorities, no legalities. She stole from me, and I want my pound of flesh. In exchange for your services, I will pay you twenty thousand pounds."

"That's a great deal of blunt over a hundred-quid necklace and a runaway governess."

Ah, the necklace. It didn't exist; at the time he'd needed to provide a motive for Miss Newbury's misdeeds and flight, and jewelry had seemed both logical and believable. "The necklace is secondary," he said aloud. "She killed—murdered—my wife. I have no proof, but I don't require any. The courts would. Hence my wanting to deal with her myself."

Extending one finger, Rycott drew a lazy figure eight on the polished tabletop. "Twenty thousand pounds. How much did you offer Nate?"

"Half that. I'm willing to wager that you're twice the man he is, so I'm doubling my offer." There. Flattery always worked, even on hard-bitten sorts like Jack Rycott. "And time is shorter, as well. I'm marrying in three weeks. You're to find her before then."

"And if she's not in the country?"

"I looked for her three years ago. Spent a great deal of money over it. She hadn't headed for any of the ports then. I doubt she'll have done it now, when she thinks she's safe. A stiff-spined chit like her wouldn't favor living like a red Indian in the Americas, anyway, and the Continent was at war. In addition, Westfall found nothing to indicate that she'd left England, either."

His guest nodded. "That makes sense." He kept his

finger moving for another long moment. "We'll shake hands on it. I want nothing in writing."

"I prefer that, as well. You'll do it, then."

"Aye. I'll do it." With that discomfiting abruptness of his, Rycott sat forward. "And I'll give you my opinion in advance of any coin. Nate Stokes would never admit to failure, especially by quitting a task unfinished. I'd wager every quid of my fee that he found her, and decided he didn't want to turn her over to you."

A shiver of anticipation ran down Ebberling's spine. He'd been suspicious, but this confirmed it. If the chit had talked to Westfall, convinced him of her story, then he would have to be dealt with, as well. Once she was finished, though, any direct witnesses would be gone. He could deal with the earl at his leisure. The fool couldn't walk without a cane. Hunting him would be simple. And . . . amusing.

"I want no mistakes," he said aloud. "Show me proof before you grab the wrong woman."

"I can do that."

He stood. "Then shake my hand, and get on with it," he said.

Rycott rose smoothly as a panther. Shaking Ebberling's outstretched hand, he grinned. "Get that blunt ready for me, my lord. This shouldn't take long."

Nathaniel backed Blue a few steps farther beneath the trees when the front door of Velton House opened. Ebberling himself walked Rycott down the granite steps to his horse. For a few moments after he'd returned the marquis's money he'd nearly convinced himself that Ebberling would give up the hunt, but he wasn't surprised at all that Jack had been summoned.

At best he could only be thankful that Ebberling

hadn't been able to persuade Jack to leave Brighton at the beginning of all this. Because if he'd been able to find Rachel Newbury, Rycott would also have been able to do so. And Jack was less sentimental than he was.

He'd learned over the years that fate was a bloody fickle mistress, but the lady had been kind to him up to this point. And to Emily, as well. Clearly now Ebberling meant to end all that, and he'd certainly found the right man for the job.

Rycott rode past on a grand bay stallion, and Nate stayed motionless until his employer, recruiter, and friend was well out of sight of Velton House before he kneed Blue in pursuit. He'd donned a groom's clothes and a floppy brown hat, together with worn work boots. Dressed this way, and without his spectacles or cane, Ebberling likely wouldn't have recognized him from more than three feet distant.

On the other hand, Jack Rycott had likely known him from the moment he'd stepped out through the marquis's front door. Even so, he kept his distance until Rycott cantered into St. James's Park. A few moments later he found Jack standing in the shade of a grand oak tree while the big bay grazed close by him. Taking a deep breath, knowing he was as prepared as he could ever be and hoping to God it would be good enough, Nate swung down from Blue and walked up to his fellow spy.

"Nate. You look like shit," Rycott commented, leaning one shoulder against the tree and chewing on a long stem of grass.

"That was the idea. You look well."

Jack shrugged. "Pretending to be retired sits well with me. Ebberling said you were a buffoon. I hate recommending people who don't do the jobs I send their way."

With a brief smile, Nathaniel inclined his head. "The game has a way of changing, as you well know. How much did he offer you?"

"Twice what he offered you. Evidently I'm twice the man you are." He narrowed one sky-blue eye. "I told him you'd likely found the chit after all, and had a change of heart."

His changed heart thudded. "Nothing but the truth, then. Do you want to meet her?"

Rycott straightened, tossing aside the grass stem. "The woman who stole Nate Stokes's iron heart? Of course I do. Where do you have her stashed?"

"The Tantalus Club."

"I've heard of it. Is it true the women running the gaming tables are naked?"

Nate snorted. "No, more's the pity. Even so it's the club adolescent boys' dreams are made of."

"And not-so-adolescent boys, as well, I wager." Rycott walked over to his bay and swung into the saddle. "You're dressed as the groom, so I suppose I lead the way."

"I don't know that he'll have you followed, but he might. Twenty thousand is quite the investment."

Remounting Blue, Nate fell in behind the spy. "What's that beast's name?" he asked, eyeing the big bay.

"Osiris. Wellington gifted him to me last year in lieu of a pay increase. Came from Sullivan Waring's stables."

"He's a brute."

"Wellington, or Osiris?" With a grin, Rycott kicked the bay into a trot. "So tell me, do I get to know what you've planned, or do I have to figure it out on my own?"

"I thought you already would have it deciphered from my letter."

"Your damned letter said 'Ebberling will ask to hire

you for my job. Do it, and inform him that I've found Rachel Newbury. Nate.' That isn't much to go on, even for me."

"I couldn't risk writing it down. After we get to the Tantalus I'll tell you everything."

"You'd better. I'm bound to lose twenty thousand quid over this, after all."

"Perhaps not."

"Even better."

When they arrived at the crowded front drive of the Tantalus, Nate took charge of both horses. "Tell the butler you're here to see Haybury," he told Rycott in a low voice. "I'll go in through the servants' entrance at the back and meet you inside."

Jack nodded. "Now I'm truly curious."

"One more thing."

Stopping, Rycott turned to face him. "What is it?"

"The redhead from Lourdes. I think I've found her."

For the first time, Jack looked surprised. And not entirely pleased. "Where?"

"Inside there." Nate gestured at the club.

"Damn me. This is a hive of subterfuge."

Nathaniel watched him go inside, then went to the stable yard and turned the horses over to Clark, the head groom. If the fellow recognized him, he didn't say anything about it. He would be one of Emily's friends, though, so Nathaniel wasn't surprised that she had that servant's loyalty, as well.

As for Rycott, well, Em wasn't the only one with a peculiar and indisputably loyal set of friends. And thank God for that. Continuing past the stable yard, Nate walked around to the side of the house and pulled open the kitchen door. The ladies there had been told to expect him, and after a glance or two, completely ignored him.

They might have had this meeting at Teryl House, where he had more control over who came and went, and more specifically, about how safe Emily remained. But he couldn't be entirely certain that Ebberling didn't have someone watching either him or Jack—and while anyone would be foolish to attempt trailing either of them more than once, it was that once that worried him.

It made more sense that Rycott would follow his own trail, which did, after all, lead to the Tantalus. And here a group of titled men and their former Tantalus-girl wives could also meet without raising any undue suspicion. Trotting up the back stairs, he walked down one of the narrow hallways until he reached a plain, heavy door with the plaque reading ADAM HOUSE beside it. Lord and Lady Haybury's private residence, though from what he'd learned from Emily the entire establishment was actually old Adam House, with several rooms built on both the front and the rear to extend the property.

He'd been told to wait there, and though it chafed him that Emily might be directly inside, he did as he'd been bid. These people were assisting him, and her, and so he would respect their rules. To a point. A few moments later Jack appeared from the other end of the hallway, on the heels of Juliet Langtree. She looked from one of them to the other, then knocked three times at the door and left.

"I think they're taking all this spying faddle too seriously," Jack commented with a slight grin.

Nate shrugged. "It's their house, and their rules."

"Ah, I do not miss civilian life."

He hadn't, either—when he'd inherited the earldom he'd seriously contemplated asking for an assignment that would take him to America. All these aristocrats with their petty prejudices and petty grievances and concern over who wore the same gown twice in a Season simply drove him mad. This though, today, made sense. And if he'd fled, he would never have met Emily.

The door opened. Jenny Martine stood there, her light blond hair pulled back in that bun of hers so tight he was surprised she could blink. She wasn't looking at him, though. Her gaze was on Jack Rycott, and her pretty green eyes narrowed just a fraction, for just a moment, so briefly that if he hadn't been looking for it, he never would have noticed.

"Bonjour, Mademoiselle Poof-Poof," Jack drawled in an impeccable French accent.

"It was Peaufoure, not Poof-Poof," Miss Martine corrected. "And you never appeared for dinner."

Jack shrugged. "I'm only five years late, and you're not a redhead. May we come in?"

"Yes, of course. The second door on the left. The drawing room."

This second meeting of the conspirators was more crowded than the first one, and although they all knew most of her secrets by now, this time Emily felt even more nervous. If anything went awry because of this, she might not be the only one to pay the price. And if everything went the way they hoped, she would have to listen to Nate finally tell her that as fond as he was of her, the most he could do was offer to set her up as his mistress, because, well, earls didn't marry the daughters of washerwomen.

She sat by the window, only half listening as Sophia and Camille chatted with her. Both of them had found refuge at the Tantalus, and both of them had managed to find love and marriage. She was happy for them, of course, genuinely so, but part of her couldn't help also feeling terribly jealous.

That feeling only deepened when Nathaniel strolled into the room in the company of Jenny and a tall, black-haired man who looked as though he'd just come from luncheon at White's. So that was Jack Rycott. Three spies present now, all of them bent on aiding her. She only hoped it was enough.

Nate made the introductions, leaving her for last. Finally he walked up to her. "And this, Jack, is Emily Portsman. Or Rachel Newbury, where Ebberling's concerned."

Deep blue eyes took her in from head to toe. "Miss Portsman. You seem to inspire a great deal of loyalty."

"Thank you for coming, Mr. Rycott." She turned her attention to Nate, to find him gazing at her. "Hello, Lord Westfall." She wanted to say more, to fling herself into his arms and kiss him senseless, but then everyone else in the room would know that she loved him. Whether they would still wish to aid a common thing who dared to crave a man far above her station, she didn't know. He didn't approach her any closer, either, however, so he might well have had the same concern.

"Emily. Let's get to it, then, shall we? Unless you've come to your senses and will let me see to this for you."

"I did come to my senses," she returned, "which is why I'm not about to sit idly by and watch."

"What is the plan?" the Duke of Greaves asked, "for those of us not making protestations over the degree of our involvement?"

Nate kept his gaze on her. "You're certain, then?" he murmured. "You'll have to trust me to a rather alarming degree."

"I trust you," she returned. How could she not? He'd had innumerable chances both to turn her over to

Ebberling and to simply turn his back on her, and instead he'd both kept her secrets and shown her parts of London she'd never thought to experience. Above all that, every time she looked at him, with his spectacles or without them, her heart beat a happy tattoo in her chest. Her, in love. It was ridiculous and hopeless, and she couldn't help it, even so. She loved Nate Stokes with all her heart.

He smiled, as if he could read her thoughts. "Very well. Let the games begin."

Chapter Fifteen

"Y ou spent three years hiding from this man," Sophia, the Duchess of Greaves, whispered, her arm wrapped around Emily's. "And now you want him to see you? This is simply mad."

"She's wearing a disguise," the Duke of Greaves put in with his deceptively lazy drawl. "It's a risk, but a damned fine plan, if you ask me."

"You're not the one whose life is at risk, Adam."

The duke lifted an eyebrow, then waved a finger toward the far end of the large ballroom. "If I were Ebberling, I'd be worrying about my own life."

Emily followed the direction he indicated. A young tiger stood there, his mask gleaming with imbedded glass of orange and black and red. Even more impressive to her eyes, though, was the tall, lean, silent wolf beside him, silver and gray and black, with piercing blue eyes of glass. Beneath them, shadowed by his masque, an even more dangerous pair of light green eyes gleamed. And they gazed directly at her.

"Ebberling won't give up the chase, Sophia," she said quietly, willing her hands to keep from shaking. "And I don't want to leave England because of something he did." Especially now, when she'd finally found a reason to remain.

"Your Westfall said he could simply make the man disappear," her friend whispered back. "Given what he's done, I'm beginning to think that's the best solution."

Greaves kissed his wife on the cheek. "So blood-thirsty, you are," he murmured. "I have no objection to doing away with the murdering bastard, myself, but I gave my word to let Westfall attempt his game first. Now come along, my dove."

Sophia chuckled. "I'm a swan; not a dove."

"And I'm a duke, not a lion, yet here I stand."

The three of them passed by the long windows overlooking the garden of Tremaine House, and Emily caught a glimpse of herself reflected in the chandelier light. Ebberling still saw her as a stiff-necked governess, she knew, so they'd costumed her as an owl, feathers sprouting from her brown hair, and a brown and white glittering half-mask across her eyes. She felt terribly exposed, but that had been the plan. The beauty patch Jenny had affixed to one cheek itched, and seemed the worst disguise in the world but that was the point.

Nathaniel had asked if she trusted him, and she did. Even so, she hadn't felt so apprehensive since her first days spent running from Ebberling Manor. He would see her tonight. And only some very careful plotting would keep him from grabbing her right there in the middle of Lord and Lady Tremaine's ballroom and dragging her off either to jail or to kill her outright. After all, who could blame a man caught up by sudden rage after abruptly finding his wife's killer?

They stopped close by the refreshment table, and Greaves took both his wife's hands in his. "We are here because you insisted, Sophia," he said in his low voice, the humor missing for once in his tone, "but you are carrying my child. Do not make me regret this."

Sophia smiled, the expression rendering Emily distinctly jealous. "So fierce, you are," she said, repeating his words of earlier. "And you're more likely to regret having your ill-born wife at a ball than anything else."

He lifted his lion's mask and bent down to kiss his ill-born wife full on the lips. "Dance a waltz with me, and see how much I regret it."

They'd arrived early intentionally, so that Greaves and Nate and evidently Laurence Stokes could find the best vantage points and so they could avoid being surprised when Ebberling arrived. All that meant at the moment, however, was that every new pair or trio of guests who arrived at the masked ball could look at Sophia and mutter, then look over at the owl beside her and wonder who she could possibly be.

"Thank you for going through this for me," she said, squeezing her friend's hand.

"Nonsense. If I feared making a scene or having people look at me sideways, I would have fled to a nunnery years ago." She grinned. "And I certainly wouldn't have looked for employment at The Tantalus Club."

The wolf turned to say something to the tiger, and the two men strolled toward them. Another kind of shiver entirely went through her as he approached. Sophia had called him "your Westfall." That wasn't so, but oh, she wished it could be. Perhaps if she'd never told him about Eloise Smorkley, if she'd made up something about being a baron's long-lost granddaughter, she could claim him as she wanted. But living with lies as he did, he valued the truth above everything, and she could never lie to him. Not about that.

"Good evening, Greaves, Your Grace, Emily," the tiger said, inclining his head.

"You sound nervous, Laurie," Greaves noted. "I promise not to invite you drinking anywhere tonight."

"I'm only terrified I'll say something stupid while I'm sober," Nate's brother returned. "I'll have no excuse for that, at all."

"I wouldn't have asked for your assistance if I didn't think you could manage it," Nathaniel commented, and bent down to take Emily's hand. Slowly he lifted her fingers, brushing his lips against her knuckles. "I do hope that of all those things you've learned, dancing is among them."

"This is my first grand ball," she said, her voice not quite steady as she looked up at him. "But yes, I learned how to dance."

"Good."

"If you two are ready to stop mooning over each other," Greaves broke in, his gaze focused past Nate's shoulder, "your panther is here. Waiting by the door for his escort."

The panther. That was Rycott. She shuddered, but Nathaniel tightened his grip on her fingers. "I swear that no one will harm you," he murmured, his light green eyes fiercer than those of the wolf mask he wore.

"I know. It's only that I'm aware that he's here and I'm simply . . . waiting for him to approach me."

"Just don't overreact. Tonight we only want him suspicious; not certain. Remember who you are."

That was more difficult than it sounded, but out of everyone there, he would understand that. Emily Portsman. Tonight she was Emily Portsman, just as she had been for the past three years. She nodded. "I'm ready."

"Then relax. You look stiff enough to shatter. You don't expect to see him here. It's meant to surprise you, love."

That last word distracted her more effectively than any words of support or promises of safety could possibly have done. Did he love her? It didn't matter, she supposed, except that it would be . . . She didn't have the words to describe what it would be like, to know that he felt the same way for her that she did for him. It would all hurt more later, but this was tonight. And tonight she could imagine that the man she loved, loved her in return.

Belatedly she rolled her shoulders. "Don't worry about me."

"Impossible."

The butler had been announcing the names of the viscount and viscountess's illustrious guests as they appeared, though as small and proud as the ranks of Mayfair's aristocrats were, she couldn't believe that they weren't already well acquainted with one another. She, of course, had been "and guest," but as that was connected with the announcement of the Duke and Duchess of Greaves's arrival, it been more than enough to garner her dozens of curious looks.

Of course being a washerwoman's daughter made her nearly as scandalous as being a Tantalus girl or an accused murderess, but that was all beside the point tonight. She carefully kept her back turned, using every ounce of willpower to avoid spinning around and looking toward the wide double doors.

"Lords and ladies," the butler droned for the fortieth time, "may I present the Marquis of Ebberling and his betrothed, Miss Harriet Danders, and Colonel Jonathan Rycott?"

Her back stiffened; she couldn't help the abrupt wait for a knife to pierce her spine. Nothing happened, though; the level of noise and conversation in the increasingly crowded ballroom didn't alter a whit. After a moment she realized she'd been holding her breath, and she forced air out of her lungs and back in again.

"He's masked as a lion, and Miss Danders as a peacock," Nate informed her, though as far as she could tell, he'd never glanced in the marquis's direction.

"Not as pretty as my lion," Greaves commented, his tone disdainful. "Social climber."

No one had ever spoken so dismissively of Ebberling in her hearing before, and it was surprisingly comforting. If he could be mocked, even jokingly, he could be defeated. She squared her shoulders, then turned around.

The tall, broad-shouldered lion half-mask turned his gaze about the room, clearly looking for someone. The marquis was well dressed, as he always had been, tonight in a dark brown jacket to complement his mask, with a black waistcoat and trousers with polished Hessian boots and an amber pin through his impeccable cravat.

This man had tormented her dreams for more nights than he had any right to. He'd ruined the proper life she'd set out to make for herself—indeed, if he hadn't murdered her employer, she would have been perfectly content to remain as young George's governess for as long as she was needed. After that, a good recommendation from Lady Ebberling would have seen her to another fine household, and so on until she'd earned enough money to retire to a small cottage well away from Derbyshire and any remnants of her old life there.

Instead she'd been forced to begin all over again, with a different name and a different past. If not for The Tantalus Club, she had no idea where she might have ended up. Certainly not at a grand masked ball in the company of a duke and a duchess, with an earl currently touching her fingers with his.

As the face beneath the lion's eyes turned in her direction, she quickly looked away. Tonight he was supposed to be suspicious, not certain of her identity. Rycott would have done what he could, but a great part of it was up to her, to play the part of a duke's guest, of a former governess, but not too well.

The tiger handed her a glass of Madeira. "If you don't drink that, Em, I will," he said tightly.

She gripped the glass, and made herself take a shallow swallow. "Thank you, Mr. Stokes."

"God, please, Laurie," he returned with a forced smile, flushing beneath his mask.

They were all trying so hard, and just for her. She smiled back at him. "Laurie, then. Thank you."

"You're welcome."

"They gave you a dance card, yes?" Nate put in.

She pulled it from her reticule. "Yes. I'm not certain I can dance with him, Nathaniel. I can look at him, but—"

"We'll make it a country dance. That way he won't get a good look at you."

He'd become the spymaster, she realized, more concerned with tonight's outcome than with how nervous she might be. That was the man this venture needed, but she couldn't help wishing he would offer a few more words of comfort, pitiful as that might make her.

Swiftly he wrote his name beside two dances, handed the card and pencil for Greaves to do the same, then to Laurie for another two. That left three dances. Rycott was to take one, and Ebberling one. They needed another partner for her, or Ebberling would attempt to take two. She knew it, because he would want another look at her.

Nate seemed to come to the same conclusion, because he cursed under his breath. Before he could write his name a third time, something that would raise the eyebrows of everyone in the room, Sophia put a hand on his arm. "Leave it to me," she said, and took both the card and Emily's arm.

"Where are we going?"

"Hush. Greaves, with me."

"Yes, Your Grace," her husband said obediently.

Together they walked toward a small group of gentlemen standing by the windows. As they drew closer Emily recognized at least three of them as members of the Tantalus, and she balked. "What are you doing? If they know I'm a Tantalus girl, Lord and Lady Tremaine will have me thrown out."

"Hush," Sophia repeated, then released her husband's arm. "Greaves, go fetch me Francis Henning."

He grinned, but the glitter in his eyes said something entirely darker. "Order me about all you wish, love, but you'll pay for it later."

Sophia gave him a slow smile. "I know it."

The exchange forcibly reminded Emily that as nervous as she was tonight, this was not all about her. Her friends were risking their reputations, and Sophia barely had one of those to begin with. If her husband hadn't been a duke, and a very wealthy and powerful one on top of that, Sophia might well have found herself not invited to a great many events of the Season. In fact, there were places she wasn't welcome, as it was.

"How goes you and Almack's?" Emily asked, as Greaves's appearance among them caused the small herd of men to begin bobbing and chittering like parrots.

"We remain enemies," her friend said easily. "It sounds dull as dirt, and I have no real desire to ever set foot there, but Adam's offended by that stupid letter of regret they had to send, when I never even requested an invitation to the assembly in the first place."

"He loves you. The idea of anyone slighting you infuriates him."

Sophia sighed. "Yes, I know. And I know he's been slighted a few times recently because of me, which . . . annoys me excessively. But I've resolved to dislike the people who dislike either of us, and I just wish he would do the same."

Greaves rejoined them, the round-pated Francis Henning in tow. Henning had donned a hawk's mask, though the narrow-faced predator seemed an ill match for the wide-faced, jovial fellow beneath it. He bowed. "Sophia. It's marvelous to see you and Greaves again. I had, well, the most magnificent time ever at Greaves Park over Christmas. My grandmama was near to bursting when I told her about it."

Smiling, Sophia took his hands. "I'm so glad you stayed after all the chaos erupted."

"Heh. I'm only glad Greaves didn't kick me out on my arse like he did most of the rest of his guests." He looked over at Emily. "Greaves said you're up to a prank, Miss Em," he whispered, "and I'm happy to play a part. Might I have a dance with you?"

She grinned, more touched than she could say. "Thank you, Mr. Henning. Any dance you please."

Sophia handed him the card, and he wrote his name down beside one of the two remaining quadrilles. "I'll see you then," he said, bowing again before he trundled off to rejoin his friends.

"That man is supremely underestimated," the Duke of Greaves stated, as the music for the first dance of the evening began. "And I have a dance with my wife. Are you ready to be intercepted?"

Swallowing, Emily nodded. If everything went as planned, Nate would be close by, ready to step in. And he was correct; this needed to be done, or she would never have a moment's peace, or a good night's sleep. "As ready as I ever will be."

"Good." Unexpectedly, the duke took her arm. "I did some checking on your friend Westfall," he said in a low voice. "He's a good man."

"Yes, I know," she returned, and with a nod he released her to escort Sophia onto the dance floor.

She stood where she was for a moment, watching her friends step gracefully into a waltz. Nate had said counting slowly would calm her as she waited for her doom to arrive, but he was far more experienced at this sort of thing than she was, and she'd already flown past seventy on her way to ninety when the hairs on the back of her neck prickled.

"Excuse me," the deep voice of Jack Rycott came, at the same moment a hand touched her shoulder.

She jumped, not having to feign her startlement, and at the same time she was grateful that he'd been the one to speak rather than the man she knew would be standing beside him. Emily took a breath and turned around. And her voice froze in her throat.

Three feet away from her, a demon in a lion's mask looked at her. Stared at her, dark eyes seeming to rip the mask from her own face, the rich gown from her shoulders, as he tried to see through them. As she panicked, her thoughts went automatically to Nate. He'd sworn that no harm would come to her. He'd sworn that he would protect her. And he would. He would.

"Y-yes?" she managed, tearing her gaze from Ebberling's face and looking at Rycott's black panther.

"You may not know me, Miss . . . Portsman, is it?

But I'm a friend of Nate Stokes. Jack Rycott. Has he mentioned me?"

She forced a nervous smile. "Rycott? Yes, yes, of course. He said you were a good friend of his from when he went looking for old books on the Continent."

Rycott shared a glance with Ebberling. "Indeed. And I was wondering if you, as a friend of my friend, would consent to a dance with my other friend and myself. This is the Marquis of Ebberling, by the by. Ebberling, Miss Portsman."

"Miss . . . Portsman," the marquis echoed, the sound of his voice sending another tremor through her.

"I . . . Yes, I would be happy to." She made herself lean closer to the king's spy. "You know I'm not truly supposed to be here. Sophia—the Duchess of Greaves, I mean—said it would be fun."

"You're a friend of Nate's. Where you came from is of no consequence to me." Rycott took the dance card from her stiff fingers, smiling warmly at her as he wrote his name by the remaining quadrille.

Ebberling didn't look overly pleased with his remaining spot, but he scrawled his name by the country dance, nevertheless. When he handed her card back to her their fingers brushed, and for a heartbeat or two she thought she might faint. But she didn't. She couldn't, or Nate would have likely rushed in and stabbed Ebberling and both of them would end up in prison—or rather, he would end up in prison, and she would be hanged.

"There you are, Em," Nate said, and his warm hand wrapped around 'hers. His voice, though, was anything but warm. "Rycott. I didn't know you were in London."

"Just arrived yesterday. Th—"

"Ebberling. Excuse us. We have a waltz."

Nate didn't wait for Jack to finish, or for the marquis

to comment at all. If he had, he might have leveled the fiend, and then all of Emily's courage would have been for nothing. No, he'd asked her to do this—for her own sake, but against her wishes—and so he would follow the plan, as well.

But he didn't have to like it. "Are you well?" he breathed, drawing her closer against his side as he hurried them to the dance floor.

"I don't know," she squeaked, her face white beneath her owl half-mask. "Just keep talking to me for a minute."

"Certainly." Sliding an arm around her waist, he stepped forward, half lifting her until she began to match his limping movements in the waltz. "What shall I talk about? I heard a rumor that Wellington might appear tonight. Would you care to meet him?"

"Wellington?" she gasped. "You are trying to make me faint!"

"Then I would have the excuse to sweep you up in my arms and carry you upstairs. I'm certain Tremaine would be happy to give over a spare bedchamber to us for an hour or so. For your health, of course."

That made her smile, as he'd hoped it would, and the color began to return to her cheeks. "You're a wretched man, you know."

"And you are a supremely brave woman." He gazed into her deep brown eyes, wishing time would slow so he could hold her like this, dance with her in his arms, forever. "I seem to be in constant want of you, but at this moment, love, I suggest you stay very close to me."

She chuckled, the sound lighting his heart. "How could I ever have believed you were a bookish slug, Nate?" she whispered.

"First appearances can be deceiving. I think we both

know that. My present and forever opinion of you, for example, is the one that matters to me."

"And what is your present and forever opinion of me?"

He hesitated. "Ask me that the next time we're alone."

"That poor, is it?" she asked, still grinning, her dark eyes dancing in the candlelight.

"Yes, excessively, I'm afraid. I don't wish to embarrass you in public."

"Mm-hm. Likewise, my . . . dear."

That hadn't been the word she'd been about to use. Even if he hadn't been accustomed to looking for hesitations and glances, for what they meant, he would have heard it. What was the missing word, though? He knew what he wanted to hear her say, and if it was as he suspected, he also knew why she'd altered her choice.

With him in the superior position socially, perhaps he needed to stop hinting about and simply say it to her. No bandying about or teasing or hinting. It would only take all the courage he'd ever had, shoved into one terrifying moment. Surely he could do that.

Not here, though. One or both of them might end up in a dead faint on the floor. Curving his lips upward, he glanced over her head. Rycott and Ebberling were deep in conversation. Neither of them looked happy— and the marquis's betrothed looked positively annoyed beside them. Would the chit be happy to have her fiancé removed? Was she looking forward to the marriage? Did she have any idea what had truly become of the first Lady Ebberling?

"I feel sorry for her," Emily said, echoing his thoughts.

"Harriet Danders? She might well be perfectly safe from him. A man would have to be both vicious and a

fool to murder two wives, after all. And I don't think
Ebberling is a fool. Arrogant, yes. But foolish? I don't
see it."

She danced a shade too precisely; no doubt she'd
made a point of learning the steps, whether she ever
thought to be able to make use of the lessons in public,
or not. "He's greedy. And sometimes arrogance is all a
man needs to bring him down." She sighed. "I've seen
that more times than I can count at the Tantalus's gaming tables."

"We're depending on that arrogance of his," Nathaniel pointed out, happy to return his attention to the
matter at hand and away from the question of what
he meant to do about her after all this mess was over.
He had the distinct feeling that the former would be a
much easier task than the latter. "Otherwise he would
never expect to find you within a day of hiring Rycott."

"You found me within a day," she reminded him, a
brief smile touching her mouth again beneath the feath-
ered owl mask.

"I wasn't certain at first, though. You knew something you didn't wish to share, but it took me a time to
figure out for certain what that was."

"And is that the only reason you went upstairs with
me, then?" Emily asked, her half-hidden eyes lowering
to his mouth.

"I could say yes," he returned, wondering whether
all the party guests in the room would be more scandalized to know a murderer walked among them, or
that a Tantalus girl did so. And he thought he knew the
answer, which disgusted him. "It would be a lie, though."
He leaned a breath closer. "I wanted you."

Her soft smile faded. "Why do I have the feeling
that you'll help me with one disaster, and cause me another?" she asked softly.

Nate tightened his grip on her hand. "I believe I told you that you're mine, Emily. I wasn't jesting."

"I didn't think you were, Nathaniel. But I've spent all of the past three years among lords, when they come to the Tantalus to wager. Some of them have lowborn mistresses, but none of them claimed them in public."

She didn't say the rest of it, but he heard it, anyway. *None of them married a lowborn girl.* No, they hadn't. And given his own rather precarious place in Society, marrying her would not be the wisest choice he could make. If he did so, this could well be the last grand ball he ever attended. And no one would task him with finding their lost baubles when they couldn't even tolerate looking upon his scandalous person.

"You are Emily Portsman, my dear. I don't believe I've ever asked anything of you other than your choice of name. The rest doesn't signify."

Emily looked down. "Not to you, perhaps. Not now. But it will."

He swept her in a close circle, attempting to remember to limp. "Now is now. If we earn a later, we shall discuss it. Agreed?"

For a long moment she stayed silent. "You are a very unusual man," she finally murmured, a sigh in her voice. "I'm all for putting later off as long as possible. Agreed."

"Good." That only left the challenge of her surviving the night, and him somehow managing to let Ebberling close enough to touch her without killing the man out of hand.

Chapter Sixteen

"Might I ask you a question, Laurence? Laurie?" Emily asked as Nate's brother circled around her.

The country dance was already half over, the evening three quarters so, and she'd survived dancing with Jack Rycott and even Francis Henning—though her toes were still undecided. But the next dance was the *one,* and every second brought it closer, and her hands were already shaking. Since the idea was to make Ebberling half rather than completely convinced of her identity, she needed to calm the devil down.

"I'm not answering any questions," he returned with a scowl, taking her hand and then moving by her again. "I've learned my damned lesson. Blasted lesson. Beg your pardon."

She forced a grin. "No need for that. I've served as croupier at faro tables when the players lost hundreds of quid. I doubt there's a word I don't know." She closed her mouth again as Stuart, Lord Dashton, took her hand in turn and then moved down the line. At least she thought it was Dashton—the elk with the large antlers had his jaw, but as the viscount hadn't been granted a Tantalus membership; he'd only visited on occasion as a guest of some member or other.

When Laurence returned, she curtsied and danced up the line with him. "I only wanted to ask if your brother often entangles himself in the troubles of scandalous women," she said in a low voice.

Somehow Rycott had managed to keep Ebberling out of this dance, but he wasn't the only one who could arrange trouble for her tonight. She'd spent the evening avoiding most conversations, and being Danielle Flagg when someone insisted on an introduction. Even if Emily Portsman hadn't killed anyone, she was still a Tantalus girl. And no aristocrat would forgive anyone who'd allowed her presence in their midst.

"Not that I'm aware of," he commented, sending a glance past her shoulder in his tall, lean brother's direction. His tiger mask glittered orange and red in the chandelier light as he moved. "Before the last few weeks, we spoke at holidays—some holidays—and over a fortnight when he came home to take the title."

"But you two seem so close," she exclaimed, surprised.

That made him shake his head. "I'm only in London because I got sent down from Oxford. Nate was . . . furious. I think he worries that I'll follow him into espionage, and so he wants me to excel at my studies and be happy here in England."

They parted, then joined up again. "You've been helping him with my . . . difficulties, though," she pursued.

"Yes, well, you've set him on his ear, which has made cracking his damned armor a bit easier." He grinned. "Thank you for that, by the way. It's actually rather grand, having an older brother."

Was that it? Had she cracked his armor? It was a rather nice sentiment, actually, even if it implied that he would not otherwise have let her so close to him.

Perhaps it would have been better if they hadn't become close, but she'd never expected to fall in love ever, and however it turned out she couldn't regret it. Later, she might, but not now.

"He admires you, you know," Laurence said into the relative silence. "Nate does, I mean."

"And what is it that he admires me for?" Emily returned. "It seems to me I've spent a great deal of time and effort fleeing from the facts of my life."

His grin was young and lopsided and infectious. "I think it's because you surprise him. I know not many people can do that. I never can; and you have no idea how annoying it is when your own brother knows exactly when you're lying, and he's already deciphered what the truth is."

Well, that was rather nice to hear. And however much she might be a surprise to him, he was even more of one to her. An aristocrat with a mind and the ambition to utilize it, a man with morality, and one who seemed willing and able to judge a person based on their actions rather than their breeding. She wondered if he had any idea just how rare a specimen he was. It would kill her to lose him. However fairly he might judge her, though, his peers would be far less kind.

"I don't know if you've realized it, Laurie," she said after a moment, "but you've very nearly been standing toe to toe with the Duke of Greaves and Keating Blackwood. And Lord Haybury. Do you know how many men twice your age have been leveled by any of those three? Many more than have successfully navigated a conversation with them."

This time he ducked his head, his cheeks darkening. "That's damned fine of you to say, Miss Emily."

"Just Emily, if you please. Or Em."

"Em, then," he returned. He looked as though he

wanted to say something more, but with a rousing crescendo the dance ended.

She couldn't even join in the applause. They'd arranged it so Nathaniel wouldn't be the one handing her over for her dance with Ebberling, which made sense. It also left her without a parting word reminding her to be brave and that he would be close by, or that he'd promised no harm would come to her. But she knew all that. Or she hoped it desperately, anyway. And it needed to be done. The more she'd thought about it, the more strongly she'd come to the conclusion that she would never have peace in her life until the Marquis of Ebberling had been dealt with. She only wished that she didn't have to be the one with the largest part to play. But then she supposed it could never be any other way.

When Laurie escorted her to the edge of the dance floor, Ebberling was already standing there, waiting for her. His betrothed stood at his side, her expression not at all friendly. If Miss Harriet Danders thought they were rivals of a sort, that Emily was in competition with her for her fiancé's favors—well, the girl couldn't have been more wrong. Emily only hoped the banker's daughter would eventually appreciate what they were doing, and what they might well be saving her from.

"Miss Portsman," the marquis drawled, as the orchestra began to play the first notes of the country dance. "Our dance, I believe." He held out one hand.

It took every ounce of willpower Emily possessed to reach out and wrap her fingers around his. For a bare moment she thought he might lock his grip and drag her from the room and into the waiting chains of Bow Street and the magistrates, but he only gazed at her for several long, hard beats of her heart, then walked with her onto the dance floor.

She could do this. She'd been prevaricating about

her identity since she'd been twelve. This was just one more time, one more man who wanted something from her. Emily lifted her chin. "I was surprised you wished to dance with me, my lord," she said, as they took their places.

He bowed, and she curtsied, and they began winding through the line of other dancers. "Rycott and I are old friends," he commented smoothly. "As he's friends with Westfall, I thought to do them both a kindness."

"A great kindness," she returned, noting that his gaze through the glittering lion mask never seemed to leave her face. How much could he see? Her mouth, her cheeks, the tip of her nose. Would it be enough for him to definitively identify her? She didn't think so—after all, governesses didn't dance at grand masked balls.

Of course, neither did Tantalus girls, unless they wanted to make trouble. Rachel Newbury had never wanted to make trouble. She'd only wanted to earn a good income, live in a fine house, and not have to scrub other people's clothes or sleep with strange men in exchange for a roof over her head. That was all she'd wanted, and the moment Ebberling had strangled his wife, he'd ruined two lives.

"How long have you been a Tantalus girl?" he asked, circling her.

With Laurie dipping and swirling amid the other dancers had been an amusing way to attempt to converse. With Ebberling, she felt as if he was a lion circling a gazelle, looking for a weakness so he could strike. "I've been employed at the Tantalus since before the club opened," she returned. She was supposed to give hints to her identity, and the more truths she could tell, the easier it would be to remember her story for later.

"So that's what, four years?"

"Just over three years, my lord." She met his gaze, trying not to shiver. "Have you visited the club?"

"I've been there once or twice. It's a damned scandal, really. But that's what makes it so popular, I imagine."

She forced a smile. "Even so."

"What did you do before you became a Tantalus girl?"

"Oh, we all did what we had to. You'll find former actresses, governesses, bankrupted lords' daughters, scandal-ridden ladies of good birth—all sorts."

"Yes, but what did you do? Specifically?"

Forcing a laugh, Emily twirled away from him. "So many questions, my lord. Why is it you've only visited my club once or twice?" Even though she knew it was only once, arguing with him over that would certainly not be helpful.

"I've been away from London for a time. My wife was murdered, and I've been seeking her killer."

Her face paled; she couldn't have stopped it if she'd wanted to, but Nate had figured that her deep dismay would only further the mission, as he called it. To her it felt more like a suicide mission, but she'd promised to trust him. "That's awful!" she exclaimed belatedly. "Did you find the culprit?"

"I believe I may have," he said slowly. "It's taken a good deal of time and money and effort, but I believe I've tracked her down."

"Her?" Emily repeated, in a squeak.

He nodded. "And if she knows what's good for her, she'll simply confess and save us all the trouble of a trial."

Was that truly what he wanted? For her to say she'd killed Lady Ebberling? They would hang her for it for certain, and he would be free to do as he pleased. Even murder his next wife. "It seems to me, my lord, that expecting someone to confess when that means facing a hangman wouldn't be in his or her best interest at all."

"It would be, if protesting her innocence would only cause harm to her friends and family."

The nervous tremors running through Emily stopped abruptly, heating into something far darker and more angry. So he would threaten the Tantalus, would he? And all her friends, the family she'd found there? Nate? "Perhaps a trial might clarify events to everyone's satisfaction," she heard herself say, her voice surprising level.

"Oh, it wouldn't," he returned. "There are several witnesses, including myself and my son, who would testify to her guilt. And then her present employers would be forced to admit that they'd hired a murderess. What a scandal that would be, and not at all the same sort of scandal that causes men to flock to The Tantalus Club, for example."

"Well. It seems to me you should be telling her all of this," Emily finally retorted. "Has she been arrested?"

"Not yet. Tomorrow, I think."

"Then perhaps you should wait until tomorrow to boast about how this murderess, as you call her, will do precisely as you say. You may be boasting overmuch, my lord."

"It's only a boast if it isn't proved true." He took her fingers, and they pranced down the center between the other dancers. "And I don't boast."

For the next few minutes they danced in silence. Let him think she was trying to decide whether to flee and how to go about it, or whether it would be better for everyone concerned if she simply confessed to a crime committed by one of her betters and let them go on with their far more important lives. In a sense it was ironic, that this was the first time she'd actually ever wanted to murder someone.

The dance ended, but when she'd curtsied and would have turned away, he seized her hands. "I'll be calling at the Tantalus in the morning. Ten o'clock. You either meet me out front, or I shall come in after you. And I will have the authorities with me."

She yanked her hands free. "You presume too much, my lord. I don't know what you're talking about."

"I suppose we'll discover the truth of that in the morning."

Walking with as much grace and dignity as she could manage, Emily moved away from him. She wanted to keep going, to walk out the door and out of London and all the way to Dover where she could take ship and disappear to the Continent, or to America. But that would mean giving up what she'd earned and beginning all over again. And that, when she hadn't done anything wrong. That, when she'd finally found what she wanted.

A warm hand slipped around her arm, angling her toward the hallway beyond the ballroom. "You look ready to shoot someone," Nathaniel's low voice drawled, as he fell in beside her.

"It would be better for me if I confessed," she murmured. "Better for me in that none of my friends would be dragged into the public eye and ruined for harboring me."

"Did he accuse you directly?" the wolf asked quietly, pushing open a door and ushering her through it.

"No. Very nearly, though. He said directly that he would be calling on the Tantalus at ten o'clock in the morning and that I should be ready to meet him there or he would send the authorities in to drag me out."

Silence.

Emily turned around to see Nate pulling the wolf mask from his face. "Well? Say something reassuring."

"He's moving faster than I would have liked. He must be very certain you're Rachel Newbury."

"I *am* Rachel Newbury. If he has me arrested, I will have to confess to killing Katherine or he'll see the Tantalus and my friends destroyed. And what do you mean, 'faster'? You expected him to attempt to drag me off to prison on Thursday instead of tomorrow?"

"You knew it would come to this." Eyeing her for a moment, he walked over to the windows at the far end of the room and pushed one of them open.

She swallowed down the bitter panic rising in her throat. "I'm not reassured, Nate. You know I won't allow the Tantalus to be harmed. They've given me refuge. I won't repay that by having it said they've been harboring a murderess."

Nate faced her again. "Come here." He held out one hand.

Emily crossed the room, and he folded her into his arms. "I'm not a spy, Nathaniel," she whispered, tears gathering in her eyes as she clutched at his lapels. "I don't know if I can do this. Running is so much easier, except—" She stopped herself.

"Except what?" he pursued, lowering his face to her hair.

"Do you need to know everything?" For heaven's sake, the next hours would be difficult enough without putting what lay between them and in their future beneath a magnifying glass.

"Where you're concerned?" he returned. "Yes."

"Well, forget it."

"Stubborn chit."

For a long moment she remained in the solid,

unexpected comfort of his embrace. She found him so infinitely arousing, to her body and her mind, that it surprised her when he could also provide her with such peace. Safety. She couldn't ever remember feeling safe, and she should be feeling nothing of the kind under tonight's circumstances, but she did. With him, she felt safe. And warm, and loved.

Finally, he put a finger beneath her chin and lifted her face to his. "We have to go tonight."

"I know."

Slowly he kissed her, his mouth warm and anything but comforting. "There's more to all this than you know, and I wish . . . I wish I could tell you."

She smiled. "I know, I know. Spies and your secrets. You asked me to trust you, and I do."

For the longest time he gazed at her, as if he was attempting to memorize her face. As if he never expected to set eyes on her again. "There is one thing I can tell you, though I likely shouldn't." He took a breath. "Promise me you won't protest or argue or reason or smack me across the face with logic."

Well, that sounded interesting. "Very well."

"Good." Tilting her face up again, he kissed her once more, slow and deep and breath-stealing. "One more of those, just in case," he muttered, that slight, sensual smile of his touching his mouth. "I love you, Emily, Rachel, Eloise, whatever you choose to call yourself. I love you with every ounce of my soul."

For several seconds she couldn't speak. "How . . ." she began, then cleared her throat. "Well. You're at least as logical-minded as I am," she tried a second time, her voice shaking, "so you know how abysmal the odds are of us finding a happy ending."

He shook his head. "I've spent most of my life being

logical, Em," he murmured, running a finger along her cheek, brushing away a tear she hadn't realized she'd shed. "But then this morning I realized that logically I should be dead. Most spies do not survive the end of a war; we know too much that even the winning side would rather no one else learned. And as for you— logically your life should never have brought you to London, much less to me. So tonight logic can go fling itself off a cliff, with my regards."

A short laugh burst from her chest before she could stop it. "Well, then. I suppose I love you as well, Nate Stokes." She straightened in his arms, brushing a stray lock of hair from his forehead, and kissed him. For a few heartbeats she allowed herself to believe that this could be the rest of her life, in a quiet room with the man she adored holding her close. Then, before that image could sear itself into her mind and lodge there, ruining everything else it touched, she pushed free of him and stood. "Enough. If we need to move more quickly, then I suppose we'd best get on with it."

Nate didn't like it; another day or two would have given him—and more importantly, Rycott—time to set a few more players onto the board, to see that the game progressed as they intended. But if Ebberling had gone so far as to announce that he meant to see Emily in prison in the morning, they'd run out of time.

"I'll go first," he said, sitting on the windowsill and swinging his legs around into the darkness of the garden outside. Opening his battered old pocketwatch, he checked the time. Three minutes of midnight.

In the past he'd always preferred working through the hours of darkness; physically sneaking about was so much easier than doing so mentally. Tonight they would be doing both, and though he hadn't a doubt that

Emily was game for it, she didn't have the same experience of operating when failure could mean death. That troubled him. A mistake could upend everything, and even if all went perfectly there would still be a price to pay that she likely hadn't yet considered. He had, and he was willing to pay it—and he hoped she didn't realize what it was until it was too late for her to interfere.

He felt her warm hand on his shoulder, and then he pushed off from the window, catching the reaching limb of the old elm tree outside and hurriedly swinging from there to the ground. Once down, he turned and held up his arms. "Come along," he whispered.

It would be a frightful jump from above, but Emily never even hesitated. Instead she sat on the sill and pushed away much as he had. Her falling weight in his arms sent him to one knee, but no one broke anything, and his first thought was how proud he was of her. "Well done," he breathed, setting her back onto her feet and rising with her.

"And now?"

"Wait for just a moment," he said, checking the time once more. Any second now, and—"

"There!" Rycott's voice came, at the same moment he leaned out the window they'd just left.

Without looking, Nate grabbed Emily's hand, and they fled into the darkness of London at midnight. Or at least as far as the street, where a sleek black coach without any marking on the doors awaited them. He boosted Emily inside, then climbed up after her. Before the door was even closed they went rattling up the street at a full gallop.

"Well done," he said, nodding at the petite French woman seated opposite him. "I thought we'd have to be doing this on foot."

"Rycott sent me a note an hour ago, that Ebberling

was already convinced they'd found Rachel Newbury, and that he meant to act in the morning. I've been here for twenty minutes. We have moved up our plot, yes?"

"Yes."

"But what of the others who were supposed to be waiting for us at Newgate?" Emily asked, twining her fingers with his. "If Rycott can't stall Ebberling, then there won't be enough time. If no one believes me . . ."

She looked terrified, and he couldn't blame her. "I swore that no harm would come to you, love," he said, squeezing her hand. "If you would prefer that we simply left England, I believe I can convince Miss Martine to drive us to Brighton or Dover."

"No! You are not fleeing England, Nate. You're an earl, for heaven's sake."

Her gaze searched his face, and he was glad of the years he'd spent learning not to betray his emotions or his thoughts. Even so, he held his breath until she faced Miss Martine. "Don't worry about heaven's sake, or mine," he returned. "This will work."

"I do think you could not have better allies than these men," Miss Martine put in, though the glance she spared him told him quite clearly what she thought of him lying to Emily.

If Emily knew the truth, though, the complete truth, she would do something abysmally noble like confess to a murder she hadn't committed. She would die for it, too, and he would not allow that. Never. No matter the consequences to himself. He forced himself to relax, to sit back in the well-sprung carriage and draw her up beside him.

"They say confession is good for the soul. I suppose we're about to learn if that's so." And he hoped she would forgive him for the rest of it.

*   *   *

By the time dawn came about, damp and gray, Peter Velton, the Marquis of Ebberling, was in a black rage. What the devil was he spending thousands of pounds for, if damned Jack Rycott couldn't do a simple thing like find a pair of people with whom he was already acquainted? If he couldn't follow the trail of a man he'd trained in the art of spying? A man who had had a head start of but a moment?

He paced his front drive, refusing the cup of tea his butler had been stumbling behind him holding for the past twenty minutes. This would be resolved by noon, or they would see how an infamous spy held up to a pistol discharging full in his chest. He'd paid for results, damn it all, not an idiotic chase through the countryside where she might find any number of sympathetic ears ready to hide her from him again. Rachel Newbury. Emily Portsman. Whatever she chose to call herself, no one could hide from him. He'd proven it once, and he would do so again if need be.

Hooves pounded up the street beyond Velton House, moving far more swiftly than was permitted in the heart of Mayfair. He faced the foot of the drive as Rycott pounded into view, his mount winded and sweating in the chill morning. "Tell me you found that murderess," Ebberling demanded. The more he said it, the more truthful it sounded. By the time she went to trial—if he couldn't see to her, himself—he was certain even he would believe it.

"I found her," the spy returned, swinging down to the cobbled drive and grinning. "They were halfway to Newgate and I had to put a ball through Stokes—Westfall, I mean—but she's good and caught."

Ebberling felt a chill run down his spine, cold and unpleasant. "You . . . shot an earl? I thought Westfall was your friend."

Rycott shrugged carelessly. "Friends betray and are betrayed. Money always spends."

"Then he's . . . dead?"

"Before he hit the ground. It's not wise to give Stokes a chance to pull a pistol."

Previously he'd thought Rycott looked somewhat like a dandy, well manicured, precisely dressed in the latest and most expensive of styles. Now that he looked more closely, though, he could see the hard line of his jaw, the glitter of amusement in his eyes caused by the murder of a friend. There was nothing dandyish in the way he appeared now—only death on two feet.

Belatedly the destination Rycott had named sank in. "They were on their way to Newgate? Why, in God's name, would they flee to a prison?"

The black-haired spy shook his head. "Not Newgate. They were headed for the Old Bailey. Or so she admitted, when I asked her very nicely. They meant to attempt to convince some judge or other that you were the one who killed Lady Ebberling, and Miss Newbury witnessed it." His grin deepened. "That Nate always had some scheme or other up his sleeve."

"Where is she now?"

"I found her a nice, cozy room in Newgate. I'd have done for her myself, but you said you wanted her, and then all the guards who'd heard the shot came piling out into the street, so I had to hand her over."

"I don't want a trial," Ebberling stated, his uneasiness deepening to anger. "And now that you've killed a member of the peerage, how the devil am I supposed to dispose of her quietly?"

Rycott tilted his head, a strand of black hair falling across one intense blue eye. A mad eye, Ebberling thought belatedly. He'd hired a madman.

"I have some . . . acquaintances in strategic places," he drawled after a moment, "one of those places being Newgate. As a favor to me, one of these acquaintances saw Miss Newbury stashed in a dark little cell beneath the men's ward. No one else will know to find her there, and I imagine between the two of us, she'll be happy to say whatever you want her to, just for the favor of seeing daylight when they march her out to the gallows."

Evidently he'd hired a clever madman. But then, Ebberling reflected, he'd always had a penchant for succeeding at whatever task he'd set before himself. "When might I see her?"

"As soon as you have a horse saddled, my lord. Though you might wish to dress in something a bit less fine. I believe there to be rats and dank water where poor Miss Newbury is waiting your convenience." Rycott chuckled. "When last I saw her, she was having some difficulty keeping her skirts out of reach of the lunatics in the cell next to hers. Almost a shame, her being as pretty as she is." He shrugged again. "Almost."

"Wait here, if you will," Ebberling ordered, striding for the house. Yes, it would be better if he didn't look so much like himself, anyway, when he called on Miss Newbury. Then no one would be able to say that he'd influenced her to confess in any way. And a confession would be the best resolution to this, even if choking the life out of the troublesome little flea would have been more satisfying.

"No hurry." Jack snatched the cup of tea from the butler's hands, then gestured the servant to follow his fool of a master into the house. He took a sip. Barely warm, but an expensive brew, fine and earthy to his taste. "She isn't going anywhere."

Once the front door slammed he turned his back to the house. Only then did he allow himself a brief, genuine smile. Most people were bloody fools. Nate still seemed to hold out a small degree of hope that better hearts and better minds would win the day, but Jack wagered on the cleverer man every time. And fortunately, between Stokes and Ebberling, Nate was the cleverer man.

His smile faded again. Even clever men had to pay, from time to time, and Nate's bill was about to come due. Jack only hoped the damned chit was worth it. His friend certainly seemed to think she was, but if Stokes turned out to be wrong about her, well, he would still be just as dead. And dead and heartbroken was a bloody poor way for a man to spend the rest of his life.

Chapter Seventeen

S ome poet—ironically named Lovelace, as she recalled—had once written that stone walls didn't make a prison, or iron bars a cage, but at the moment Emily had to disagree. She felt very much as if she was trapped in a small cage within a large prison, and no promises or protestations could ever make her other than utterly terrified.

They'd finally stopped howling in the cell next to her, but the quiet was even worse. The drip of water from the damp, moldy ceiling, the clank of chains and rattle of bars—if she never had a sleep free from nightmares ever again, she would know precisely why.

How long had she even been down here? Logic said an hour or so, but even so it already felt like days. It already felt like forever. How long would they wait? What if Ebberling decided simply to let her rot there? What would happen then?

The door at the far end of the crumbling old lower ward screeched open, and immediately the howling began again, louder than before. She wanted to cover her ears at the bloodcurdling, mad screeching and yowling and barking. At the least, she didn't have to feign her misery and fear; she was cold and wet, and would likely perish from being in such close proximity to whatever it was that rotted in the corner of the cell beside her.

Underground as they were, there weren't even any of the tiny windows she'd glimpsed on her way down to these neglected cells. Orange torchlight, uncertain and flickering, provided the only illumination as the trio of men emerged from the doorway and approached her cell. Two were plainly dressed, while Jack Rycott still wore his fine, if disheveled, evening attire. From twenty feet away she recognized the guard who'd locked her in earlier, but all of her attention was on the third man.

Lord Ebberling walked as if he was half convinced that corpses waited just beneath the floor to rise up and grab his ankles, but he'd come. And as he saw her huddled in the far corner of her iron-bar cage backed by the old stone walls of the main prison at the top and bottom and back, he smiled. It wasn't a pleasant smile, either.

"Well, Rachel," he drawled as the three of them stopped before her cell door, "who would have thought either of us would be here? Not I, certainly, and I wager you, even less."

"Go away," she spat, shivering.

Ebberling angled his chin toward the far door. "Yes, you two may go. I want to chat for a bit."

The guard nodded. "Pound on the door when ye want out, then."

"I'll be just on the other side, there, waiting for my payment," Rycott seconded, blowing Emily a kiss before he sauntered off. The door closed a moment later with a creak and a heavy thud, echoing in the large chamber like the crack of doom, itself. Whose doom, remained to be seen.

The marquis leaned forward against the bars separating the two of them, and not for the first time Emily wished her cell had been a bit larger. She shifted backward against the cold, damp stone. "I know what you did," she stated, her voice smaller than she intended.

"Yes, so do I," he returned, sending an annoyed glance at the mad rabble in the common cell adjoining hers. "Do they ever stop making that noise?"

"They quiet down a little when the guards aren't here, but that awful Rycott said they were amusing. He said they would keep me company."

"I imagine they will, and for a very long time, poor mindless brutes."

"I'm not the one who belongs in here," she attempted again, raising her voice to be heard over the yowling.

"Say that as often and as loudly as you like," the marquis commented, smiling. "I doubt they care. And your voice seems to . . . excite them."

Indeed, several of the filthy lunatics were reaching through the bars for her—or for Ebberling. "Why are you doing this?" she asked him, pushing stiffly to her feet. "I didn't do anything wrong!"

"But you did, Miss Newbury. Or is it Miss Smorkley? A very unfortunate name, really." His grin deepened at her wince. "You were very chatty with Colonel Rycott, it seems."

"I hoped he might listen to me. And I told him everything, so he knows you killed Katherine." Tears welled in her eyes, and fell down her dirty cheeks as she blinked. "Did you tell him to kill Nate, too? He was only trying to help me get away from you! I would never have told, if you'd just left me alone!"

"I had no idea the colonel would kill Lord Westfall. I think we've already established that you did it, however. Just as you'll admit that you killed dear Katherine."

"I won't!" she screamed. "You killed her!"

"Hush now, my dear. You're beginning to sound as

mad as your companions, here." He pushed still closer to the bars, so that she was grateful he hadn't asked to be allowed into the cell with her. "And if you don't want to spend the remainder of your natural life right here, you'd best admit to both killings, Rachel. Or whoever you are. You tricked Katherine, didn't you? You lied and said you were a well-practiced governess, and she hired you. She even thought you were friends."

"We *were* friends," Emily shot back. "And she told me how you liked to hit her."

"Only when she misbehaved." He cocked his head at her. "I think you would have improved your own character after being corrected in the same manner."

" 'Corrected!' " one of the lunatics repeated, giggling, then resumed picking at the lice in his hair.

"Well, isn't that unsavory?" Ebberling commented, making a face and miming an ape's dance at the ill-washed madmen, then laughing when two of them lunged against the bars toward him. They laughed back at him.

"You hit her when she misbehaved?" Emily retorted, drawing his attention back to her. "What did she do to warrant you pulling her off her horse and strangling her?"

He shrugged. "She threatened to tell her father. It wouldn't have worked, because no grandfather would cut off funds that went to support his grandson. But she threatened me. What husband would stand for his wife spewing such filth at him and not react?"

"She said something of which you didn't approve, so you killed her?" Emily repeated incredulously. "It wasn't the threat, but the fact that she threatened?" For the past three years she'd thought it had been because Ebberling feared what his father-in-law might do. But it had only been because Katherine had dared to speak up. And only because Emily—Rachel—had encouraged Katherine to do so. "It *was* my fault," she said aloud, half to herself, her stomach roiling.

"Ah." He gazed at her for a moment. "Then you won't mind terribly much saying that to a judge. You will leave off the other bits, and just stay with 'it was my fault,' if you don't mind. Surely a swift hanging would be preferable to a lifetime in here."

"I don't know," she returned, hearing a faint, high-pitched squeak as the door to the lunatics' cell swung slowly open. "Would it be? That's something you'll have to decide, my lord."

"Good. Then you should definitely confess, my d . . ." Ebberling trailed off as he caught sight of a pair of the lunatics shuffling toward him, out of their cell. "My God," he hissed, stumbling backward and hurrying away, toward the main door of the ward. The solid wooden one. "Get away from me!"

By now most of the madmen were in the corridor, and Emily belatedly noted how very quiet they'd become. She'd been so absorbed in convincing Ebberling to speak that she hadn't noticed before. She supposed the marquis could say the same, but he didn't seem in the mood to chat any longer. Rather, he was pounding on the wooden door, swearing at the lunatics and screaming for Rycott to come open the door. The six-inch-thick oak didn't budge.

He swung a punch at the closest of the lunatics, but the tall, raggedy man dodged the blow with deceptive speed and instead lurched beneath the swing to grab Ebberling by the shoulder and fling him face-first into the door. Before the marquis could straighten and push away, the lunatic yanked his right arm backward and pinned it between himself and Ebberling's spine. "That's enough of that," Nate's low voice came, hard and clipped.

"W-Westfall? What the devil is—let me go! Rycott! What is—"

"Shut your damned mouth, Ebberling," Nate growled. "We've all heard quite enough from you now."

"You? And those lunatics? And that lying chit? Who cares what you've heard? No one! That's who! Rycott, open this door!"

Reaching back with his free hand, Nate knocked three times on the door. "Jack, open up."

The key turned in the lock, and the door swung open as Nate shoved Ebberling upright and out of the way. The marquis would have sprinted through the opening, but Rycott was there to block him. "Not so fast, m'lord," he drawled in a soft Scottish accent. Was that his own? Emily wondered briefly. "A few of these fine fellows would like a word with ye."

"You can't lock me up in here!" Ebberling said shrilly. "No one will believe a pair of spies and a common chit! I'm a marquis!"

"And I'm a duke," Greaves's low voice came, as one by one the lunatics began shedding their rags and hats and wild wigs for the far more conservative clothes and neatly trimmed hair beneath. "I win."

"I believe a Wellington trumps a Greaves," another deep voice announced, and Emily couldn't help smiling at the expression dawning on Ebberling's face as the Duke of Wellington stepped out of a pair of ragged, oversized trousers.

"And I believe a prince beats a pair of dukes." Prince George shed a large jacket to reveal a fine blue, equally large jacket beneath it. "Well done, Colonel Rycott.

I've not had so much amusement in ages." He chuckled, then let loose a particularly fine howl.

"Your Majesty. I believe the thanks should go to Lord Westfall. It was his idea, mostly. I merely called in all my favors to accommodate."

Arm in arm with the Duke of Greaves, Prince George left the ward, while the rest of the witnesses, which included a judge of the Old Bailey and Mr. Danders, Ebberling's almost father-in-law, and Lord Garrity, his former father-in-law, shoved the marquis out the door ahead of them.

Once only Wellington and Rycott remained behind, Nate took the keys Jack proffered and walked up to Emily's cell. "Well done, Emily," he murmured, unlocking her door and yanking it open.

She threw herself into his arms. They were both ragged and disheveled and dirty, and she didn't care. He'd said he would save her, and he had. "Prince George?" she exclaimed, and then couldn't talk any more because he was kissing her.

"I was meeting with him when Jack's note found me," the Duke of Wellington said, sketching a slight, stiff bow. "He insisted."

"I do apologize, Yer Grace," Jack drawled, "but we had little choice."

"When did you become Scottish?" Emily asked, eyeing the colonel.

"When I was born in Glengarry," he returned with a grin, then looked past her toward the ward door. "If it isn't Madamoiselle Poof-Poof," he said, his smile deepening.

Emily turned as best she could with both Nate's arms still close around her. Jenny pranced through the doorway, then curtsied elegantly at Wellington. "Your

Grace. I had no idea stupid Rycott would bring you into this mess."

"I owe stupid Rycott and stupid Stokes—Westfall—one less favor now, my dear," he said, lowering his head over Jenny's hand. "And Nate is about to owe me one."

Emily looked from the duke to Nathaniel. Something was afoot, something neither man was surprised over, but from Nate's hard expression she couldn't imagine that it was anything pleasant. "What are you talking about, Your Grace?" she asked.

"You're going to have to come up with another name," Nate answered, sliding his hand down to grip her fingers. "There will be a trial, because Ebberling will not lose his title or his income or his standing without one. He has no incentive to confess. Which means you—"

"I will have to testify as to what I saw," she finished, that cold lump in the pit of her stomach stirring again. "As . . . myself. Everyone will know that I'm common."

"I find that there is nothing common at all about you, my love," Nathaniel said.

She whipped back around to face him. "Stop humoring me, Nathaniel. I *am* common, and I *will* have to leave the Tantalus. No peer wants to knowingly flirt with or play games at the table of a common chit. Especially one who will be speaking in court against one of their own." Warmth ran down her face, and she wiped at it, angry that she was crying. "I hate that man. He's ruined everything."

"Perhaps," Nathaniel returned. "And perhaps not. We've worked one miracle here tonight. Perhaps we can manage another."

Whatever he was thinking, it would be for her benefit rather than for his own. "You've done enough for me, Nathaniel. More . . . more even than you know. But I can't stay here. Not without hurting all the people who've helped me." All the people who'd loved her, she'd almost said, but for heaven's sake, the Duke of Wellington was standing there watching her. She cleared her throat. "Jenny, will you see me back to the Tantalus? I'll need to gather my things and then find a place to stay until this is finished with."

"Em—"

"No," she broke in, putting her fingers over his mouth. "Just stop it. I may have attempted to bend reality to my will, but that time is past. I need to accept who and what I am."

Nathaniel would have pursued her, but Jack put a hand around his arm and held him back. "Nothing you can do about it now," the colonel said, frowning.

Ignoring that, Nate watched until she was gone, until he could no longer hear her footfalls on the stairs leading up to the main part of the prison. He'd asked for her trust, and she'd certainly given it to him. The only protection he'd been able to guarantee had been to lock her into a prison cell and to promise to remain nearby. The rest had been up to her, and by God, she'd gotten the Marquis of Ebberling to confess to killing his wife.

"I don't want to lose her," he said finally. "What do I have to do to remain in her life?"

"You're an earl, Westfall," Wellington commented, leading the way toward the stairs. "You have an obligation to your station and your peers."

"I didn't ask to be an earl. I'm asking for this one thing to work out as it should."

"Nate, Prinny and the others here'll make certain everyone in London's talking about what happened here today. You 'n Emily and how an earl helped a common girl arrest a marquis. You had enemies before. What d'ye think they'll make of you now? They'll know the man with the different names and different faces all add up to being Nate Stokes, the not-so-bookish book collector."

Wellington was nodding. "Ebberling has friends. Every one of them would be more than happy to point a finger in your direction when someone comes looking for you, knife in hand. Add marrying Miss . . . Whoever-she-is into that, and you won't be able to leave your house without having rotten fruit thrown in your direction."

"If you're attempting to recruit me again, the answer is no." If he knew one thing, it was that becoming a spy again would destroy what was left of him. He wasn't Jack, who seemed able to set aside with rather alarming ease his conscience and his friendships in favor of his work. Every bit of it ate away at his soul, and if not for Emily, he wasn't certain how much of him would be left by now.

"And you think your solution is an improvement?" Jack cut back at him. "You'd be a no one. With nothing."

"That's all I ever wanted, Jack."

Slowly Wellington walked up and offered his hand. "You can't tell her, you know. She'll be in the center of the storm, and while she did admirably today, she's not trained to deceive so many people for so long."

Nathaniel didn't like that at all. Emily had had so many blows dealt to her in her life, and she would blame herself for this, just as she did now for Lady Ebberling's death. "What of my brother?"

"He's just a lad, Nate. He shouldn't know, either."

The frustration that had been eating at him for the

past few hours heated further. "And how about if I decide who knows what, and when they find out, and you help me because it's the damned correct thing to do?"

"Nate, y—"

"No." Nathaniel cut Wellington off, so abruptly that the duke's mouth snapped shut. "And you'll help her, too, because once this is over she shouldn't have to begin her life over again. She did nothing wrong, and I know that both of you have the resources to do a good deed."

"You're making a mistake, Westfall. If you don't cut ties with her now, you'll be obligated to stay with her."

That made him smile. "Yes, I know, Jack. Tell me you'll help."

Jack blew out his breath. "I never figured ye for a sentimentalist, Stokes, but it's yer funeral. Literally."

"Thank you. And you, Your Grace?"

"I've a soft spot for impossibilities. If you tell anyone that, however, I'll see you exiled to Russia."

That done, he shook hands with the two men. And then he went to find his brother and his love—to tell them that he needed to disappear from Society. Permanently, this time.

Chapter Eighteen

By the time Emily swore out a statement—for the second time—it was late afternoon. She had no idea why she needed to repeat her tale yet again, except that now more people were inclined to believe her since Prince George and Wellington and Greaves and Judge Mathers and Lord Garrity and Mr. Danders could corroborate that what she'd said was indeed true. If she'd been less relieved she would have felt insulted. As it was, the idea that she no longer needed to look over her shoulder or be ready to flee at any moment should have made her weak-kneed with relief.

All it took, however, was one look at the mob of men crowded on the steps of the Old Bailey for her to realize that she'd escaped one sort of peril only to plunge headfirst into another kind of trouble. "Reporters, friends of Ebberling," Jenny whispered, putting herself between them and Emily as they descended the steps to the waiting coach.

"When did you know Lord Ebberling murdered his wife?" one man called.

"Devil take you for turning on your betters!" the next one yelled, his face red and angry.

"I hope Haybury knows what a traitor you are!"

"Ignore them," Jenny said concisely, ushering her into the carriage and then climbing in behind to close the door and pull the curtains closed. "You did what was necessary."

Emily wasn't entirely certain that was the truth of it. "If he hadn't come after me again, I likely would never have said anything," she returned quietly. "What does that say about me?"

"It says you were frightened to lose the life you've made for yourself. So would I be, in your shoes."

"But you aren't in my shoes, Jenny." Emily looked down at her hands. "I truly do have to leave the Tantalus now, don't I? None of the members will want me about. Not after I helped see one of their peers arrested. Especially not after I testify at the trial."

"Yes, you will. I'm sorry, but you know the truth of it, Emily. I don't think you've ever tried to lie to yourself in all this. Beginning now would be a very poor decision."

"Do you think Diane will be angry? Not that I lied about my background, I mean. That I'm exposing it now to all the world."

Jenny took her hand and squeezed it. "Some of the girls might be angry, but Diane will not be. Nor am I. If you'd been a man, you might have joined the army and won honors for your bravery and courage. Females have many fewer choices, and you found a way to alter your fate that not many others ever would have dared. I admire that."

She forced a smile. "Thank you, Jenny. I believe that you will be in the minority, however."

"Yes, I likely will be. I don't envy you, or Westfall for that matter. It's one thing to be in a foreign country and by your actions stop a man from doing harm. It's quite another to accuse a peer of murder after you've agreed to help him."

Emily sat up straighter. "Nathaniel only wanted to know the truth."

"And in so doing, he betrayed one of his own." Genevieve patted Emily's fingers. "Rycott will disappear back to his duties, no one knows of my part, or of Greaves's or Haybury's, but they know about you and they know about Westfall. Someone must be blamed."

"They can blame me! I have to leave, anyway. Nate shouldn't . . . It isn't fair."

"I cannot argue with that. And you shouldn't waste your time arguing with the facts of a thing."

When had this all gone from something she had to do in order to free herself, to something that was now ruining at least two lives? And that didn't even take into account poor Harriet Danders, who might have been perfectly safe, or poor young George, who would now have to lose a second parent. Emily wanted to scream and cry and rail at the sky—but mostly she wanted to see Nate, to hear his voice and have his arms around her while he said wondrous things like "I love you" and "No harm will come to you." He'd likely known all along that her troubles would also come to bite him, and he'd stepped forward anyway. And no one would call him hero for it this time, either. No one but her.

When they stopped at the head of The Tantalus Club carriage drive and Diane herself pulled open the carriage door for them, Emily knew for certain that her life was being upended once more. "You can't come in," the marchioness said, her deep green eyes somber and sad. "I'm sorry, but if you do, half our membership will walk out. Even the ones who believe that Ebberling's a killer detest the idea that someone they flirt with might betray a confidence. And it's even worse that you're not highborn."

Emily nodded, her throat closing and her eyes filling with unshed tears. "I understand. I . . . I'll find somewhere to stay. Will you have my things sent to me?"

"I will. And we've arranged a place for you." She handed up a piece of paper to the driver. "Harry, see her here safely and then return for her things."

"Yes, my lady."

"I'm so sorry, Em," Diane said, leaning up into the coach to take her hand. "If it were up to me alone, you could stay as long as you liked."

"I understand. You help so many of us, Diane. I would not jeopardize that for anything. Thank you so much for everything you've done."

The marchioness straightened briskly, brushing at her cheek as she did so. "Nonsense. And I'm certain I'll see you again. You haven't been abandoned. Only shifted elsewhere."

Emily knew it was a lie, but she was glad to hear it, regardless. She was learning to appreciate kind lies. She wondered which one Nate would tell her, when he came to part company from her, as well. Unless he'd already done so.

When Jenny kissed her on the cheek and climbed out of the coach to join Diane, Emily clenched her hands to keep from crying. At one time she thought she'd learned the lesson that she could rely on no one but herself. Three years at The Tantalus Club had softened her, made her decide that friends were a good thing, that her life was better when she could include other people in it. At least she would have time now to learn to be on her own again. And to swear once and for all that she wouldn't forget that lesson again.

The coach rumbled out of Mayfair and to a small house on the edge of Knightsbridge. "This is it, Emily," Harry called out, reaching down to flip out the coach steps and open the door.

Refusing to hesitate, she descended to the cobblestone street and looked up. It was pretty, painted white with four sizable windows overlooking Chesham Street from two stories. She wondered who'd been forced to grant her its use until Ebberling's trial was finished with, and how quiet it would be inside.

As she reached the front door it swung open, though, and Sophia, the Duchess of Greaves, pulled her into a tight hug. "Oh, Em," she exclaimed, "you should have told me all of it!"

The waiting tears began pouring down Emily's cheeks. "Why are you here?" she sobbed, returning the hug. "Where are we?"

"This is Reynolds House. It belonged to one of Adam's relations. I've never been here before, either, but it's very pretty. It has a rose garden, as well."

Greaves was in the foyer when Sophia pulled her inside and closed the door. Emily looked, but she saw no sign of Nate. Perhaps those parting words of his at Newgate had been the last she would ever hear from him. The last she would ever see of him. Ever. Another fit of tears made her shake.

"Oh, good God," the duke muttered. "Both of you, into the morning room. I'll fetch whisky."

Emily had never been a watering pot, but now she couldn't seem to stop. That made Sophia cry, as well, which made her feel even worse, and then she began blathering, and then Cammy arrived at Reynolds House, and all three of them began sobbing.

"And now Nate's involved, and no one will like him for turning on Ebberling, and he doesn't like being an earl anyway, and it's my fault," she sniffled, burying her face in Camille's shoulder.

"It isn't your fault," Mrs. Blackwood returned unsteadily, wiping at her own tears. "It's Lord Ebberling's fault. Surely everyone will realize that, especially after the trial."

"It's an embarrassment," the Duke of Greaves put in from as far across the room as he and Keating Blackwood could place themselves. "It wasn't handled quietly, and—"

"It couldn't be handled quietly. Not under the circumstances," Keating countered.

"That doesn't matter. It's a sticky mess, with the involvement of commoners. Of a commoner pretending to be above her station. Westfall is going to be run out of Town on a rail. Or he might as well be, because no one of good birth will so much as tell him how do you do. And they'll all know he's not some bumbling fool they could trust with their secrets. Oh, they'll hate that."

"It won't last," Blackwood insisted. "I've gotten invitations to four parties this year, and I killed a man and married my cousin's fiancée."

"Yes, give it a decade, and he might find himself welcome back at Boodles. Huzzah."

"You're not helping, Adam."

His expression softened as he looked at Sophia in a way that made Emily's heart ache for Nathaniel. "I apologize, my love. I'll keep my own counsel, if you wish."

Emily shook her head. "No. Lying or keeping silent certainly won't change the future, and I would rather know the truth."

"But knowing the truth won't change anything, either, Em." Camille stood to retrieve a tea tray from the distraught-looking servant—likely the housekeeper—at the door. "And you are welcome to come live with Keating and me at Havard's Glen. It's in Shropshire, so you won't have to face these awful people here in Town."

"That's a lovely offer, Cammy, but I can't do that. You and Keating have your own troubles, and my presence would only make returning to Society harder for both of you. I have money I've been saving up, and I'll go somewhere far away with a new name. Another new name. Scotland, perhaps. I've always wanted to see Scotland. I could open a dress shop." It wasn't as low as being a washerwoman, but it was close enough that even the idea of it made her shudder. Even so, if nothing else, the past three years had taught her that aiming high also made her a much more visible target.

"But what do you *want* to do?" Sophia insisted.

What did she want? She wanted to marry Nathaniel Stokes and not have to worry about people finding her. She wanted to know that Nate was safe and that no one from his past would be able to find him now that her actions had put his name on everyone's lips, as well. She wanted . . . She wanted to be happy. And that meant Nate. But that would never happen, so the rest of it didn't signify, either. "I want to open a dress shop in Scotland," she said aloud, knowing her friends would accept that because it would make all of this easier on them, as well.

"You're certain?" Camille asked.

She nodded. "Yes. I'm certain. And I'll make sure you know the name I've chosen and where I'll be, so you can come see me if you like. And of course you'll write me and tell me about your baby, Sophia."

"Of course I will."

Someone rapped at the front door, the sound loud

and echoing through the small house. Emily jumped. If she had to retreat again before the trial had even begun, she had no idea where she would go.

Greaves stood. "I'll see to it."

A moment later she heard the door open and the duke's low voice. A second, louder voice replied—a voice she recognized. "You do not have the right to remove her without informing me where she's gone!" Nate didn't sound at all like himself; in fact, he sounded angry. Furious, even.

Three hard beats of her heart later, he stood in the morning room doorway. Emily rose, and he strode forward, not stopping until he wrapped his arms around her. "There you are," he murmured. "I thought I'd have to begin looking for you all over again."

"I had to leave the Tantalus."

"That's where I went looking for you. Damned Haybury could have smuggled you in the back way. No one needed to know. That's your home. You shouldn't have had to leave it."

"No. Someone would have found out. There are other girls there with nowhere else to go. I won't jeopardize that. And Greaves and Sophia are letting me use this house until the trial is over. I'll be fine."

Finally he lifted his head, seeming to notice the rest of the room's occupants. And she abruptly realized that his brother had joined them, as well, his own expression nearly as miserable as she felt. He knew, then, the social price that Nate was going to have to pay for coming to her aid.

"I need to speak to Emily," Nathaniel said. "Alone."

"She shouldn't have to stay here by herself," Sophia argued.

"She won't."

With more diplomacy than he generally showed,

Greaves took his wife's hand and pulled her toward the door. "We'll go. I'll send a plain black coach for your use, Emily. And a driver. The housekeeper is Mrs. Avery. She is at your disposal, as well."

"Thank you, Your Grace. And you, as well, Sophia." She hugged Camille again, and kissed Keating on the cheek. "You are all truer friends than I ever thought to have."

Nate waited, refusing to show his impatience, while Emily parted from her friends. She was lucky to have them, though how anyone could resist falling for her charms once they'd met her, he had no idea. Finally the front door closed, leaving only the housekeeper, Emily, and himself and his brother.

"Laurie, go see that the larder is stocked, will you? And shut the door here."

His brother had barely uttered a word since daybreak, and he only nodded and left the room, closing the door quietly behind him. *Finally.* Nate bent his head and kissed Emily softly on the lips.

"Much better," he murmured.

"You shouldn't be here," she said, when he reluctantly straightened again.

"And why not?"

"Because you'll only make things worse for yourself. And for Laurie."

He shifted his grip to her hands. "Come here. Sit with me. We need to talk."

"I'll sit with you because I find you utterly irresistible, but we don't need to talk. I know I've ruined your life. Don't try to make it sound any better than it is."

That made him smile. "So practical, you are. Very well. I won't coat anything with sugar or honey. But I do need to talk to you."

When he sat back onto the overstuffed couch she

seated herself beside him, tucking her petite form against his shoulder. For a moment he kept silent, letting the feel of her sink into him. If he didn't say the wrong thing, or if she didn't decide that the best way to aid him was for both of them to be miserable and apart, he could have this every day. He could have her, be in her life, keep her in his, for the rest of their lives. And that was what he wanted. *Her*.

"The gossips have already got the tale," he finally began. "About you being a commoner and a Tantalus girl, about me being a spy and lying to everyone about the reason for my presence on the Continent during the war. Wellington's admitted to it. Jack's already gone into hiding. It isn't so easy for me to disappear. I'm Lord Westfall, now."

"I'm so sorry. I never meant for you to get dragged into this. I never meant for you to be hurt."

He tilted her chin up and kissed her again, tasting the salt of her tears on her lips. "I wanted to be involved. I've yet to do anything against my will, Em." He took a breath. "There are people in my past who now know for certain that I've deceived them. Some of them will be quite unhappy about it. They may come looking for me. Or they may hire men to come for me."

She sat up straight, her already pale cheeks going gray. "Nate! You have to leave London. If anything were to happen to you— Dear God, why didn't you say something? I would never—"

"You would never have let me help you. I know. You would never have let me into your life. Did I mention that I'm in love with you? I'm accustomed to danger. I've never been in love before."

She punched him in the chest, hard enough to hurt. "And I love you! Does that in any way make you think

I could stand it if someone hurt you? If someone killed you?"

For a long moment he gazed at her, wanting to memorize the expression of deep worry and fear on her face—so he could make certain she never had to feel that way again. "Someone *is* going to kill me. I'm going to make certain of it."

Ripping out of his hold, Emily bolted to her feet. "*What?* Who? I'll kill them before they can touch you! I swear it, Nate. No one is allowed to hurt you! No one."

Nathaniel stood, grabbing her wrists when she flailed at him and would have pushed away. "Listen to me. Listen, Em. Please. I won't be hurt. I swear it."

She glared at him, tears glistening in her eyes and running down her cheeks. "Stop jesting with me!"

"I spoke with Wellington and Jack," he said, deciding that describing the details could wait. "Jack is going to pretend to kill me, in public. Tomorrow. I can then disappear, leaving you and Laurie and everyone else around me safe. It's a last resort, but it's the best solution."

"You'll be safe," she muttered, swaying forward.

Damnation. Nate caught her as she fainted, lifting her in his arms and kicking open the morning room door. He carried her upstairs, the housekeeper and Laurie appearing to fall in behind him.

"She took it as well I as I did, then," Laurie said.

"Shut up. Mrs. Avery, the master bedchamber?"

"Third door on the right, my lord. Oh, dear. Shall I fetch smelling salts?"

"No. Some peppermint tea, and brandy."

The housekeeper hurried away without another word. Nate liked her immediately; no fluttering or wailing or indecisiveness from Mrs. Avery. She could be handy to have about. Laurie moved past him, opening the bedchamber door and hurriedly turning down the coverlet, then piling pillows up and throwing open the windows. His brother had matured, Nate realized. He would make a fine Earl of Westfall—likely a better one than he'd been, himself.

"Thank you, Laurie."

Laurence glanced up at him, hesitated, then nodded. "She loves you. I was . . . She'll be good for you. Don't be so logical she turns you away, Nate. And make certain she knows how much blunt I'm giving you. And the Crown's donation, or whatever they're calling it. I'll be downstairs."

Nathaniel gently set Emily down on the bed. When he would have straightened, though, her arms swept up around his shoulders and pulled him down to her for a kiss. "Turns you away from what?" she asked, her face still alarmingly pale.

"In a minute."

When Mrs. Avery returned with the tea tray and a decanter of brandy with two snifters, Nate decided he was going to hire the housekeeper away from Greaves, whatever the cost. He thanked her, watched as she left the room again and shut the door behind her, then sank down on the edge of the bed.

"Now. Where were we?" he asked, handing Emily one of the snifters.

She sat up, sipping at the brandy. "Jack Rycott is going to shoot you tomorrow, you're receiving some blunt, and I'm not to turn you away from something."

"No, you're not." He grinned at her, kissing her again because he couldn't not do it. "I will be killed, Laurie will take the title, and I will assume the identity of your footman, butler, and groom while you're staying here." He'd just now decided that last bit, but it made sense, and he could keep her safe from anyone who didn't want a common Tantalus girl testifying against a wealthy marquis about a murder she'd witnessed.

Her free hand twined around his. "Nate, you can't give up an earldom. Not because you were good enough to want to help me."

"I never wanted to be an earl. And in all honesty, Em, if I remained an earl I couldn't do this." Trying to keep his fingers from shaking, he took the brandy from her and held both her hands in both of his. Her dark brown gaze lifted to meet his, and he smiled. "*This* is what I want. I want to be your husband. I want to marry you. I want to have children with you. I want you to be my wife. I want to be a gentleman farmer and not have to wear spectacles or assume a limp. I want to choose a name and make it mine for the rest of my life. I want you to choose who you want to be, and be it with me. Will you marry me?"

For a hard beat of her heart Emily thought she must still be asleep and dreaming. But his hands were shaking, and they were warm and real as they held hers. "This is what *I* want," she said, sounding to her own ears as unsteady as he had. "I want to be loved and cared about and safe. I want to be who I am without pretending to be anyone else ever again. I want to be with you for the rest of my life. Yes, I want to marry you. *You.* Whoever you choose to be."

He captured her mouth with his, kissing her until she couldn't breathe. When they separated to take a breath, Nate pushed her back down on the bed and resumed kissing her, her mouth, her damp cheeks, her ears, her throat, everywhere. Then his hands joined in, undoing the trio of buttons at the front of her gown and slipping inside to caress her breasts.

Emily sat up again to push the coat from his shoulders and open his waistcoat, shoving them to the floor as he pushed her dress down her arms to her hips. When she lifted up he stripped the dress down her legs and flung it aside, her shoes following.

"Have you thought of a name?" he asked her breathlessly, moving her hands aside so he could open his own trousers and shove them down. Together they yanked off his boots and dropped them to the floor, his trousers following them onto the polished wood. "Who do you want to be?"

"I've always been partial to Isobel," she returned, kissing him again as she lay back on the bed, tossing aside pillows and pulling him down on top of her.

"Isobel," he said slowly, drawing out the word as if he was tasting it. "I like it. Isobel." Pushing his hips forward, he slid inside her, hot and hard and deep. "My Isobel."

She gasped at the filling sensation, at the weight of him across her hips. "And what about you? Who are you going to be?"

"William. It's my middle name, and I've always liked it."

"It's a good, solid name. Like you. William."

"Then I, William, ask you, Isobel, t—"

"McQueen," she finished, groaning as he entered her again and again. "Isobel McQueen."

"We're to be Scottish, then? Very well," he returned, laughing breathlessly. "Isobel McQueen, will you marry me, William . . . Pinkerton?"

"Yes. Yes, I will marry you, William Pinkerton. But . . . oh, yes . . . but where does Pinkerton come from? It sounds familiar."

"From that damned book you were reading. *The Scottish Cousin.* The cousin's name is Bartholomew

Pinkerton. It seems a good Scottish name, don't you think?"

She'd forgotten about that. "Yes, for a Spanish troubadour's son. I like it. Nate and Isobel, oh, Pinkerton. But may I still call you Nate?"

"Only when we're in bed together, and I'm inside you."

Emily—Isobel—grinned. "Yes, Nate."